Marie Lu

'Heart-stopping action, fierce friendship, and intense romance'

Bustle

Also by Dhonielle Clayton from Gollancz

The Belles

THE EVERLASTING ROSE

DHONIELLE CLAYTON

For all the angry girls.
There's nothing wrong with you.

This paperback first published in Great Britain in 2020 by Gollancz

First published in Great Britain in 2019 by Gollancz
an imprint of the Orion Publishing Group Ltd
Carmelite House, 50 Victoria Embankment
London EC4Y 0DZ

An Hachette UK Company

1 3 5 7 9 10 8 6 4 2

A CIP catalogue record for this book is
available from the British Library.

ISBN (mass market paperback) 978 1 473 22400 1
ISBN (eBook) 978 1 473 22401 8

Printed in Great Britain by Clays Ltd, Elcograf S.p.A

www.dhonielleclayton.com
www.gollancz.co.uk

"Beauty is blood and bone and sovereignty;
a perfect smile is its greatest weapon."

—Orléansian proverb

The Goddess of Beauty chose the first queen of Orléans. Beauty searched for the one who would treasure her most sacred gift—the Belles. She knew she wouldn't be able to journey back and forth between the sky and the ground for much longer. The tension among the gods required her to pick a realm. She enacted a series of tests—the Beauty Trials—to draw out the woman who had the right qualities. The one who could nourish their precious talents. The one who would never be jealous. The one who would, above all, keep them safe. When Queen Marjorie of House Orléans emerged the victor of the Trials, she pledged that she and her descendants would forever revere the Belles as extensions of Beauty herself; to be treated as if they were as delicate and precious as the petals on an everlasting rose.

from The History of Orléans

Maman never told me what to do when the world falls apart like a dress ripped at its seams, the beads scattering into faraway corners, the fabric a storm of shredded pieces left destroyed and unrecognizable. She never told me how to battle the nightmares that creep in like icy shadows, lingering behind closed eyes. She never told me what to do when all the color leaks out of the world like blood oozing from a mortal wound.

She gave me a mirror to see truth. I clutch it, the glass warming inside my palm.

But what happens when the reflection peering back is ugly, and when all I want to do is set everything ablaze, and she's not here to help me?

The past three days are a chaotic blur, a télétrope in perpetual motion—the palace, Sophia's dungeons, Charlotte waking up, and Arabella helping us get here with false papers.

"Are you listening to me?" Edel snaps. "You've been gazing out that window for almost a full hourglass."

I don't pivot around to face her or the small boardinghouse room we've been stuffed into. I fixate on the sun as it sinks behind the row of shops across the street and watch how it turns the sky the color of a peacock's tail. Sunsets are much more beautiful this far south. It feels like the Spice Isles are at the very edge of the world and poised to float right off.

I press my nose against the frigid glass; the cold-season wind attempts to push its way through. I wish it would wrap its icy fingers around me and cool my insides. In the distance, the cluster of islands almost kisses at the Bay of Croix, and the capital city of Metairie overlooks them like a huge house-lantern out at sea, drawing ships safely near. Golden bridges connect the four isles and radiate like fireworks as evening arch-lanterns are lit. Decadent river coaches skate over the waters beneath, the light glinting off their gilded trim. Grand spice plantations stretch out in all directions with large white mansions overseeing fields of mint, lemon balm, lavender, and sage. Plant-lanterns crest over the crops, paper-thin bees carrying sunshine and nutrients.

This place feels even stranger than the palace did, so different than our home. I used to want to see every far-flung corner of this world, but now, all I think about is what it would be like to watch Orléans burn, each island turning to ash, clouds of thick smoke clogging the skies and stamping out the sun, the seas blackening from the leftover debris. Would the gods intervene?

I gaze back down at the maps littering the desk. My charts of the trade winds. My theories about how far Princess Charlotte could have gotten if she sailed west toward the Glass Isles or maybe east around the base of the imperial island.

Overcome with frustration, I throw the compass rose Rémy gave me, and it lands on the floor with an unsatisfying thud.

Edel picks it up. "Camille, I need to show you something!" She looks over my shoulder at my maps. "Come now. You don't even know if Charlotte made it out that night."

"Rémy said the queen's private schooner was spotted. Who else could it be?"

"A thief? Pirates? Some drunken courtiers who got on the wrong boat?"

I scoff. "He said no one knows who was on it, and now you're putting all your hopes into a girl who was unconscious for four years."

She touches my bare shoulder. I jump.

"Your skin's hotter than a cookstove," she says. "Are you ill?"

I want to tell her a never-ending fire burns in the pit of my stomach now, the flames fed by my rage.

"And your fingers are like ice," I reply.

I grab the compass from her and trace another potential route Charlotte might have taken, putting her north of the imperial island. "She was coughing and waking up when Amber and I rushed out."

"Let's forget Charlotte and storm the palace. We could take down Sophia ourselves."

"Then what? Rule Orléans?"

Edel nibbles her bottom lip. "Maybe."

"If Charlotte is queen, then she can return Orléans to what it used to be. The way Queen Celeste wanted."

"I don't want to go back. I won't be in another teahouse again. I won't be forced to—"

I take her hand, and she swallows the rest of the sentence. "We need to hope. If we can find Charlotte and bring her back to the palace, she can confront her sister. She can put an end to all of this." I hold her close. "Then we will find a different way forward, a different life for us. I promise."

"Fine, fine," Edel mutters under her breath and pulls away. "But I have something more important to show you . . . something that will help us when we leave this place." She's shaky and casts nervous glances at the door. "I've been waiting until we were alone."

"What is it?" I turn away from the maps.

"Watch." Edel closes her eyes, concentrating so hard she looks minutes from laying a golden egg. Veins swell beneath her white skin and a red blush sets into her cheeks. The pale blond hair at her temples soaks with sweat, which beads across her forehead like a strand of pearls. Her hair lengthens down to her waist inch by inch, then turns the color of midnight.

I scramble backward, smacking into the tiny cage of sleeping teacup dragons. They squeak with alarm.

"We're not supposed to be able to do that." I put my hand over my mouth.

"I'm calling it our fourth arcana—glamour." She takes my trembling fingers and pushes them into her hair. It still maintains the same fine texture it's always had, but the color is utterly unfamiliar.

"Our gifts are for others. . . ." My heart flips in my chest. My arcana hums just beneath my skin, eager to learn, eager to experiment with this dangerous trick; my mind fills with a thousand possibilities.

"No. *This* gift . . . this is for us. This is how—" Edel starts.

"We will outsmart Sophia and her guards," I interject. "And find Charlotte."

The possibility of success wedges itself down to my bones and mingles with the anger living there. I'd always built my life on doing the unexpected and wanting it all—to be the favorite, to be the most talented Belle, to shape what it meant to be beautiful in Orléans—and now I'm presented with doing the biggest thing I've ever had to do and with the risk of danger far greater than I could ever imagine. All of it breathes life into my ambition.

A full grin spreads across Edel's face. She takes a deep breath, and the dark shade of midnight in her hair lightens as if morning sun pushes through each strand.

"How did you learn to do this?"

She glances at the door. "It was an accident. Madam Alieas was yelling at me, laying out all the things I'd done wrong. She barked about how I needed to be nicer, and how she'd wished she'd gotten Valerie instead. I was twirling my hair around my finger." She lifts one of the strands. "Growing angrier and angrier, thinking of our sister, and then it darkened to Valerie's brown shade."

"What does it feel like?" I stroke Edel's hair again, and it shrivels back to its previous shoulder length.

"Remember when we'd sneak up on the roof at home before the first snow? Our fingernails would be purple and blue. Our nightgowns would catch the wind, the fibers almost freezing."

I nod as the memory flickers through me. All of us on the roof after Du Barry and our mothers had fallen asleep, waiting for the clouds to release their crystals, waiting to catch a snowflake on our tongues, waiting to see the white mounds frost the tops of the dark forest behind our house.

"It feels cold like that. I panicked at first. I didn't think it was real. Thought my arcana was low, my eyes playing tricks on me.

So I experimented with sections of my hair." She walks in circles. "Adding a wave or a highlight, and testing how long I could hold it."

My stomach flutters. Trusting untested aspects of the arcana feels like trying to harness a windstorm. "Did it make you sick?"

"Nosebleeds, headaches, the chills."

"Then maybe—"

She puts a hand up, sweeping away my worries. "That lessened as I got stronger. It just takes practice. I moved from my hair to aspects of my face."

"Does it weaken you like after we've done beauty treatments?"

"Yes. I use the sangsues and chocolate to help me hold a glamour and to feel better after using one." Edel takes my hand. "Quick. Let me show you."

I stretch across the thin mattress Edel, Amber, and I share. The springs dig into my back. Maman's mirror sits just under my breastbone on its chain. I press my hand to it, wanting its truth and wisdom to push down inside me, fill me up, and make me feel like Maman is still here, ready to fight alongside me. What would she think of all this? The things I've done. The things I'm about to do.

"Close your eyes," Edel directs.

A tremor pulses in my stomach.

Edel pushes my curls away from my sweaty forehead. Is this how our clients feel on our treatment tables? Tiny, exposed, vulnerable?

She takes my trembling hand. "Are you afraid?"

"I'm angry."

"Good. That will make you strong." Her soft fingers graze over my eyelids, forcing them closed. "Now, think back to when we were little girls first learning our second arcana, and Du Barry made us do all those lessons on visualizing our clients like paintings or sculptures. Remember?"

"Yes."

"Instead, try to see yourself."

Du Barry's childhood warnings are sharp echoes inside my head: *"Belles must never be vain, for the Goddess of Beauty shall punish those who hoard their gifts. The arcana are favors from the Goddess of Beauty to be used in service."*

I push her words away, bury them deep down with the rest of the lies.

Edel squeezes my shoulder. "Go back to Maison Rouge. You'll see."

I take a deep breath, let my muscles relax. Edel describes the home where we spent our entire lives until we turned sixteen last year. The pale white trees growing out of the bayou like bones, the rose-shaped bars on the house windows, the crimson-and-gold-papered walls leading into the lesson rooms, the Age chambers with their terrariums of dying flowers and bowls of rotten fruit, the Aura rooms with their treatment tables and Belle-products, the nursery full of crying babies, the black forest—a shadow behind our house.

"You're tensing your muscles," Edel says, stroking my cheek. "Let the arcana wake up. Focus on that."

At the mention of the word *arcana*, their power throbs inside me, rising quickly to meet my request. All three skills—Manner, Aura, Age—are threads ready, able, and eager to be tugged and bent to my will.

The veins in my hands swell beneath my skin. My nerves prickle with thick energy.

"Think of your own face," Edel whispers. "Your curly hair and your high forehead. Your full lips. The shade of your skin is the brown of the almond luna pastries Rémy brought us this morning for breakfast."

When I would see clients for beauty work, a familiar warmth would race through me like someone had let a candle flame graze across my skin. But now, a deep chill settles in, replacing that feeling. My teeth chatter, and a shiver makes me jerk.

"You're all right. Keep going," Edel says. "Change your hair to match one of the crimson Belle-roses from our home solarium with petals as large as plates."

The flower sprouts beside the image of my own face in my mind. Its color bleeds into the strands of my hair, twisting around the coils like ribbons of blood. A headache erupts in my temples. My lungs tighten like I've just raced up a winding staircase.

"It's working," she says.

I sit straight up.

"Don't break your concentration."

"Why does it feel this way?" I ask, out of breath.

"I don't know. But you're doing it." Edel rustles through the beauty caisse Arabella sent with us, retrieving a small mirror and thrusting it into my hands. "Look!"

I gaze into it. The frizzy curls at the crown of my head are a deep fiery red like Amber's, like Maman's. I play with one curl and twist it around my finger to examine it more closely.

"How long does it last?" I grimace through the cold. It grips my bones, a radiating ache splintering my insides.

"As long as you can hold it in your mind and your levels stay strong. I've been able to maintain it for almost five hourglasses when I'm rested and focused," Edel boasts. "But I know if I push myself or drink Belle-rose tea or elixir, I could go longer."

"I can't concentrate any longer."

The red fades away and the brown appears once more. I crumple on the bed.

The door snaps open. Amber marches in, her presence a landquake. A nest of red hair peeks out from under her hood.

Edel stands. "You're back early."

"There were too many guards, and I lost the mask you gave me," Amber reports, then surveys the room. "What's going on?"

"Edel was just teaching me how to—" I start to say.

"Quickly refresh your arcana." Edel's eyes burn into mine.

I purse my lips and flash her a puzzled look.

"Where's Rémy?" Edel asks, taking a porcelain bowl from a nearby table and fishing out two wiggling sangsues. She wraps one leech around my wrist like a cuff, and in a whisper says, "Don't say anything."

"He's doing one of his rounds before coming upstairs." Amber rushes to the dragons' cage and lifts the blanket. They're tangled together in a pile and remind me of jeweled bracelets made of pearls, emeralds, sapphires, rubies, and gold. "I brought them some pig meat and found these sweet necklaces." She dangles the collars from her fingers and sets them in front of the cage.

"Why'd you spend our money on those?" Edel snaps. "You were supposed to get hair dye for all of us."

"I did." She yanks two pot-bellied jars from her pocket and throws one at Edel.

Edel catches it.

"All she had left was evergreen."

"That's going to help us blend in," Edel replies sarcastically.

"The whole city is at a shortage of Belle-products with the teahouses shut down. And she gave me those collars at a discount.

The dragons need leashes for their training." She hands me a crumpled page. "Found this on the lobby table."

Four cameo portraits stretch across the page: Amber, Edel, Rémy, and lastly, me.

My own eyes stare out, looking haunted. The animated portrait shifts through a series of my most notable looks: one with my hair in a signature Belle-bun full of camellia flowers; another with it down and around my face in a big, curly cloud; and the last with the strands all ironed straight and resting on my shoulders. The text calls us dangerous, cunning, and traitors to the crown. Sophia has promised 850,000 leas and 275,000 spintria for our capture. That would make a person instantly one of the wealthiest individuals in all Orléans, ready to join the circle of the kingdom's finest.

WANTED: ALIVE AND IN GOOD CONDITION.
SUITABLE FOR USE.

What does that mean? Are we cattle headed to the slaughterhouses on the Isle of Quin?

Amber places fresh food in the teacup dragons' cage, then plops down in one of the wooden chairs. "I hate this place."

Edel starts to cough. "I need water," she says.

"Are you sick?" Amber asks.

"Thirsty," Edel replies. "Can you grab some?"

"Why can't you?" Amber's eyebrows lift with suspicion.

"You always get the water. You know how to work the house pumps." They lock eyes. "Plus, I'm not dressed, and you are."

"Amber, please. The teacup dragons need some as well," I add.

She shrugs, then leaves the room.

As soon as the door closes, Edel stops coughing and turns to me. "Don't tell her about the glamours."

"Why?" I ask, feeling Edel's distrust of Amber like a flash of heat.

"She's too weak to try it right now. We should wait until we know exactly how it works. We both have always been stronger and more willing to experiment than she is."

"But we'll need to show her soon." I study Edel's face.

"Of course," Edel says, avoiding my eyes. "When the time is right."

2

The sun hasn't risen when I sneak out of bed and dress to go out. Rémy is off on one of his night-watch rounds. I don't bother using the cold water in our basin for fear of waking Amber and Edel. I'm getting used to the dirt. The memories of onsens full of clawfoot tubs and rose-shaped soaps and sweet oils and honey scrubs, perfume blimps leaving behind their scents, and beauty-lanterns dusting us with perfect beams of light are clouds drifting out to sea never to be caught again.

I put in the eye-films that Arabella gave us, then blink until they settle, and I can see the small room again. We've fallen into a synchronized rhythm like the dancing koi fish that used to live in our fountain at Maison Rouge: Amber fetches fresh water from the house pumps every morning and even scrounges up small pieces of lime soap so we can make an attempt at bathing; Edel keeps the room tidy by stealing the house mistress's broom each afternoon; Rémy watches every movement in and out of the boardinghouse;

and I nurse our teacup dragons, teach them how to fly, and secure our nightly meals.

At times it feels like we could go on living this way if we wanted. Move from boardinghouse to boardinghouse to evade the imperial guards. Take care of one another. Fold into the regular population of Orléans and live in secret. But my desire to see Sophia fall has become a whispered refrain making my body restless, as if my limbs and heart know that this isn't the place for us. That I must face her. That I must make her pay for what she's done. That I must do what Queen Celeste would have wanted.

Amber and Edel are still a mess of legs and arms and quilts in the bed we share. I have only a few moments to get out the front door of the boardinghouse before Rémy returns. I ease down the staircase, careful not to hit any of the squeaky wood planks. This is the second time I've sneaked out since we arrived.

In the main salon, a few night-lanterns putter low along the ground. Three teacup cats wander across the long tables in search of crumbs. One meows at me.

"Shh," I whisper. "Don't ruin my plan."

I tie the ribbons of the mask Edel gave me. It's made of rich black velvet and lace, and hugs the contours of my face and neck like a soft glove. *Guaranteed to protect one's makeup from the cold-season weather.* Or shield one's identity. The southerly winds make these popular here, creating the perfect locale for staying hidden.

I unlatch the hook on the front door and close it gently behind me.

An early-morning mist covers the city, choking the buildings with fog. The day after Maman died, the world outside the windows of Maison Rouge looked the same. Through the rose-shaped bars, I watched the dark forest catch rain clouds, trapping them down from the sky. I always imagined them as the Goddess of Beauty's tears, shed over the death of another one of her gifts to our world. I wanted to race out the back doors and venture deeper into the forest than we'd ever been allowed to go before, scream for Maman to be brought back, and wait for the Goddess of Beauty to answer me.

I gaze up at a wakening sky. The plum darkness cracks open like an egg, releasing ribbons of orange and yellow and tangerine.

"Are you up there, Beauty?" I wait to hear her voice boom down from the sky. "Were you ever there? Or are you a lie, too?"

Nothing.

A milk vendor and her cart plod along, leaving the noisy trail of clinking glasses. "Fresh pints to go with your morning pastries. Get them here!"

Her calls hasten me forward. Last time I sneaked out, the streets were empty.

Black mourning-lanterns drift about, casting their shadowy light over the cobblestones. Portraits of the departed Queen Celeste hang from banners and populate nearby avenue boards. The sight of her beautiful face wrenches my heart. How upset she'd be about what has happened, her warnings about Sophia now prophetic. Blimps snake through tall towers and post-balloons zip around their large frames. Their bulbous underbellies leave behind swaths of darkness and shadows.

A woman exits a shop.

My heart beats against my rib cage.

A warning. A sign to turn back.

I duck into a nearby alley, waiting for her to pass. She slows down and stops to look in my direction. She wears a peculiar mask that curves around all the edges of her face, neck, and chest, reminding me of a gilded mold for a bust or statue. The moonlight exposes its delicate iron edges and intricate etchings.

I press myself farther into the shadows.

The noise of the milk vendor pulls her attention. She abandons her curiosity about me and runs off.

I should go back to the boardinghouse, but I count to twenty, then leave my hiding spot, and press on. I turn onto the Imperial Mile that stretches from Metairie's royal mansions and empties out at one of the island clusters' many bridges. Gauzy arch-lanterns scatter strips of light like bars of gold. I've memorized each street and avenue and alley near the boardinghouse under Rémy's guidance and his expert maps. *You must know how to get out of here without me,* he'd said right after we'd first arrived. *If anything should happen, I need to know that you'll be able to navigate.*

The avenue boards don't even shimmer at this time of the morning, my lonely presence not strong enough to animate them. Orléans's most famous singer stares back at me with bright eyes and a frozen grin and rich light brown skin like hazelnut butter. The shops wear CLOSED signs and burned-out night-lanterns float over their doors like stormy, ominous clouds. In a few hours, these avenues will bloat with bodies.

I hook a right down the street that ends with a perfume shop. A trio of eccentric-pink flowers glows in the front windows. Almost there.

"Lost, dearie?" a voice hisses.

I whip around. Red eyes flash at me from beneath a hood. The Gris woman bares her teeth, yellowed and crooked and meant to be a smile, but it looks more like a threat.

"No," I say, steadying my voice.

The woman's shriveled gray skin catches the moonlight. "Any leas to spare?"

"Sorry, I don't have anything."

"You look like you have spintria. I'll take that, too."

I wish I did have something for her. I used to have a pocket full of beauty tokens and possess enough bags of spintria to easily fill a thousand safes. But her words are a surprise. We were told many of the Gris choose to remain that way, the madness pushing them to the edge, erasing any desires to pull themselves up and earn enough spintria to join regular society.

"I have nothing," I say, rushing ahead, but she follows, muttering nonsense. Fear crawls over my skin. I remember the first Gris woman I ever saw. My sisters and I had just turned thirteen, and the older girls were practicing using their arcana in the lesson rooms. Hana and I sneaked into the Aura chambers and hid beneath the treatment tables when women as gray as a thunderstruck sky were marched in. We pressed our faces against lace tableskirts as the women were laid over us, their screams quelled with mouth bandages. The tussling melody of their fighting bodies was stamped out with thick leather straps pinning them down as vial after vial of Belle elixir was administered in an attempt to calm them.

"Only spiders come out this early," she says.

"Leave me alone," I whisper hard.

"Out past curfew," she screeches and wags a crooked finger at me.

"Go away." I try to dodge past her. Panic races through my veins like it's replaced the arcana.

She slaps me and knocks my mask askew.

I scramble to fix it and swallow the cry of shock and pain clawing its way up my throat.

"I know you. I've seen you before."

The heavy stomp of soldiers' boots echoes in the morning quiet.

She grabs my wrist, digging hooked fingernails into my skin. "You're the one they're looking for."

"I don't know what you're talking about." My heart speeds up.

Her throaty chuckle becomes a wheeze. "Who are you fooling?" She points her other finger at me as I jerk away. "Not me, that's who." Her eyes narrow. "Guards! Guards!" she shouts. "I shall be rewarded. The newsies told us we could change our stars if we made sure to pay attention for the fugitives. I didn't believe them. They tell so many lies. But now, it's true."

Sweat pours down my back despite the chilly air. I shove her, but her grip tightens. We crash into a window box of cold-season flowers. The arcana almost hiss beneath my skin. An instinctual reminder. I tug at the fibers of the holly plant, forcing them to grow like hair. The roots burst through the wooden sides of the box and tumble along the cobblestoned street. They coil around the woman's arms and legs, yanking her away from me. Her red glare burns into me and she screams.

I force the leaves to grow and cover her mouth, silencing her protests. She thrashes until she clobbers her head against the wall and loses consciousness.

My heart plummets. What have I done?

I touch her face. Cold. Clammy.

The noise of the soldiers grows louder. They run in our direction.

She wouldn't stop, I tell myself.

I had to.

Is she dead?

The sound of my pulse thrums in my ears. I dart left off the Imperial Mile and run the rest of the way down the avenue. Only a single shop boasts a morning-lantern over its glass windows—a signal that it is open for business. Glittering rose-colored lanterns bear apothecary symbols—a snake curled around a mortar and pestle. The wind bats them like balloons.

Nerves flutter like tiny wings inside my chest. Maybe it's from being recognized. Maybe it's from using the arcana. Maybe it's from interacting with a Gris person up close for the first time. Maybe it's from hurting someone.

I gaze through a gold-trimmed window. Three apothecary bulbs sway and glow in shades of ocean blue and emerald green. Spiderwebs climb over them and glisten in the light. Day-lanterns cruise about the store. The walls are alive with color and hold endless shelves of glass containers that twinkle like bottled stars. A beautiful sign hangs above the doorway, and in cursive lettering announces: CLAIBORNE'S APOTHECARY.

I glance behind me at the now empty street before ducking inside. The scent of a crackling fire and medicinal pastilles meets my nose. The large room has three stories of mahogany cabinets separated by curled iron balconies and sets of spiraled staircases. Bottles wear handwritten labels and lea prices. I recognize many by sight—foxglove, belladonna, poppy, bay laurel. Others contain blue-glass poison bottles, bei powder, wafers, metal instruments— saws, scissors, knives, lancets—and patent medicines boasting cures for fever, lumps, and other illnesses.

Mr. Claiborne, portly and close to losing his eyesight, pops out from behind a curtain. His light brown skin is covered with freckles and moles, and I wonder why he chose to have so many. "Is that you, little flower?" he says. The sound of his voice puts me at ease.

"What if I said no?" I reply.

"I would say that someone was walking around in your skin. There's a natural perfume you have. Different than ours. You might want to mask it with pomander beads. Le Nez should be releasing their new year's scents soon. If you don't, you could be easily caught by a soldier with a keen nose." His mouth lifts with a smile. "But not to worry, I have several new formulas if you care to take a look."

"You could've turned me in days ago," I say.

"Why would I do that?"

"The reward," I counter, taking off the mask.

"I'm in no need of leas. My father left me a boon and this shop. What I needed was a challenge—and you've provided it. This is a once-in-a-lifetime type of exploration. Furthermore, my wife—if awake—would have none of it. She's longed to spend more time with Belles. Always been fascinated by your kind. I think every person in this world believes at one point or another that they'd love to switch places with you all."

"Only because they don't know the truth."

"What is the truth anymore? With the papers profiting from lies and people scrambling to outdo one another. The truth is whatever you say it is." He turns and whistles. His teacup peacock struts along the counter and places gold lea coins on a set of scales. "Good work, Sona. Well done," Claiborne praises.

I roll up my sleeve before he asks me to. "You need to dust off your window bulbs. They're full of cobwebs."

"Spiders are always welcome here," he says. "Now . . . on to the reason for your visit." He rummages through cabinets beneath the counter, retrieving a small wooden case. He opens it and exposes a set of gleaming needles. "I have some not-great news for you, little flower. I'm loving this puzzle but finding it difficult to crack."

I sigh with disappointment.

"Well, rather . . . a challenge to get precise, and I require precision above all else. The items in my apothecary contain promises, and I want this tonic to fulfill your wishes. I've mixed nightshade and hemlock, even a bit of strychnine extract, with your blood, and found our elixir continues to be unstable. Too little of my tonic and it does nothing to the arcana proteins in your blood. Too much and it kills them and any other healthy ones around it."

"What should we do?" I try to keep the desperation out of my voice as part of my plan becomes a post-balloon set off in the wrong direction, unable to be caught and re-sent.

"Let me show you the conundrum first." He fixes a monocle to his left eye, then takes an optic-scope from a nearby shelf. The apparatus resembles a large beauty-scope—a slender end to gaze through and its opposite stretching out like a horn plugged with glass. "Ready?"

I nod.

He pushes a needle into the crook of my arm and draws a vial of blood, adds a few drops of it to a sliver of glass, and slips it into the base of the optic-scope.

"Look into the oculus," he directs.

I press my eye to the slender tip. My blood. The blood Arabella said had the strength to grow the next generation of Belles. "It looks like a glittering net holding rose petals."

"Quite the poet you are," he replies. "Those oblong-shaped objects—the petals, you call them—are what make up your blood.

The net is your arcana. If you were to look at mine, the threads wouldn't glow. That is your gift from the Goddess."

"A curse."

He chortles. "I suppose now it is one." He uncorks a small bottle and uses a metal dropper to draw out its contents. "Now pay careful attention. One pearl-size bead or so..." He squeezes the top, and a fat drop slides onto the glass, mixing with the blood. The net of arcana threads hardens like bone, then shatters into pieces.

I gasp.

"Keep watching. A little more..." He adds a half drop, and the red circles shrivel and darken like raisins. "Too much of this and someone could die." He looks up and taps the oculus to get my attention. "You have to be very, very careful, my flower."

His warning wraps around me and squeezes tight.

He pats my hand. "I will package it with specific instructions while you go and visit my wife."

"Has she woken?" I ask while glancing into the oculus one more time. Now, the red circles resemble black pebbles.

"Only briefly. But I'm certain she will regain her wakefulness soon. She falls into those deep fits of sleep from time to time. I have to get her balanced and my patent medicines do that. Me and my trusty assistant Sona here." He ruffles the peacock's tiny feathers. "We'll work it out. When she does wake for a longer spell of time, she'll be happy to see her beauty maintained. I only have you do this for her benefit, you see. I don't care how she looks, as long as she gets well."

"I understand."

"But it'll keep her invigorated to recover fully and maybe avoid the things that put her in these sleeping spells to begin with."

I nod at him.

"Sona, will you lead our guest like a good host?" He sets the peacock on the floor and lifts the curtain separating the front of the shop from the back. "Don't mind the mess, little flower. I've been busier than usual."

The little bird trots forward down the long hallway. Night-lanterns bathe her in soft light, catching the rich blues of her tail. I follow, stepping into a world of cupboards lined with bottles of every shape and size, liquids the color of honey, amber, and licorice; bulb-shaped vials and vases of curious construction; and shelves featuring flasks of pickled items, delicate glass instruments, and piles of drying herbs.

We climb a winding staircase up to the second floor. Healing-lanterns bob and weave through the room, scattering balls of cerulean-tinted light. Madam Claiborne's long frame swallows a too-small bed. Her arms and legs hang off of it like dead branches discarded by trees as the windy season comes to an end, and her skin struggles to hold on to the alabaster color I gave her two days ago. The gray pushes through, and her veins resemble threadbare yarn ready to unravel. Stick-straight hair cascades over her chest like spools of midnight, and she has the beautiful curves of an hourglass. Thick, sinewy, and full.

I made her look like a blend of Hana and Valerie. My heart squeezes at the thought of what they both might be going through; what all my other sisters must be experiencing. The newsreels report that those from my generation are being held hostage. Hana in the Glass Isles and Valerie at Maison Rouge and Padma in the Bay of Silk. An angry knot coils tight in my chest, the desire to rescue them competing with the need to find Princess Charlotte.

The handmade beauty caisse Mr. Claiborne made for me rests on the nightstand beside mourning tablets for Queen Celeste.

Belle-products sit on tiered trays—miniature skin-paste pots and rouge-sticks and bei powder. Shiny rods lie on a velveteen cushion like cylinders of silver and gold.

I run my fingers over them, then hover above her bed.

"Madam Claiborne," I say. "It's Camille. Can you hear me?"

Her chest moves up and down in a soft rhythm. It makes me think of Charlotte—the memory of her body jerking and the sounds of her cough. I try to hold it in my heart like a precious jewel that I never want to lose. She's out there somewhere.

I sprinkle the bei powder over Madam Claiborne's arms. I close my eyes. The arcana meet my command. I touch her again and think of Queen Celeste. I deepen her coloring to match the departed queen's luscious black skin and add a rich gloss to her dark hair.

Mr. Claiborne enters the room. "She'll love this look you've given her." He gazes down at her. "Thank you."

"You are helping me, remember? This is the least I could do," I reply.

He holds up a velvet pouch. "It's ready. As much as it will be."

My heart lifts with relief.

"Now, little flower, this tonic is essentially a poison." He places it in my hand. "Are you sure you still want this? You weren't completely honest about why you wanted it in the first place."

"I need to know that if I'm ever captured, I can't be used. That I can kill the arcana in my blood."

His jaw clenches, but he nods. "In the Matrand Dynasty during periods of unrest, powerful houses had small armies to guard their land, and many were given tiny poison pellets to ingest if taken prisoner. Information required protection at all costs." He closes my hand around the pouch. "But please only use it if you must.

23

I'd love to see you again when all of this is over, and I know my wife would like to properly meet you under other circumstances."

I look down, staring at the swollen veins beneath my skin, pulsing like green serpents as the arcana proteins rush through my bloodstream. I think about all the things that they can do: make others beautiful, grow Belles, and now, change me.

If all goes well, I'll never be taken or used, never have to ingest his poison, never have to take this risk, but I somehow feel comforted as I slip the vial into my pocket.

The weight of it contains the promise of freedom.

3

I make my way back to the boardinghouse through a wakening city. The aurous glow of Metairie's gilt-lanterns freckle the salt-white buildings with golden leaves as they're lit for the morning. The port bells ring, and the first ships move into the harbor.

Carriages start to fill the avenues and lanes. Many empty themselves of well-dressed passengers. Women parade about in billowing gowns made of fur and wool, wearing headdresses and holding all manner of objects for sale. Men wear frock coats with tails that drag along the snow-dusted streets. Heat-lanterns are miniature suns following behind people. Some disappear into glamorous shops and others stop at sweets pavilions offering cold-season treats: spiced teacakes, chrysanthemum-shaped marzipan, snowmelon meringues, hot beignets piled high with sugar, and bourbon tarts. Tiny wisps of steam trail hot mugs of molten caramel and chocolate.

Passersby wear grim expressions, their lips pursed, brows furrowed, as imperial soldiers swarm the crowds, stopping to interrogate people at random. They rustle up merchants and shoo away Gris beggars. Their heavy footsteps create a terrifying melody, and their black armor glistens beneath the cold blue market-lantern light, severe as a murder of crows. Sophia has deployed her entire arsenal to find us.

I lingered too long at the apothecary. I hurry past vendors shouting slogans through slender brass trumpets.

"The Spice Isles grieve. Get the best mourning cameos of Her Majesty Queen Celeste."

"Vivant scarves that change color—silk, cotton, wool, even velvet. Only sold here!"

"Get your very own replica of Queen Celeste's mortuary tablets for your family altar."

"Invisible post-balloons—undetectable for the utmost privacy. Leas-back insurance guarantee. We have the best price."

I adjust the mask on my face. Sweat soaks through the lace and velvet.

A trio of guards steps into my path.

I avoid them, making a sharp left into the seedier areas of the market—the part Rémy warned us to avoid. Gris women and men hold signs begging for food, leas coins, and spintria. Others with skin nearing gray and hair poking like straw out of their hats skulk about toting tattered baskets and peddling shoddy wares. Shopkeepers and stall owners chase them away to make the passageways clear for customers.

"Make way for the Orléans Press Corps," someone yells. "The morning reports are in!"

Newsies swarm the market like the rush of snow flurries that have started to fall. They thrust their papers about, the animated ink scrambling to hold on to their headlines, and their screams assault my ears.

"From the *Orléansian Times*," one shouts. "Must be indoors at three hours after sunset! Imperial curfew moved up until dangerous fugitives caught!"

"The *Daily Spice Sentinel* states if the poor can be beautiful, what's the point?! Beauty lobbyists petition new queen for spintria increase," another hollers.

I press my hands to the sides of my head as I rush through the throng of bodies but can't block out their voice-trumpets.

"The *Trianon Tribune* first to report. New imperial law decree straight from the Minister of Law and Her Majesty. Any person caught with beauty work that mirrors the looks of the criminals will be fined and jailed."

"The *Imperial Inquirer* is holding the most lucrative kingdomwide lottery," one boasts. "Place your bets! Guess the date when the fugitive Belles will be caught. Pot is up to twenty thousand spintria for the most accurate prediction. A bonus of five thousand for location of capture."

"The *Chrysanthemum Chronicle* has the exclusive—Queen Sophia's wedding to Minister of the Seas' youngest son, Auguste Fabry, will take place on the first warm day of the new year!"

The sound of his name is a punch to the chest.

I stop. Bodies shove into me.

"Move out of the way," one complains.

"Keep going!" another says.

"No standing here," a third barks.

Memories of Auguste—the clever smile in his eyes, the way his too-long hair always escaped the knot he put it in, the taste of his lips—flood through my arms and legs and stomach, creating a circle around my heart where the warmth of it all hardens like glass ready to shatter.

I remember his touch. I hear him whisper my name. I can almost see him standing there before me in the masses: shoulders arrogant and pulled back, the pitch of his voice full of confidence, and everyone turning to listen to every word he has to say.

The thoughts fill me with rage.

"Get away from my stall," a cardamom merchant shrieks, startling me. "You're blocking customers." She thumps a porcelain spice scoop on my shoulder, and her sharp voice stamps out Auguste's image like a candle extinguished.

I step back into the crowd. A second wave of newsies gluts the market.

"We've got Her Majesty's favorite paper, the *Herald of Orléans*. In eight days on the first day of our new year, the queen is to present the body of her beloved sister, Princess Charlotte, before the court and the people of Orléans. It will signal the start of her Coronation and Ascension celebration. The deceased princess will lie in honor and remembrance."

My heart all but stops. But Charlotte isn't dead. What body will she present? A look-alike? How will she forge the identification ink on Charlotte's neck? Or did Sophia find her before I could, and kill her?

No. I refuse to believe that. This is just one of Sophia's games. Still, dread rattles me. We have to leave right now and find Charlotte before this lie becomes truth.

I hurry down the street where Pruzan's Boardinghouse sits. This news bubbles in my chest, ready to spill out. A blimp skates over my head with fluttering silkscreen banners that hold portraits of my sisters' faces as well as my own and Rémy's. They sparkle and flash like lightning trapped on parchment, the sky candles creating bright pictures even in the daylight.

Soldiers choke all the alleys. "Out of the way!" they shout.

"There's been a sighting of the fugitives!" someone hollers.

My stomach plummets. I push through the bodies and sprint up the creaking staircase into the boardinghouse. Other boarders dart to their rooms as the noise of the soldiers grows louder. I leap up the stairs two at a time to the second floor and rush into our room.

"They're everywhere," I whisper, yanking off my mask. "They know we're here!"

Rémy pulls me inside and presses a finger to his mouth, signaling me to be silent. He goes to the window, glancing out at the street below.

Heavy footsteps reverberate through the house.

"We have to get out of here." Edel scrambles to pack our things into satchels.

"How did they find us?" Amber asks.

"I don't know. Maybe the housemistress reported us," Rémy says. "Hurry."

I tie my waist-sash around me and tuck the sleepy teacup dragons into it. Shouts echo through the walls.

"Eye-films in and mask on, Amber," Edel directs.

I fumble to put mine back on, my fingers shaky with nerves.

Rémy touches my shoulder and nods, his quiet confidence a temporary balm.

Amber jams in her eye-films. "I can't see anything."

"Blink and they'll settle," Edel replies.

Amber struggles to tie on her mask, her eyes watery, her

fingers fumbling. The ribbons rip as she pulls them too tight, but there's no time for me to help her before we're slipping into the hall behind Rémy.

"All boarders are summoned to the common room," a voice commands.

"We'll leave through the kitchens," Rémy whispers. "Pull your hoods tight."

The boarders swarm the space with confusion and chaos, allowing us cover to sneak down a back set of stairs. My heart thumps with each step I take. Soldiers rummage through rooms, flipping up beds and snatching open closet doors.

"Any of you found to be harboring fugitives will face the maximum punishment allowed by the Courts of Justice," a soldier barks. "That's fifteen days in a starvation box. The Minister of Justice will not be lenient."

We ease into the kitchen.

A soldier steps out of the pantry. "And just where do you think you're going?"

Rémy shoves straight through, knocking him to the ground. Another soldier appears in the doorway behind us. I grab the nearest cast-iron skillet and hit him on the head. He crashes into the table.

"Run!" Rémy yells.

Edel pushes through the back door first.

I stumble out with Rémy at my side. We duck behind a carriage just as a scream cuts through the air.

Amber.

Instinctively, I turn back toward her, toward my sister, toward my best friend. She thrashes about in the arms of two soldiers, writhing in their grip.

"We've got one of them!" a soldier hollers. "The others must be nearby!"

The world slows around me.

Amber's wails pierce the air; each one hits me like the stab of a knife.

I start to go to her. Rémy grabs me by the waist. "We have to leave. We've already been seen. The longer we linger, the more of them there will be."

"No." I wrestle with his tight grip. "We can't."

"Camille, he's right. We'll all be captured. And they want you the most." Edel squeezes my chin, forcing me to look at her. "We can't help her right now. If we're taken, too, it's over. We can't find Charlotte. We can't fix all of this. We can't do anything."

Tears storm down my cheeks.

"We'll find a way to get her back."

Edel tugs me forward, toward the dark shadows of the alley, as the guards drag Amber away and she disappears, like a post-balloon snatched by its ribbons.

4

We weave through Metairie's network of markets, moving as far away from the boardinghouse as possible. My heart swells with heaviness. What will Sophia do to Amber? Will she torture her? How bad will it be?

"We need to go back for her," I whisper to Edel. "We should follow them and see where they take her."

"She lingered behind us," she replies. "I don't understand why she'd do that."

"What do you mean?" I ask. "She was struggling to get her mask on."

Rémy shushes us. "Not out in the open. Too risky. Whatever happened, we'll discuss it later."

I turn to him. "Where are we going?"

"To a place where people rarely ask questions." He pulls his hood tighter, reassembles his mask around his face, and leads the way forward through the crowd. We venture deep inside, headed for its edges, where the city lanterns darken from blues to plums. The cobblestones trail off. Stalls and shops are pitched at strange and rather worrying angles, each having sunk a little too far into the muddied ground. Signs advertise beauty-scopes featuring nude men and women, products claiming to steal another's beauty, and tonics with the promise of love, money, and fame.

"Prisms for good fortune when the rainy season returns. Trap a rainbow, get good luck from the God of Luck," a vendor says.

"Wish dolls sold here. Best in the marketplace!" another shouts through a voice-trumpet. "Best in all of the Spice Isles. Exact your revenge. Or make your dreams come true. My pins will unlock it all. I've collected the metal myself from the Goddess of Death's caves!"

"Care to know your future?" A masked woman cuts off my stride.

I almost slam into her. Glass beads dot the veil she wears, and her mask is etched with a curious pink flower. She lifts it and whispers, "A new year and a new moon is coming. The threads of danger slowly thickening. You should draw from my cards." She fans them out, exposing their hand-drawn faces.

I flinch. Spiderwebs stretch across them. Why does it seem like spiders are following me everywhere this morning?

"No, thank you," I say, sidestepping her to keep up with Rémy and Edel.

"There is anger around you. I can lift it," she calls out behind us. "Come back."

No one can get rid of this fiery cloud.

Rémy heads for a salon that can't make up its mind if it's a teahouse, a shop, or a limestone mansion. A tiny door holds a porthole-shaped window and red sill-lanterns sit behind two pairs of windows like glowing eyes. The lip-shaped sign RED VELVET SALON flaps from a gust of wind.

"Is this..." I start to say.

Rémy clears his throat and doesn't meet my eyes. "A place where no one will search for us. And if they did, the soldiers would be easily distracted."

"Smart," Edel says, patting him on the shoulder. "I knew you were good for something."

He stiffens. "Wait here." He pulls his mask tight and vanishes up the stairs.

A nervous tremor pulses through me. I look around, alert with adrenaline. Women push a variety of pavilion carts advertising the strongest bourbon pies and the savoriest meat skewers and the perfect ale to warm one's belly. Men and women stumble in and out of the buildings along the street—some holding bloated purses ready to gamble in the card salons, and others looking for love and companionship. Many readjust their masks to cover garish makeup and hold on to their face embellishments, the trend of jewel-embedded skin very popular here. Gris beggars rush to every available person asking for spare leas and spintria.

"We need to go look for her," I repeat.

"No," Edel spits back. "I'm not risking my life for Amber."

"She's your sister!"

"She's *your* sister." Edel crosses her arms over her chest. "As far as I'm concerned, she's changed."

A few newsies parade through with their voice-trumpets. Their shouts hit us in heavy waves.

"Buy the *Daily Orléansian* for exclusive first pictures of construction on Queen Sophia's new prison being built in the middle of the Royal Harbor," one cries out.

"Power of Belle blood discovered."

Edel and I freeze and lock eyes.

"Royal scientists give first interviews about the breakthrough to the queen's favorite newspaper, the *National*." The newsie waves around a reel. "Watch it now."

"Disgraced Guardian of the Belles, Madam Ana Maria Lange Du Barry missing. Report just released via the *Orléansian Times*."

The sound of Du Barry's name sends a shudder through me. I step forward to buy the paper, but Edel grabs my arm and shakes her head. I stand frozen beside her as the newsies' headlines hit us one after the other. "Did you hear that? About Du Barry?"

"She could be found at the bottom of the Rose Bayou for all I care." Edel points up. Blimps skate overhead with silkscreen banners holding our pictures. No longer Amber's portrait. The leas reward has doubled.

The sight of it makes my heart somersault.

It happened so fast.

"We should buy the papers, then go back for Amber. I know you and she have never been the closest, but she—"

"I saw what she did," Edel says.

"What?"

"A leaked newsreel circulated after Sophia's lady-of-honor Claudine died. I watched that arcana challenge Sophia made the two of you participate in at her dinner party. The tattlers had it until Sophia threatened to shut down the press and made them come before the Minister of News."

The memory of that night hits me in waves:

Claudine's vacant eyes.

Claudine's slack mouth.

Claudine's dead body.

"I saw how she acted. She wouldn't stop. She was the same old Amber. Always needing to win. You tried to stop her. I saw the pain on your face."

My heartbeat quickens with each accusation Edel lobs at Amber. I'm unable to defend her.

A vendor stops to stare at us. "Care for a bourbon pie?"

Edel runs her off.

We step a little away from the Red Velvet Salon staircase.

"We were both at fault. I should have refused," I whisper to her.

"She should've helped you both get out of that game. But Amber has always, *always* had to win above all else." Edel balls her hands into fists. "The one with the best marks from Du Barry. The one who got the first pick of dresses and desserts. The one who had to go first with every group lesson given to us. I thought it was just a bad habit from when we were little. Her maman spoiled her. I thought she'd grow out of it—"

"She—"

"No excuses. The rest of our sisters don't behave like that. You don't do that."

"Sophia tortured her during her time as favorite. You can't—"

"I don't trust her anymore."

Another blimp crests overhead, bathing us in a dark shadow.

Rémy reappears at the top of the entrance stairs. Edel rushes up toward him, leaving me and our conversation behind.

I climb the stairs and step through the door. The space reminds me of the candy houses we'd built as little girls to celebrate the new year and call sweetness from the God of the Ground. Red-and-gold-papered walls hug us inside a decadent living room that looks up to five wraparound floors. Blush-pink lanterns putter about, bathing each level in pale shades of light. Perfume blimps squirt rose water. Velvet chaises and tufted chairs hold glamorous powdered and primped women and men.

We follow Rémy to a hall that smells like dried flowers and clove smoke, then up a flight of stairs and down another hall. My body is tense, my nerves coiled up like a spring. My argument with Edel replays over and over again in my head. Her words—"*I don't trust her anymore*"—drumming through me like discordant music on a stringed misen.

He opens a door and ushers us inside. Night-lanterns float through a pleasant bedroom. Two beds are pushed against opposite walls. A gold-striped couch and matching armchair sit beside the solitary window. Mirrors hang above a modest vanity.

"I'm going to go buy the most recent papers and get a sense of where the guards are," Rémy says as he leaves the room.

I let the teacup dragons out of my pouch. They stretch their tiny wings, then hiss and tiptoe through the room, sniffing every object in their path. I call out the names Amber gave them—Feuille for the green, Poivre for the red, Or for the gold, Eau for the blue, and Fantôme for the white.

Edel flits them away as they circle her, begging for attention. "We were tracked. Had to have been," she mumbles angrily.

"I think it's my fault," I say with a shrug. "I've been sneaking out."

"What? Where have you been going?" Edel demands.

I drop my hand in my dress pocket, the raised glass grooves of the poison bottle finding my fingers. I almost show it to her, but a twinge in my stomach makes me bury the secret.

"I couldn't take being stuck in that tiny room all the time. I needed air—some space to think," I lie. "Maybe I was followed?"

"That's too easy." Edel brushes her hand along one of the bed frames, then sits. "They would've just arrested you on the spot. Why follow you to the boardinghouse? Why interrogate all the boarders and do a search?"

The green teacup dragon, Feuille, climbs into my lap and curls into a tiny ball. "Maybe one of us was spotted while running errands, but they didn't know which boardinghouse we'd returned to."

"Someone like Amber?" Edel asks, arching an eyebrow.

I take a deep breath. "What do you think she did, exactly?"

Edel snaps upright. "Look! I know you've always loved her more than you love the rest of us."

"I have not. You're all my sisters." I set Feuille on the floor and rush to sit at Edel's side. I touch her, and she yanks away.

"We all felt it. Hana, Valerie, Padma, and me. It was always the two of you. . . ." She purses her lips. "You can't see it. Or maybe you don't want to see it. But she's hiding something . . . I know it."

The door snaps open. Rémy returns with an armful of newspapers and the latest newsreel.

Edel stands and turns to Rémy. "What are the papers saying?"

"Find the room's télétrope," Rémy says.

Edel riffles through the nearest bureau and retrieves a dusty télétrope. She opens the machine's bottom compartment, fishes out a wobbly matchstick, and lights the tea candle in its base.

I take one of the papers from Rémy's stack. Poivre tries to nibble its edges, but I wrestle it from the teacup's tiny fangs, his mouth warm with the promise of fire.

I think of Amber. Edel's words linger, sinking into my skin. A whisper echoes inside me: *What does my and Amber's closeness have to do with her not trusting Amber?*

A knot squeezes in my throat, thickening with regret and threatening to choke me.

Edel takes the film from Rémy and inserts it into the télétrope. "Close the curtains, and blow out the night-lanterns."

Rémy extinguishes them. I bunch the curtains closed. The tea-cup dragons squeak and flutter about, protesting the dark until the newsreel projects on the wall. An image of Sophia appears. She's seated on her throne surrounded by her teacup animals—her monkey, Singe, at her shoulder, her elephant, Zo, in her lap, and a small bunny on her scepter. Her grating voice drifts through the télétrope's tiny voice-box. "The time of the Belles is over. Orléans has been at the mercy of their powers for too long. They've been able to lord it over us. But never again, now that I am queen."

Edel paces.

My cheeks warm as if the arcana are waking up. "We've lorded it over them? No! They beg for our help. They work us until we're sick. Du Barry was the one who profited—not us!"

Sophia continues: "We will take back control. I will regulate the entire beauty system—it will cater to all our needs when we're at the very heart of it. Those who don't cooperate will meet a deadly fate. The Fugitive Belle Act has just passed without a single protest vote in my new cabinet. I'm going to round up all the runaway Belles. They will live in my prison, the Everlasting Rose. They will be raised and trained there, and prepared for their duties to our great country. They're dangerous and aggressive, and need to be watched and controlled for their own benefit. My loyal subjects, the reward for bringing me Edel Beauregard has risen from eight hundred fifty thousand leas to one million leas."

Edel gasps.

"And anyone who brings me Camille Beauregard, my disgraced favorite, the Belle who killed two of my most beloveds: Lady Claudine, Duchesse de Bissay, and"—her voice breaks in mock-upset—"and my best friend, my sister, Princess Charlotte . . ."

"What?" I cry.

Tears fall down her cheeks as the people in the crowd before her shout in agreement. My pulse is a throbbing drum, counting down the moments of this newsreel like racing sand in an hourglass.

"Yes, it has been confirmed that she experimented on my sister's weak body and stopped her heart," Sophia says. "And she *will* be punished. Two million leas for anyone who brings her to me. And if she is delivered by the time of Princess Charlotte's viewing and the coronation, I'll give you your own small palace. My mother's favorite summer one on the Isle of Minnate. You have seven days. An auspicious number revered by the Goddess of Love." She smiles, showing the perfect sliver of teeth. "My dearly beloved mother was a passive queen. I will not be."

The newsreel ends. The sound of its tail flapping cuts through the silent room. I hear my own heartbeat thrumming and each of the deep breaths Edel and Rémy take. I let out a guttural scream. Rémy rushes to me, clamping his hand over my mouth.

I snatch away from him. "Don't."

"People can hear—"

"I know . . . I know . . ."

"There's more." Rémy reads from one of the papers. "After the Coronation and Ascension ceremony, no sitting queen can be deposed or challenged according to imperial law."

A tense bubble engulfs us, its edges charged, ready to smother all three of us.

He opens another paper, the *Orléansian Times*. A two-page spread showcases a massive structure floating in the middle of the Royal Harbor.

The headline reads: QUEEN SOP HIA'S NEWEST ENDEAVOR—THE EVERLASTING ROSE—HALF-COM P LETE.

The animated portrait of a circular building flickers like a chandelier-lantern the size of Trianon's Coliseum. The picture flashes and takes onlookers on a tour. Outer window bars twist in the shape of Belle-roses. Our older sister, Ivy, stands on an enclosed lattice balcony spanning the structure's entire circumference. Half her face is masked; the other battered. Pale pink sill-lanterns bathe her cheeks in soft light. Her falling tears glow; she looks trapped in the gilded filigree of a jewelry box. The portrait pans out, showing a thorny garden growing around a great tower in the center where Sophia waves and blows kisses.

"A cage for us. Like rabid animals," Edel says.

My eyes scan the article:

The construction of the Everlasting Rose, affectionately named after the eternal "everlasting" roses that bloomed in the Goddess of Beauty's garden, has been under way day and night, with labor teams toiling without pause. Located on the edge of the Isle of Chalmette, its glow can be spotted from the rooftops of Trianon's limestone mansions. Newsboats sit in the Royal Harbor reporting on every moment of construction and every coming and going of visitors to the site. The newly titled Minister of Belles, Georgiana Fabry, said, "We'll be opening the building soon. The citizens of Orléans will be able to enter the world of the Belles. No more secrecy. We're starting new traditions."

The Rose, as it's been nicknamed, will replace Maison Rouge as the locale where all Belles will be trained to serve Orléans. Tours of the building are slated to begin after the Coronation and Ascension of Queen

Sophia. Tickets will go on sale during the auspicious festivities. Citizens will be able to reach the structure via special rose-coaches and lavish wire carriages currently being built.

I shove the paper away. "This is where they're going to take Amber. She's going to be tortured. We have to help her."

"And risk all of us getting locked in that prison?" Edel snaps. "No, I won't do it."

"Edel—"

"Stop arguing," Rémy says. "And look at this last paper."

It's one I've never seen before. The pages are black as night and the ink white as clouds. The articles and headlines appear and disappear depending on where I touch it. The border contains webs holding beautiful seedlings, unfurling and blossoming into tiny teardrop leaves, curls of stems, and oval petals in soft lavenders and magentas and pinks. I remember these from the solarium at Maison Rouge.

Cleome flowers. Maman's favorite.

I thumb the top.

"What is it?" Edel peers down over my shoulder.

"The *Spider's Web*. An underground paper," Rémy replies. "The publication the Minister of News doesn't regulate because he doesn't know it exists."

"How'd you get it?" Edel's eyes grow big.

"They circulate in this part of the city. I admit, I've never seen or read an issue before. I've only heard about it. I didn't think they were real. The Minister of War taught us that people don't resist." Rémy removes the tea candle from the télétrope and waves it over the paper. "The newsie said to hold the light over it and the ink will settle and sharpen."

The letters rise on the black parchment like drizzles of cream in steaming hot coffee. The headlines sparkle and snap like whips.

QUEEN SOPHIA IN TALKS TO START RANKING BEAUTY
WORK KINGDOM WIDE, USING THE MEASURE TO ALLOCATE
LAND, JOBS, TITLES, AND FAVOR WITH THE MONARCH

DON'T BELIEVE THE MORBID DEATH LIES!
PRINCESS CHARLOTTE IN HIDING DESPITE
FALSE REPORTS FROM PALACE OFFICIALS

DECEASED QUEEN'S PARTNER, LADY PELLETIER,
SPOTTED IN VARIOUS APOTHECARIES. PERHAPS
LOOKING FOR PRINCESS CHARLOTTE'S CURE?

AFTER UNFORTUNATE CAPTURE OF FIRST FAVORITE
AMBROSIA BEAUREGARD, QUEEN'S GUARD CONFOUNDED
ABOUT LOCATION OF OTHER FUGITIVE BELLES

IRON LADIES GATHER MORE NUMBERS AS THEY PLOT
TO END QUEEN SOPHIA'S TYRANNICAL RULE

"Who are the Iron Ladies?" I demand, anticipation rising inside my chest.

"The Resistance," Rémy replies.

5

Each time I close my eyes and try to sleep, Sophia lures me into a nightmare. She's always in a long white nightgown like a spirit that's escaped the Goddess of Death's caves, and she leads me down a twisting corridor with no end in sight. She glances back with a sly smile that reveals a hint of teeth; her pupils dilate so big her eyes are two gigantic black pools.

The dream darkness fills with smoke and ash, the world burning around me like a rose set aflame, each petal shriveling and whitening, furious at being stripped of its color and perfume. The cameos of her courtiers appear along the walls, shifting and morphing within the angry fire. The frantic pulse that lives inside her ripples out like waves, crashing into me, while the screech of her laughter pierces the silence like a thunderclap.

I wake up soaked every time.

"Can't sleep?" Rémy asks, his heavy whisper bouncing off the walls like a skipping stone across the bayou waters at home. He shifts in a high-backed chair beside the door and lights a small night-lantern, setting it adrift in the room. His rich brown skin glows when beads of light find him.

"How can you?" I sit up and pull my sweat-soaked curls into a low bun before they start to frizz. Beside me, Edel turns over and sighs in her sleep.

"I barely sleep. You know that," he replies.

I sigh. "Right."

I gaze out the window. The sky looks like it's in mourning— the dark streaks of blue mirror tears and the gashes of purple bruises. Maybe the heavens are troubled by what's happening below. "What time is it?"

"The evening star rose about two hourglasses ago. Only a few more until dawn," he says. "Want some tea? Maybe it'll help."

"Yes," I reply.

I slide out of bed.

Rémy quickly stands and turns his back to me. "Tell me you're changing next time." His shoulders tense.

The cotton sleeping-gown hugs my edges. "Yes, all right," I whisper, blushing. We're still finding the rhythm of being in small spaces together.

I slip on my traveling cloak. "I'm ready."

He inches open our door, so it doesn't groan.

We tiptoe into the hall. Shabby night-lanterns pockmarked with holes and covered in nets of dust struggle to reach the ceiling or to provide us with light.

"The kitchens are empty right now," he reports, leading me down a back set of stairs. Deep snores escape from behind nearby doors and mask the noise of our footsteps. The red sill-lanterns have been extinguished, and the ladies of the house have all gone to bed. We've only been here a few hours, but Rémy has started a detailed ledger of their movements.

Thin walls allow the wind to find its way inside. Its icy, sharp fingers send a shiver through me.

"Are you cold?" he says.

"I'm fine."

"Your teeth are chattering."

"Do you hear everything?"

"I guess you could say that. My maman used to say I could even hear the smallest mouse pee."

"That's ridiculous!" I laugh, then try to swallow it.

His face lights up like the time I saw him talking to his sisters. He lets out a deep chuckle, full-throated and from the very bottom of his stomach. It vibrates across my skin. It's the sort of laugh that makes you sit up and pay attention and wish you were always the one to laugh with him.

I think about how long I spent hating him, and blush with regret.

We arrive at the kitchen. He motions for me to wait, then ducks inside, stalks around in the dark, and reappears tugging the strings of a night-lantern.

"No creatures waiting to eat me?" I ask with a smile.

"Looks fine," he says. "And I'm shocked you stayed put."

"I guess I've learned to listen."

"Or to trust me." He leads the way and sets the night-lantern afloat. A fire burns low in the hearth. A monstrous stone stove hulks in the corner like the fire-breathing bayou bird Maman used to tell me stories about as a child. Jars of bits and bobbles and thing-amabobs clutter the shelves. Shoddy cabinets hold cracked glass panes. Dishes are stacked in perilous towers in a sink. Remnants of the cook's stew sit in a pot on the long worktable, calling out to any critters looking for a meal. A stack of night-edition newspapers blinks their headlines.

"You walk like you own the land beneath your feet." His laughter fades, but he doesn't stop smiling. "Like my sisters. I could always tell when one of them would enter the house. I knew them by the sound of their footsteps. Mirabelle, quick and light, always a little too excited. Adaliz, heavy and demanding, ready to order someone around. Odette, jumpy and timid, looking for something coming around every corner." He sighs.

"You miss them?"

"Desperately," he replies. "I'm used to being away on assignment or for training. But this feels—"

"Different," I say.

He nods.

"What do you think they're doing?"

"Getting prepared to celebrate the new year despite being worried about me," he says. "They're also anxiously checking the newspapers and watching the reels every day."

"I should've never dragged you into this," I say. "I'm sorry."

"If I recall, I got myself into it by helping you escape." He smiles.

"You could be doing so many other things right now."

"Like what?" he says as I lean back against the kitchen counter.

"Taking your sisters for a cold-season holiday in the mountains of the Gold Isles."

"Fine."

"Or off training somewhere."

"I could be doing that."

"Maybe getting married," I say, and as soon as it pops out, I want to press it back in. I don't know why I thought of it. Or I do know but push it down inside, tucking it away like the poison bottle heavy in my pocket. Always with me, but never taken out into the light. A heavy warmth blooms in my cheeks.

He scoffs. "I've never had much luck with courting. My sisters say I'm not charming enough."

"I wonder why," I tease, thinking for the smallest moment what he might be like in a relationship. Would he always be so protective? Has he ever loved someone romantically? Or been kissed? "Tell me about the Iron Ladies," I say to brush away those feelings.

"I don't know much." He shrugs. "When I was training on the Isle of Quin, there were rumors about one of the generals who'd been passed over by Queen Celeste to be the Minister of War. She disappeared—like a spider, hence the title of the paper—and wasn't seen again. She's thought to be the leader of the Iron Ladies."

Could they help us? Would they want to help us?

"Most of it always sounded like fairy tales. A whole civilization of people living away from the cities, learning to survive with the grayness, plotting and planning to change things."

"What if it is true?"

"Then, maybe they'll help. But I trust nothing that I read in the papers." He motions in the direction of the stack. "It's too easy to make things up, use parchment and ink and words to distort opinions."

"Do you trust anyone? Do you trust me?" I ask.

The question crackles between us like the fire in the hearth. Each letter of that small and complicated word an ember.

"Why do you want to know?"

"Well, you did stab me." I touch my side where his dagger pierced me only a week ago.

"For good reason. It was part of the plan."

"You could've told me about it."

"And have you ruin it?" Rémy says. "No. You didn't have confidence in me at that point. Barely even liked me. You hadn't had a chance to test me with that mirror of yours."

I press a hand to my chest. "How do you know about that?"

"I'm supposed to know about everything when it comes to you."

"I . . . don't even know what to say to that."

Rémy leans closer. "I'm not him. You don't have to hide things from me. I'm not watching you or trying to find things out only to hurt you with them."

The word *him* lands hard.

Auguste.

I bristle at the mere thought of his face.

"My mother left the mirror for me, but it was Arabella's," I whisper.

"Does it always show you the truth?"

"Yes." I fish it out from under my nightgown and show it to him.

He runs the pad of his thumb across the grooves, his hand so close to my chest that maybe he can feel my heartbeat. The perfume of his skin is different than Auguste's—almost like warm-season rain and fresh Belle-rose leaves. "It's beautiful. Will you show me how it works?"

"Soon." I take it from his grasp and tuck it back under my nightgown, the metal now warm from his touch.

He stares at me, but I don't meet his eyes. His long arm reaches over my head to rescue a plump white teapot from a hook.

"Are you skilled in the art of making tea?" I ask.

"Add leaves to boiling water." He lifts an eyebrow.

I sigh at him and roll my eyes.

His brow furrows, crinkling like the brown ridges in a molasses cookie.

"Step aside." I swat at his shoulder.

He smirks. I wash out the pot, fill it, and set it on the stovetop. He hands me a fire-stick from the hearth, and I light a flame beneath the pot's round body, then open a cabinet of tea tins. Worn labels advertise their contents—mint, chamomile, almond, lemongrass, and Belle-rose. I run my finger over the last label, remembering how many pots I'd made at the Chrysanthemum Teahouse and the palace until Bree took the process over.

I close my eyes, seeing Bree's delicate hands at work: her small frame hunched above the tiny hearth on the treatment carts, her scooping out dried leaves and making tiny mounds in tea nets before dropping them into the porcelain pots, or rolling up Belle-rose petals plucked from the solarium garden to steep in piping-hot water. The memory of her tugs at the walls I've built inside, and bring tears to my eyes.

"What's wrong?" Rémy asks.

"Just something in my eye." I turn my back to him and wipe away a tear before it falls. "It's nothing."

"All your thoughts show up on your face, Camille. You can't hide anything." He approaches the stove, his shadow looming over me.

"Everything is fine."

"Something is bothering you. I can tell." His eyes study me, pricking my skin, sharper than needles. "You keep biting your bottom lip and your left eyebrow is all twitchy. And you're scowling."

A wave of embarrassment hits me like he's seen me without my clothes on. The presence of his body feels like Auguste's did once—inviting and a little dangerous. A lump of thick, hot betrayal simmers in the pit of my stomach.

I fuss with the teapot. He puts a hand on mine to still it.

Rémy fishes for my gaze, his eyes big and brown with the tiniest bit of red pushing through. His words sink into my skin like warm water, the heat going right through muscles and tissue down to my bones.

"I must've done something. What is it? I didn't even yell at you for disappearing this morning while I was on my perimeter check. I didn't even ask you what you were doing out at that hour."

"Lucky me." I pull my hand out of his grip. It drifts into my nightgown pocket where the tiny poison bottle sits. I can't tell him about this yet. Though I desperately want to.

"I had every right to. Had a whole speech planned out."

"I need to refresh your irises," I say. "And remove that stripe from your hair. It makes you too recognizable."

His hand finds his soft, tight curls and the silver streak down the middle marking him as a soldier in the House of War. "You've been telling me this, but—"

"You're stubborn."

"I'm just not ready to let it go yet. The hair powders you gave me have been covering it for now."

"We will run out soon. I should change your skin color, too."

"Only when you tell me what's wrong."

"You'd risk becoming a Gris again?"

The teapot screeches. I remove it from the flame.

Rémy places two chipped teacups on the table. "I'm not afraid of the grayness."

"What's it like?" I ask, and remember one of Du Barry's lessons about the Gris: *The madness overtakes every part of you, itching to be free.*

"I haven't experienced it since I was a child. People say it's painful. Like a long-lasting sickness. The sweats, a headache, vomiting, and rabid, racing thoughts..."

"We would see little Gris babies, shriveled, angry, and hot from escaping their mothers' wombs. But they only stayed that way for an hourglass's worth before we'd mix Belle-rose tea into their milk and they'd endure their first transformations." I stir a spoonful of honey into each of our cups. "I've seen more Gris people in the Spice Isles than ever before."

"The House of Orléans continually expels them from the imperial island. Rounding them up to disperse, to the irritation of other powerful houses. You must be on high alert."

I think about the Gris woman who attacked me while I was on the way to see Claiborne.

"They aren't any worse than Sophia," I say. "Nothing can be."

"You will get rid of her," he says. "It'll show the world how to resist tyranny."

The image of the *Spider's Web* newspaper drifts into my head. "Du Barry only taught us how to obey."

"And it seems you've learned that lesson well," he chides, pulling a reluctant smile out of me.

"There are so many things I don't know."

"You'll learn them."

"We spent our entire lives being lied to."

"And now, you're waking up. You're lucky. Some people never do."

I turn away from him to avoid his gaze. I stare at the night edition of the *Orléansian Times*. A familiar face winks at me. The Fashion Minister. He's beneath a headline: GUSTAVE DU POLIGNAC, BELOVED FASHION MINISTER, IN THE SILK ISLES PREPARING TO PRESENT DRESSES FAVORED BY QUEEN FOR HER CORONATION AND ASCENSION.

I tear out the article, fold it, and slip it into my pocket with the poison bottle.

"What is it?" he asks.

"Nothing."

He spins me around by the waist and takes my hands. "I know when you're lying."

Our fingers are wrapped together like sweetcanes of chocolate and caramel. He doesn't look up at me, his gaze fixed on them. The firelight dances across his beautiful dark skin like the glow from the red bayou flies at home.

He leans down so our foreheads kiss. "Tell me."

"I'm formulating a plan."

"All right," he whispers.

"We will find Charlotte. We will take down Sophia," I whisper to him.

"Sophia won't go away easily, and the damage she's done will linger—"

"I will kill Sophia if I have to."

"Taking lives is hard."

"She's ruined so many."

"That may be true, but the act of it..."

"What do you think we should do?" I pull back.

"What do you want to do?" he asks.

"I want to find Charlotte. I want my sisters to be all right. I want Sophia to not be able to hurt anyone again."

He squeezes my hand.

"You don't have to kill anyone to accomplish this," he says. "It's not as easy as you think."

"I don't think any of this is *easy*. And if you believe what I want to do isn't right, then what should we do? You usually have so many opinions. So many directions for me."

"Not this time. You've got to figure it out," he says.

"I will do what I must," I say. "Whatever it takes."

6

A knock pounds the door in the morning. It startles Edel and me awake. Rémy signals for us to go into the closet.

We squeeze in. A quiver starts in my feet, traveling up my legs to my stomach and chest. I can't still myself. A landquake is erupting inside me. My heart might never find the right beat again.

Edel leans against the wall, her jaw clenched, and fists balled. "They've found us again," she mutters. "I can feel it."

"You don't know that," I reply.

But her words suffocate the small space. If there are guards at the door, how will we get away from them now? What if Rémy were taken—or hurt? How would we be able to help him from in here?

I press my ear to the door and catch three words: *morning paper delivery.*

"You can come back out," Rémy says. "It's all right."

My whole body deflates, my knees buckling, the worries sputtering out like wind. We ease out of the closet. The teacup dragons squawk and push their faces against the bars of their cage. Rémy holds the tail ribbons of a pearl-white post-balloon dragged by a plum-colored teacup dragon.

"I thought it was the papers," I say.

"So did I," he replies.

"Who's it from?" Edel asks. "No one knows we're here."

I take a piece of dried pork from our food pack and whistle. The teacup dragon dives toward me and lands on my shoulder. Rémy grabs the ribbons, breaks open the post-balloon's back, and retrieves an empty perfume bottle and a miniature porcelain jar with several sangsues in it.

A cold stone drops into my stomach. "There's no note."

"The lid is engraved." Edel crouches over my shoulder.

I squint at the tiny script, and read the word *Listen*.

I uncap the perfume atomizer. The sound of a woman's voice echoes through the room. "You only get a single chance to hear this. Pay attention."

"What's that?" Edel asks.

"Shh." I lift the bottle to my ear.

Edel and Rémy huddle closer. My heart trembles. The identity of the speaker crystallizes in my head.

Arabella.

"*Camellia and Edelweiss, meet Ryra, my teacup dragon. Please take care of her well. Listen closely. Track the headlines, though we all know they don't tell even a fraction of the story. With Sophia as queen, we cannot trust them to publish the truth unvarnished, but they furnish clues to the storm she's trying to create. There are newsies doing her bidding, spreading the things she wants everyone to believe.*

"*Sophia has taken all the generations of Belles—Ivy and her sisters, plus yours, Valerie, Padma, Hana, Amber, and the new little ones.*

*They're in the most complete wing of her new prison, the Everlasting
Rose. She's growing new Belles here at the palace. I must feed my blood
to two hundred fifty pods, with more to come. Sophia intends to start selling Belles to the highest bidder as soon as these new ones are big enough
to do beauty work.*

*"You must stay as far away as possible until I can figure out the rest
of what she's up to. Here's what I need you to do: feed a teacup dragon—
Ryra, if she's rested, or any of yours—one of the sangsues I've sent, which
hold my blood. Doing this will tether the dragon to me, so it can find me
wherever I am, and we can send messages back and forth. Send word that
you're safe. Be careful."*

The memory of Sophia's threat about building a golden auc-
tion block in Trianon or the Royal Square coils around me like
the silver chains and jeweled collars she'd use. The ones Madam
Claire looped around the throats and wrists of the other Belles at
the Chrysanthemum Teahouse.

"Who was that?" Edel asks.

"Arabella," I tell her. "She's an elder Belle. She lives at the palace and helped Rémy, Amber, and me escape."

"What does she mean *growing*? She said something about
pods." Edel must have a million questions about how this was
possible. "What is she talking about?"

The image of the clear vats in Sophia's palace nursery, the Belle
babies floating in gilded cradles, being fed Arabella's blood, takes
horrifying shape in my mind. "Belles are different from Gris," I
tell her. "We're grown . . . in vessels."

"I don't understand." Edel shakes with rage. "Babies develop
in their mothers' wombs."

"Not us. Belle babies are more like flowers in bulbs." The
words coming out of my mouth feel thick and laden with lies.

Unbelievable, even though they are the truth. This is not what Du Barry told us about our births. She said that the Goddess of Beauty sent us here in a rain of stars to be her vessels. But I've seen it with my own eyes.

I shake the bottle, waiting and wishing there was more.

"We have to go to the palace," Edel says.

"Arabella told us not to."

"So? Who put her in charge?" Edel presses. "We need to break our sisters out of prison and end this."

It's not lost on me that she had no interest in this line of thought when it was only Amber who'd been captured.

"Let's send her a message saying we're safe, as she asks, and tell her of our plan to find Charlotte. Based on my maps, I believe her to be—"

"We can't *only* chase Charlotte. She could be a spirit for all we know. Sophia's setting up a grand reveal of her body. What if she's actually dead? What if this plan of yours is doomed?"

"What if she isn't? Arabella would know if this was one of Sophia's lies. We can ask her."

"And how long will that take? Waiting around for another three days for a reply?" Edel says. "Sending messages and charting winds isn't getting us anywhere." She throws her hands in the air. "It's taking more time that we don't have. The closer we get to the Coronation and Ascension, the less opportunity to challenge Sophia. She's rushing a ceremony that should take months of planning. Tradition and rules will allow her to—"

"We can't just storm into the palace, Edel. We have to have a precise plan. Every move of it certain and calculated. I want to take Sophia down as much as you do. Maybe even more so. I want to get our sisters. But we can't afford to make any mistakes." I pull out the night-edition newspaper clipping to show Edel the head-line about the Fashion Minister. I feel the heat of Rémy's gaze, but don't look at him. "I have an idea. I want to go—"

"No!" Edel strides angrily between us. Her dress, now tattered at the bottom, catches the splinters in the wooden planks. Her anger is loose like the snap of a newsreel spinning out of control. "While you two are playing with compasses and writing letters, I'm going to do something about it."

Rémy clears his throat. "Edel, if you would simply—"

"Don't tell me what to do. Go back to staring at Camille and watching for guards!" she barks.

He flinches.

"That's unfair and rude," I say, reaching for her.

She snatches away and stalks to the door.

"Wait! Edel!" I shout. "What are you going to do?"

"Not sit around and wait for a pretty post-balloon."

She stomps out and doesn't look back.

7

Rémy and I walk through the crowded stalls near the salon in search of a vendor who sells invisible post-balloons. Two of the teacup dragons—Fantôme and Poivre—squirm in my waist-sash, attempting to peek their heads out and sniff the air; the scent of roasting meat and mulled cider mingle in this section of the Market Quartier.

"Are they still restless?" Rémy asks.

I lift my mask a little to answer him. "Yes. It's probably because I fed Fantôme the leech Arabella sent. She and Poivre seem close. Connected. They affect each other."

"Like you and Amber?"

I shrug, thinking of what might be happening to her right now. If she's all right. If she's surviving Sophia's torture. If she will ever forgive me for not coming to her rescue.

"Your mask is loose," he says, reaching around the back of my head to tighten the top ribbons. "I saw a headline about how they're going to ban these soon, force people to take them off, and check identification marks."

His fingers flick my hair, and it sends a rush along my scalp.

"Then I should change your skin color and facial features."

He scowls as he ties the bottom ribbon. "Maybe. Soon. I am getting tired of the mask. Too hot."

"But you need to protect your makeup and make sure you don't get caught in the scandal sheets without maintaining your beauty."

A small chuckle escapes his mouth.

"Also, I'm sorry about what Edel said."

"It's not your fault."

"But it is. She's taking out her frustrations with me on you. She's just..."

"A lot."

"Always has been."

He finishes knotting the ribbon and shifts back to my side. "You know that I don't stare at you. I'm not—"

"I know." My cheeks heat up beneath my mask. I want to tell him that I look at him, too. That I love it when he looks at me, his eyes carrying an energy I don't fully comprehend, one I'm not sure I want to, one I enjoy. "Let's get these post-balloons and hurry back so I can deal with her."

He turns into a narrow alley. "What's your concern with Arabella?"

"It's complicated."

"So, tell me what you're thinking. It might help you work through it."

I shoot him a skeptical look.

"Truly. It's something I used to do with my closest friend at the academy. We'd discuss our plans when the Minister of War would give us challenges. Sometimes, it helped me see ways forward that I hadn't before."

Snow begins to fall. Delicate white flakes crest the market lanterns with tiny coats and collect on windowsills and inside garden boxes full of cold-season flowers.

"That was definitely Arabella's voice, but I need to know if she sent it on her own or if it's one of Sophia's sick games. Arabella could've been threatened—forced to say what she said."

Rémy nods. "Smart."

"Indeed, I am," I spit back.

"No one is questioning that. Least of all me."

"Edel is. She doesn't agree with my plans."

"I get the sense that she wouldn't agree with anyone's plans."

I let out a laugh.

"Where do you think she went?" Rémy asks.

"Wherever it is, I hope she doesn't get herself caught." The worry of losing another sister sits like a limestone brick in my stomach.

"It doesn't matter what she thinks. Or even what I think. I always trust my instincts. Soldiers are trained that way. And if you need to have the information verified, then we'll do it. But invisible post-balloons aren't perfect and can often be intercepted." He points at a shop called Ombre and a window sign boasting the best invisible post-balloons for sale.

"But it's all we have. Hopefully, Fantôme will deliver it safely and bring back a reply."

The shop looks nearly desolate—only a worktable littered with post-balloon wire nets, ribbons, parchment, a series of empty shelves, and a single dusk-lantern whizzing around a beautiful woman.

"There's nothing here," I say to Rémy.

"Ah, don't be so hasty," the woman replies, popping up from a high-backed chair. Half her head is shaved close to her scalp, but on the other side, her hair falls over her shoulder like a river of fire. Her smile is crooked in the best way possible, intentional and making her look clever, and her skin is a soft shade of beige—like honey and caramel swirled together in steaming milk.

"Wait here," Rémy whispers, leaving me at the shop door.

I turn my back to the shop, pretending to watch skittish people who don't want to be spotted in this part of the city move through the narrow market alleys.

"Come in. Don't be afraid," she says to Rémy, almost purring. "Our post-balloons are the best. We truly have the highest success rate."

I steal glances over my shoulder at the woman. Her eyes are filled with light and excitement as she takes Rémy in, a smile curving across her lips.

Rémy steps inside the shop and jumps as if he's been touched.

The proprietor chuckles. "Be careful, the post-balloons are everywhere. I should've warned you, handsome," she says. "So, how can I help you? What exactly are you looking for? With some blessing from the God of Luck himself, it'll be a wife."

Rémy's shoulders stiffen and he clears his throat. "I don't see any post-balloons for sale."

"I can't hear you very well. Mind removing your mask? Or does your makeup need protecting at this hour?"

My panicked thoughts trip over one another.

He flips up the bottom of it. "I'm ill and contagious."

She leans back. "Oh."

A smile tugs at the corner of my mouth.

"Where are your post-balloons for sale? Since you say you have the best," he says.

"You felt them when you first walked in. Let me show you." She unhooks the tail ribbons of her dusk-lantern, drags it forward, and closes the shop's drapes.

I yank the curtains back open.

She eyes me. "Can I help you?"

"She's with me," Rémy blurts out.

"Well, then, come in. You're messing up my show." Her eyes flicker over me, assessing every inch of my body, tallying and deciding if I might be beautiful under my layered winter dress and cloak and mask. I've watched the women do this at court.

Seemingly unimpressed, she turns back to Remy. "Watch."

As the dusk-lantern circles the woman, it reveals the outlines of dozens of post-balloons.

I gasp.

Rémy tries to catch one, but it disappears again.

"Impressed?" she says.

He huffs. "How much?"

"By the looks of you, I'd say you have leas to spend. But maybe if you let me see your face or throw in a kiss, I'll give you a discount." She sidles closer to him.

An unfamiliar feeling crops up inside me. My fists ball and my feet itch to wedge myself between them. *Does he think she's beautiful? Does he like the look she's chosen for herself? Is this how people interact with each other outside of court?*

Those questions grate across my skin. She winks at him, and he smiles.

"Are you all done?" I ask, and Rémy's mouth resumes its usual frown.

The woman's eyes are fixed on Rémy. "We've just started negotiations. And he looks like he's a wealthy guy."

"Looks can be deceiving," he replies.

"Oh yes, in this world." She clucks her tongue. "Forty-two leas for one."

"I'll give you seventy-five for two," he replies.

Her eyebrows lift with surprise, and she licks her lips. "You're very clever." She runs a painted fingernail over his jacket lapel.

He steps back. "Flattery will get you nowhere with me. Seventy-seven," he replies. "Final offer."

"Offers are never final unless you're dead," she quips.

He fusses with the leas in his pocket, then glances over at me, catching my grimace. Our eyes meet. I turn away, pretending to stare out at the bustling crowd.

"Seventy-eight," I hear Rémy say.

"If you buy five, I'll give them to you for one ninety."

"I'll give you three hundred fifty leas for ten."

"Done. And only because I feel like you might be handsome under that mask, and I'm a sucker for pretty men," she replies. "Have you ever bought one of these before?"

"No," he replies.

"Let me show you how it works. If you don't follow directions, you are at risk of your messages being intercepted, so pay attention."

He takes a tentative step forward. She bats her big green eyes at him. "The secret to an invisible post-balloon is the reactive parchment. Light a candle and wait for the parchment to awaken. You'll be able to see its edges for thirty beats. Enough to run your fingers along its curves." She runs her hand across his. He doesn't move. "You already look like you're good with your hands, so this shouldn't be a problem."

I make a noise, and he flinches.

"To put your note into the back, open this flap. See here?" She leans closer to him, and I swear she sniffs him.

My stomach flips, a riot of new emotions battling within it. "We know how to light post-balloons," I grumble loud enough to be heard.

She pauses, and her heavy gaze lingers on me.

"Then, handsome, light this charcoal candle. The special oil allows it to smolder slowly and give the post-balloon enough air and energy to reach its destination, but without the brightness of a regular post-balloon candle. Add two if it's going beyond the imperial island." She hands him the parcel, but doesn't let go when he takes it. "You were such a delight to talk to, despite your guard over there." She nods in my direction. "I rarely get such interesting customers."

"Thank you," he says, tugging it out of her hands.

"No, thank *you*." She laughs. "I don't mean to be so forward, but are you married? I'm in need of a husband."

"Yes," I blurt out. A sharp warmth crawls up my chest, and my heart pounds against my rib cage. "Why else do you think I'm here?"

He glances at me, surprised. Not that I blame him. I'm shocked by what I've just said. But then Rémy jauntily opens the door for me. "Let's go, Mrs. Chevalier."

"Mrs. Chevalier?" I stammer out, my words in a tangle.

"It's tradition for one of us to take the other's last name. I guess I could be Mr. Beauregard. But everyone is looking for you. So, my name would probably be best."

I chuckle. "They're looking for you, too."

We both laugh, then get quiet.

"Were you upset?" he asks, and I can feel the smile behind his mask.

"Uh, no . . . that's not the right word. I was—"

"Jealous?"

I laugh. "No," I lie. "She was strange."

"She was flirting."

I ease this question out: "Did you like her?"

"What do you mean? Her personality was—"

"No, did you think she was beautiful? Would you have taken her up on her offer? She said she needed a husband."

"Soldiers don't marry. We take one vow—to protect the kingdom."

"And nothing else?"

"Above all else queen and country."

I don't know what I'm really asking. I don't know how to form the question or pluck it from the depths of my heart and give it breath. The silence between us feels loud in contrast to the noise of the Market Quartier.

"I'm still a soldier even though I'm here with you," he adds.

Night-lanterns are lit as the sun sets behind us. News blimps start to fill the sky, their silkscreens and sky candles scattering the first of the evening headlines around.

We turn right and Rémy stops. I crash into him.

He pulls me close to the side of a nearby building. I take a deep breath. My heart trembles. His bottom lip brushes my forehead. He looks down at me. An energy tethers us in place.

Is he going to kiss me? What would that be like?

Those questions simmer in my stomach. His eyes drop to my

lips. I lean forward a little to close the gap. I let the desire and curiosity loose from the place I'd hidden it inside. I admit to myself—*I want him to kiss me.*

"Don't move." His words graze my skin.

The sound of heavy boots clomp behind us. I glance over my shoulder. Guards march up the stairs of the Red Velvet Salon.

Panic and worry weaken my legs. I almost fall forward. His hands grip tight around my waist.

"Edel," I say.

8

We stand in the alley and watch the Red Velvet Salon until our fingernails turn blue and the teacup dragons in my waist-sash can't keep me warm any longer. Rémy's body is stiff behind me.

"What if we go into the card salon across the street? We can keep an eye out for Edel," I say.

"We should go to another part of the city to be safe." His eyes scan every person walking by.

"We can't. What if Edel was taken?"

"We'd know. I've seen no movement in and out of the salon yet."

I feel like I've fallen down several sets of stairs—the air in my chest too thin, my head spinning like a télétrope, and my legs shaking beneath me, threatening to buckle under my weight. "I can't lose another sister."

"You won't." He reaches for my hand, cupping it with his, and tries to warm it. "You're freezing." His brown eyes drift over my face. "Your nose is red as a cherry."

"How are you not cold?" I push my other hand into his grasp. He lifts them to his mouth and blows warm air over them. It streams through my knit gloves, the sensation sending a rush of tingles into my limbs. The energy from before is back, the desire welling up once again.

"The Minister of War trains us in the harshest places, conditioning our bodies to adapt to any circumstance." He turns back to the street. "I guess we could wait inside for a little. They do have private game rooms. But we'd have to spend money we don't really have."

"We must." I shove the leas purse into his hand.

He bunches his scarf around his neck, pulls down his mask, and adjusts mine to cover more of my face.

"Everyone is subject to a check," a guard yells as she harasses as many people as she can. But Rémy and I quickly duck into the Queen of Spades. Maroon house-lanterns drift over plush tabletops ringed by high-backed chairs. Men and women slam down porcelain chips or clutch cards or place bets. Laughter and excitement ripple through the room. Parlor workers push treat carts through the labyrinth of game tables.

"Wait here," Rémy says, then he goes to a speak to a man at a nearby desk. He returns with a skeleton key. "A room for a few hours, and with a view of the street."

"How'd you pull that off?" I ask.

"Told him we were just married," he says. I fight the smile erupting across my lips. "Well, you put the thought in my head!" he adds.

We scurry up a set of stairs and into a long hallway. It forms a balcony that overlooks the main room. There are a few potted plants sitting along the railing, and I crouch down and peek between them, to ensure no one followed us. Slanting shafts of lantern light dance across the ground.

Rémy opens the door. Large square windows look out onto the street. A four-poster bed swallows most of the room. At its foot sits a pair of matching armchairs and a card table with a plush red top.

He watches the movement along the street, then draws the curtain and ties a night-lantern to a nearby hook. "We have to leave the Spice Isles tonight. I'm adept at hiding, but they seem to anticipate my every move."

"We're going to the Silk Isles," I declare.

Rémy turns to look at me. "Is that where you think Charlotte is?"

"No." I reach into my pocket, giving the poison bottle a comforting squeeze, and I retrieve a crumpled newspaper segment instead. "We need to see him." I unfold the scrap to reveal the face of the Fashion Minister. "In order to find Charlotte, we need money. Gustave will help."

"Can you trust him?"

"Yes." The comfort of that truth brings back memories of him helping me as favorite: the little jokes, the advice he'd given me, the secret warnings about Sophia. I have to believe he'll be on our side. He knows what the queen truly is. "First, I need to send a letter to Arabella. I'll make sure Sophia didn't force her to send that message, and once I'm satisfied of that, I'll tell her of our plan to locate Charlotte. She might know in which direction the princess sailed the night we escaped." I release Fantôme and Poivre from my waist-sash. They fly about the room, their scales twinkling like snow and fire in the dim light.

I scribble across the page:

Arabella,

Two things:

What do I carry of yours?

How did your teacup dragon find us? We're not in the place where
you told me to go.

Love,

Camille

"Fantôme," I say.

The tiny dragon flies over to me.

"Good girl."

"The training has worked," Rémy comments. "She didn't even
need an incentive to come. That's a good sign."

"She's ready."

She has to be.

"Do you have your knife?" I sweep Fantôme into my arms and
sit on the edge of the bed.

"Always. Why?"

"I don't have our sangsues, so I need blood."

He furrows his brow. "Maybe we should wait until—"

"No." I roll up the parchment. "The night air-postmen will be
leaving the sky to obey the curfew, so this is my chance to send her
out without being detected. The skies will be empty."

"Maybe that's the biggest danger. Maybe we should wait to
send, so that there's too many things to watch. In a sky full of birds,
it's harder to find a certain one."

"We don't have a choice."

Rémy leaves his post at the window and eases down beside
me on the bed. His body radiates like a star caught in a jar. The

question eases back between us, that energy hissing and crackling like the fire in the room's hearth as each moment passes.

"Cut my thumb," I order.

He removes a knife from his pocket, the sheath white as porcelain. "Do you think—"

I cup my hand over his mouth. The softness of his lips sends a flutter through me. "Do it."

He nods.

I take my hand down and turn it palm up. Fantôme perches on my knee, watching.

His hands quiver.

I purse my lips, trying to mask a smile.

"You nervous?"

He grunts a response, then presses the blade into the pad of my thumb. I bite my bottom lip as the silver ridge pierces the flesh and the blood rises to meet it. The sting and throb of it rush in as a red stream trickles down my hand.

"I've cut too deep." Rémy cradles my wrist and frowns.

"It'll heal fast. I promise," I say through a grimace. "Come closer, Fantôme."

The white teacup dragon trundles across the folds of my dress, then leans down to sniff the wound with her hot nose.

"Go on," I urge her.

She licks the blood from my hand until the cut seals itself shut, my arcana proteins stitching me back together without hesitation.

"And you're *sure* she'll go to Arabella?" Rémy asks.

"They're instinctual. They'll find the person whose blood they've ingested first, then return to me once that's passed. I fed her one of Arabella's leeches earlier."

"And you trust it?" His eyes hold doubt.

"I have to. I have to trust her."

He runs his dark brown fingers across her scales, and she nuzzles and licks his hand.

"Can you prepare the invisible post-balloon since that woman gave you such *specific* instructions?" I look away from his penetrating gaze.

He stands and unpacks the parcel on the small side table. "She told us both," he says with his back turned.

"She only wanted to talk to you. She *liked* you."

His shoulders tense.

I bite my bottom lip, regretting saying that as the silence thickens around us.

"I didn't like her," he replies.

It makes me wonder if he could like me.

"You ready?" He turns back around.

I hand him the letter. He slides a charcoal candle inside the post-balloon. It flares briefly as it fills with air, floats up like a tiny cloud, then disappears.

I wave a hand and graze its invisible form, then run my fingers down its base to discover its translucent ribbons. Once I have a grip on the balloon, I grab the night-lantern from the wall hook and hand it to Rémy, who holds it over me and Fantôme, so I can see where to tie the ribbons along the teacup dragon's neck.

Rémy opens the window.

I set the dragon on the iron railing. "Little Fantôme, go straight to Arabella, then come to me in the Silk Isles." I kiss her nose and inch her off the perch. "Be careful."

My heart squeezes as I watch her disappear in the thick snowy clouds.

9

The street outside the Queen of Spades empties as the kingdom-wide curfew sets in. We have watched out the window for Edel all afternoon. Guards disperse in all directions, their coats shining beneath the night-lanterns like beetle shells. The laughter in the game rooms grows louder, pushing through the thin walls of our room.

Rémy closes the window drapes. "We can go back now, check on Edel and the dragons, and pack to leave for the Silk Isles. Then I'll go to the docks and see if they're still scheduling the midnight ships. Many people are already making their way to the imperial island for the Coronation and Ascension. They've allowed a certain number of ships to continue to sail despite the curfew."

I nod and tuck Poivre into my waist-sash despite his protests, and pack the remaining invisible post-balloons. We dash across the street and into the salon. The house is a chaos of flipped-over furniture, shattered teacups, and crushed lanterns. Mud stains crisscross the plush carpets. The women cry as they clean, attempting to put everything back together again.

Rémy and I try to remain calm as we walk upstairs.

I slowly open the door. My heart thuds. I hold my breath and clench my body, bracing for the worst possible outcome.

"Edel..." I say in a whisper.

She is on her knees lifting the bedskirts.

I dart over to her and hug her as tight as I can.

"All right...all right," she complains.

"What happened?" I ask.

"I'll tell you when you stop choking me. But first, help me get the four dragons from under the bed."

I crouch down and spot the rest of the teacup dragons curled up, shivering in fear. I release Poivre from my waist-sash.

"Come out from under there," I call out. "All is well now."

They bat their eyes, then shuffle forward, stretching out their wings. Edel sighs with exhaustion. She plops herself in the nearest chair.

"Tell me," I say.

"I used a glamour to throw the guards off," Edel says.

"A glamour?" Rémy replies with confusion.

Edel grins like a cat who's just caught a fish. Her hair changes from pale blond to cherry red, the straight strands twisting around each other in a storm as they turn into a mess of corkscrew curls.

Rémy stumbles backward, knocking into a chair. "How... what..." he stammers out.

Edel curtsies and her hair returns to its previous color and texture.

He turns to me. "Can you do that?"

"Barely," I answer.

"Is it dangerous?" Rémy asks.

"I haven't experienced any issues so far," Edel says.

"It doesn't mean there won't be," he says.

Edel levels him with a glare.

"Where did you go earlier?" I ask.

"I went to check on the Spice Teahouse."

"What? Why would you do that?" I almost yell, anger slipping into every syllable.

"All the teahouses are closed." Rémy strides to the table and holds up one of the afternoon papers. The headlines of the *National* and the *Orléans Globe* scramble as he shakes it.

SPICE ISLES TEAHOUSE CLOSED UNTIL FURTHER NOTICE

TRAVEL VOUCHERS TO THE IMPERIAL ISLAND

FOR BEAUTY MAINTENANCE—COLLECT YOURS;

ALL METAIRIE RESIDENTS ELIGIBLE

"Yes, Rémy, thank you for pointing out the obvious as always." She drapes her travel cloak around her shoulders.

"Edel, they will assume we'll try to go to the teahouses to find our sisters," I say, trying to keep my voice low. "That was the most dangerous thing you could have done!"

Edel's eyes flash. "You want to find Charlotte, right? And I want to get to the palace. Moving around requires money. Amber squandered much of ours. I thought if I scoped out the teahouse, we could break in and take some of the Belle-products to sell. People are desperate to hide their gray until the teahouses reopen. The items would fetch us leas."

I blink at Edel, surprised. It's actually not the worst plan. If we're to go see the Fashion Minister, we'll need to pay for tickets on the midnight ship to the Silk Isles, which will deplete what we have left, and I couldn't bear to sell one of the teacup dragons, not even Arabella's Ryra, who has folded into the pack.

"Plus, we need more sangsues to hold glamours. Ours have become weak from overuse."

"I actually—"

"I'm not going to argue about this with you," Edel interjects. "It's a good idea."

"If you'd let me finish, I was going to say that I agree with you. We need money for food, and also to buy tickets to the Bay of Silk."

"Why are we going there?"

I hand her the crumpled picture of the Fashion Minister. The headline is no longer animated, the ink trapped in the wrinkles. "We're going to go see him and ask for help."

"Oh no..."

"Yes. He will help us. I know he will. And he's one of the most well-connected men in Orléans. He must have some idea about where Charlotte might be. We can trust him."

"We can't trust anyone." She shoves the balled-up scrap of newsprint back into my hand.

"He was good to me while at the palace," I tell her. "He warned me about Sophia."

"No one in her cabinet is our friend."

"We have to try."

I start to pull off my scarf and coat.

"Don't," Edel says. "We're heading out now."

"We shouldn't risk it," Rémy adds. "There are more guards here than I anticipated. I never thought they'd be able to deploy so many and so quickly."

"In fact, you'd better get a second scarf, I can feel more snow coming," she tells me, ignoring his warning.

Rémy gazes at her, exasperated. "You think it won't be suspicious if the two of you march over there so close to curfew? You think you won't be seen? You think they're not monitoring the teahouses at all? It's possible someone spotted you earlier and they've sent a whole platoon there to lie in wait for you to come back. This is a reckless errand."

"Didn't you see my trick? We can appear how*ever* we want to," Edel says. "Are you coming? Or do you want to go fetch our tickets on one of the midnight boats while we go do this?"

He sighs and turns to the door.

"Ready?" she asks me.

"I need to practice the glamours more, Edel. I've only done it once," I say. "I'll just wear my mask."

"You're a fast learner, little fox. Always have been." She pats my shoulder and grins. "Masks on, hoods up, and scarves bunched around the base of our faces. Once we get close to the teahouse, we'll change. I don't want to waste a drop of energy on the walk over. I'm still recovering."

She leads the way out of the room. My mind is an unexpected whirlwind of worries with each step we take. What if I can't hold the transformation? What would we do if caught? The poison bottle taps my leg like a swinging pendulum as we hustle down the stairs. It may kill my arcana, it may kill me, but either way, I won't ever do Sophia's bidding again. The reality is a small, terrifying comfort.

The women share meals at long tables in the kitchen. Hunched over bowls of food and caught in heated conversations, no one notices us slink out the back door and into the falling snow. The street is empty aside from early-evening vendors selling warm ale and thick stews, before the curfew sets in.

"The new year is coming. Make it sweet, be sure to build your candy house."

"Best stew! Get it here."

Edel makes sharp turns through Metairie's Market Quartier. Plum market-lanterns fade to dark blue, then lighten to pale pinks as we cross into the aristocratic Rose Quartier of this city. It reminds me of Trianon. Du Barry taught us that every Orléansian city organizes itself similarly to receive blessings from the God of the Ground, who values order, symmetry, and the divine number four.

Ominous news blimps float overhead, their banners bathing us in pockets of gloom. Street-sweepers brush away the fresh snow with long brooms and polish cobblestones so they glisten like pearls under the light. Carriages drop passengers at beautiful mansions that hug a square edged by the Bay of Croix. Ornate river coaches sit at house piers. Newsboats bob in the shallow canals, newsies frantically organizing navy story-balloons and black gossip post-balloons to send out for the night editions or attempting to grab portraits of well-dressed courtiers heading home with their light-boxes.

The Spice Isles' teahouse perches like a glass egg over the quartier. The wind jostles brown-and-red house-lanterns above a door emblazoned with the Belle-symbol. Bronze sill-lanterns sit in dark windows. Royal buildings flank its sides like a jeweled nest made of pearl, marble, and gold. A funicular rail sends empty golden chariots to an entry platform.

"There's no way we're getting up there," I say. "The porter station is closed."

Edel points to a small alley. "We'll use the servant entrance—the stairs. I found them earlier."

Rémy gazes around. "The fewer people out on the street, the more likely we'll be seen."

"You might be spotted since you refuse to let us change your looks," Edel snaps at him. "So maybe *you* should stay down here and wait for us."

"Not happening," Rémy replies. "I'm trained to not be seen, but you two are not."

"We'll be fine," Edel says, then pivots to me. "It's time to change."

My hands quiver. The warnings we received all our lives about our gifts and the way they're supposed to be used pile into a mountain that sits upon my chest.

This is wrong.

This is dangerous.

This will have consequences.

"I don't know if I can," I reply.

"You have to. You have no choice." Edel closes her eyes and takes a deep breath. Her skin darkens from milk white to the color of sand, and her hair knits itself into a long braid—a shiny rope hanging over her shoulder.

"Hurry," Edel says. "I don't want to have to hold this for longer than necessary."

The arcana quiver just beneath my skin. My heart rattles in my chest.

I close my eyes. I try to picture myself, but only darkness greets me. The noises in the square grow louder—newsies dropping the evening papers through mail slots, the light honk of river coaches approaching house piers, a sweet-vendor pushing a cart along the cobblestones, men and women laughing as they return home, the sounds of teacup animals squeaking at their owners.

I tremble with doubt.

A hand slides into mine; a little rough and a little warm but nice.

Rémy's hand.

I take a deep breath. I think of Maman: her soft gaze, the rich red of her hair, and the curve of her cheekbones.

A headache drums in my temples. I feel myself change, my limbs frosting over, my hair straightening and landing on my shoulders, my veins flooding with cold, my skin prickling with gooseflesh, and my legs stretching and lengthening.

Edel jostles my shoulder. "You look just like Maman Linnea. And you're taller. I haven't tried changing my body size and height yet."

My eyes snap open. "I didn't mean to." I drop Rémy's hand and finger my now red hair. I look around for the nearest reflective surface and spot myself in the window of a télétrope shop. My breath catches in my throat.

I touch my face. I am almost her. The pain of wanting my mother back floods my heart, drowning it with sorrow, longing, and anger.

Rémy gawks, his eyes bulging with a mix of curiosity and horror.

"It's still me," I say.

He opens his mouth to comment.

"No time to admire your brilliance." Edel grabs my arm and yanks me forward.

We hustle into the alleyway and climb the winding staircases to the teahouse's side door. Rémy easily breaks the lock like it's nothing more than a clockwork toy, and we tiptoe inside.

The walls burst with violets and turquoises like an anxious sky tumbling into nightfall. The ceilings bloom in pinks and tangerines like a spice box of the gods. Doors inlaid with leaf-shaped jewels dot the long corridor that opens up into a grand foyer. Plush cold-season rugs stretch out beneath our feet, and bronze house-lanterns graze the floor like sunken rocks. It smells of burnt candlewicks and rancid honey and damp wood.

None of my sisters were placed here after our Beauté Carnaval. The Belle from the previous generation, Anise, remained. Dark chandelier-lanterns hold her cameo portrait. The silkscreen flutters and ripples from the draft we let in. I wonder where Anise is now and how many other Belles had been secretly kept here. Were they chained? Were they overworked?

"It looks so different from the Chrysanthemum Teahouse," I whisper.

"They're all unique to the specific islands," Edel says. "The Fire Teahouse always looked like it would burn down any minute with all the oranges and reds and yellows. If this teahouse is set up like the others, the storage rooms are in the back left corner nearest to the servant lifts." She grabs a house-lantern from the floor. Rémy hands her a matchbook before she asks, and she lights the lantern, setting it afloat. Once it gathers enough air, she tugs its tail ribbons forward.

We scramble up the stairs, tearing past treatment rooms, linen closets, and servants' quarters until we locate the glass-walled storage room. Belle-products sit on cushioned shelves and in colorful cabinets ready to be plucked for use: complexion crème-cakes, mineral powders, kohl-ink bottles with jeweled lids, perfume blocks, beads and ointments, rose water, hand pallets, beeswax resins, pomatum boxes, rouge crayons, pumice stones, false brows made from mouse fur, tooth sponges, tinted wool pads, hair powder, and more. The products bear the Belle-emblems. I thumb each one and suddenly feel a swell of homesickness.

"I wonder why no one has broken in here yet," Edel says.

"They will if the teahouses don't reopen. It's only been a few days since the queen died," I say, though it feels like a lifetime.

"Desperation will set in soon," Rémy adds.

"You get the bei-powder bundles and as many skin-paste pots and complexion-crèmes as you can carry for us to sell them, Rémy," Edel orders. "And, Camille, you get the Belle-rose leaves and some soap. I'll search for the sangsues and see if they also have Belle-rose elixir. That's all we really need."

Edel and I dig through drawers and cabinets, filling our dress pockets and satchels with the supplies. My mind unravels a series of memories—the glorious treatment rooms in the palace Belle-apartments, making women and men and children feel beautiful and their best, the clients I loved to work with the most, Queen Celeste trusting me to help Charlotte. Regret grips me. If only I'd healed Charlotte sooner, she might be on the throne right now. We might not be in this mess. Why did I resist for so long?

I hold a skin-paste pot in my hands and think of Bree. I glance out the window overlooking the Bay of Croix. Bodies are bent over like question marks in the fields. Their gray hands pluck leaves and carry baskets. Wide-brimmed fur hats crest their heads and heat-lanterns nip at their backs as they navigate the rows. I wonder how late into the night they are forced to work. I wonder how much their lives mirror ours.

"Camille, focus! Your glamour is wearing off," Edel warns. "Your hair is frizzing."

I move away from the window and try to grasp the image of Maman once more. The cold pain cuts through me as the glamour resettles itself.

A rush of footsteps echoes through the teahouse.

We freeze.

Rémy puts a hand up and motions for us to duck out of view. I press myself flat to the floor.

A lady stalks past the room, seemingly frustrated, her long dress swishing back and forth like a pavilion bell. She's hunched at the shoulders and ghastly white. Her black hair is swept into a bun similar to the one Du Barry always wore, and her mouth is painted so red you'd think her lips were coated with blood.

"The new queen wants this place up and running again," she yells at someone I can't see. "There will be more Belles than ever before. All rooms will be occupied like in the olden days, she said. As if she has any idea what the olden days were really like. As if any of us do. Complete incompetence."

Anxiety thrums through me.

I exchange tense glances with Edel and Rémy. My stomach becomes a storm of nausea. A thin trickle of blood escapes my nose. I grab a handkerchief and wipe it away.

"She's already trying to decide which of the newest generation of Belles will be favored and placed at the teahouses. They're still young girls. I went to have a look at them. They barely know how to do anything with Du Barry gone. But either way, I want top pick, so this place has to be in the best shape. I'm learning our new queen likes to be impressed, and I want to show her that *this* will be the premier teahouse in all of Orléans. Maybe she'll even let me open up a secondary one to complement it. Now is the time to expand the teahouses. It'll allow us to serve more people." The woman's voice trails off and she disappears from view.

"Your glamour is gone," Edel whispers. "You have to focus."

"I can't," I reply. "My nose keeps bleeding."

"Try again," she says.

"We don't have time," Rémy whispers. "We have to go."

"I'll lead the way out," Edel says.

"No, I will," Rémy replies. "I knew this was a bad idea."

Edel scoffs and jams the remaining vials of Belle-rose elixir into her already full dress pockets.

Rémy slips into the hall. I hold my breath until he returns. He waves for us to follow. Night-lanterns coast through the halls now, and the sounds of tinkling glass and running water reverberate within the house.

We navigate the corridors as quick and light as mice. The servant door is propped open and the moonlight is a beacon ahead.

We run.

A man steps out of a nearby room. He wears an imperial guard uniform like the one Rémy used to wear. "Hold it right there! No one is supposed to be in here," he shouts. "Just who are—"

Rémy slams right through him. The impact sends the man flying into a banister, and he passes out from the fall.

"Maybe Rémy's good to have around after all," Edel says.

"Keep going," Rémy shouts.

We tumble down the servant staircase and back outside.

Guards stand in the center of the square. They whip around and march in our direction.

"We have to split up to throw them off. Edel, go back to our room and get the teacup dragons and anything else you can't spare. Camille, go into a shop and wait until they start hollering about the curfew," Rémy says. "Once you see them harassing people about getting home, the chaos will afford you some cover. Then meet me at the docks. Pier seven. Ship doesn't leave until midnight, so we have time."

"But—" Edel argues.

"Listen to him," I snap.

Edel's mouth drops open to protest, but she nods.

Rémy squeezes my arm before ducking into the alley. Edel bolts in the opposite direction. I glance around. Many shopkeepers blow out their window-lanterns and close for the night. A chilling panic fills me as I search for somewhere to hide.

I turn to run for the Market Quartier, but guards swarm in as if from nowhere and block my path.

I'm trapped.

10

I mop the sweat from my brow and try to will my heart to slow down. I take a deep breath and pretend to be an aristocratic lady out shopping past curfew.

"Shops are closing. Start making your way home," a guard barks into a voice-trumpet. "Only those with curfew passes can remain out."

I've lost my glamour. I fumble with tying my mask. The guards call out behind me, but I don't stop or change my pace. The aristocratic women wave off their demands, seemingly unafraid. I try to mimic them and fill my motions with their confidence. I fold into a small crowd of people in line at a sweets pavilion. They complain as I push, accidentally knocking their bourbon pies to the ground.

Fardoux's Teacup Emporium sits in the center of the winding avenue. It's the only shop still alive with light. Gilt-lanterns dangle above the door like shooting stars caught by their tails.

Three WANTED posters stretch across the large glass window: one for Edel, one for Rémy, and one for me.

I turn the doorknob. A bell chimes as I step inside.

It's empty.

The room's crackling hearth sends its warmth through the space. Sunset-pink walls hold shelves full of teacup pets in golden cages. Tiny elephants sport painted chrysanthemums on their sides, little hippos wear red bow ties, small tigers and lions play with their pearl necklaces, miniature monkeys throw pastel balls to one another, and a zebra no bigger than my shoe prances through the shop. We learned that many of these animals used to be massive—oftentimes, the size of carriages or as tall as buildings—but the early queens of Orléans bargained with the God of the Ground for more palatable companions.

I find a mirror and adjust my mask, now battered from over-use, bunch my hair into my hood, and smooth the front of my crumpled dress. My outsides can't reflect the panic of my insides.

"Hoot!" a tiny teacup owl squeaks.

I jump.

The bird waddles across a nearby perch, and its eyes, big as leas coins, follow my every move.

A man pops out from behind a curtain. "Madam, may I take your coat and show you some of our newest pets? We don't have much time before the guards rush in here and remind me it's time to close to obey the nonsense curfew. I've lost so much business because of it, but I'm so happy you've found your way here despite the trouble. I have some excellent arrivals from the imperial island. And ones you can only get here. A sloth to fit in your palm. A panda for your pocket." The shopkeeper slides from behind a counter, grinning with a perfectly waxed mustache that curls into tiny spirals at the end. He's powdered and white like a fresh cream pastry hot from the oven. His waistcoat hugs his chest too tight, forcing his stomach to spill out of the bottom. "A honey bear for your boudoir."

I start to speak.

"Oh, wait. Let me guess. This is my favorite part. Matching teacup pets and owners. And by the looks of you, I think I have the perfect fit. Just in today. One moment."

He disappears into another room, and I'm grateful. Less time having to talk to him and more time to hide inside away from the guards.

I steal glances at the glass door, hoping the guards have cleared out so I can get to the docks, but they seem to be everywhere. In the windows, the backs of the WANTED posters also hold our images. There's no escaping our faces, not for any citizen of Orléans. It's a miracle we've yet to be caught. I squeeze my eyes shut and steady my breaths. I think about sneaking back out on the street before he returns. But the guards thicken in number as they shut down the sweets pavilion and step into nearby shops. In only a few moments, they'll be in here.

"It's a half hourglass past curfew. All must return home." The voice-trumpet warning echoes through the shop.

That's my cue, but there are so many guards on the street I won't be able to leave without being stopped.

The shopkeeper returns with a tiny Belle-rose-red flamingo.

"Thank you, sir, but I don't need a teacup pet."

He frowns. "Then why are you here?"

The stupidity of my statement slaps me in the face. I stutter, searching for a reason. "I need a supply of mice, or better yet, rats.

And alive, please. I have a teacup pet at home already that needs feeding."

"I can't hear you well due to your mask. Will you take it off? I don't suppose your makeup needs protection indoors, and I assure you there are no newsies hiding in here ready to snap a picture."

"I have a terrible and highly contagious illness," I say, remembering what Rémy told the post-balloon merchant.

He arches back and a deep flush colors his white cheeks.

"I just need mice or rats," I repeat. "And then I will leave you in peace."

"How many? I'll have to check my supplies. My little snakes have been eating so many lately."

"A week's supply for a newborn drag—I mean, lion. Yes, my sweet little lion." I cringe. I'm making a mess of Rémy's plan.

"Hmm, teacup lions often prefer pig meat. Mice are full of bones."

"Give me both then." I set leas coins on the counter. The purse is so light, I'm afraid if the Fashion Minister doesn't help us or we can't sell any of the stolen Belle-products, we won't have enough left to buy food.

He stares at me a beat too long, then fishes in his pocket to retrieve a quizzing glass. He scrunches his nose and puts it up to his eye to examine me. "Don't I know you from somewhere? Have you come in my shop before? I never forget a voice."

My stomach binds itself. "Impossible. My husband and I only just arrived today on the queen's tide." Sweat drips down my forehead. My pulse races. "And if you would please, sir, hurry. My pet is ravenous after the long journey."

He grumbles but shuffles into the back.

I glance at the street thinking I should just run out of here while he's gone, but the guards are hustling people in lines to check them.

I hold my breath until he returns with a small cage of sleeping mice and a paper-wrapped parcel.

"Thank you," I say, checking the guard count outside the window again.

"They'll be quiet for a while. I've given them a little lavender-infused cheese." He eyes me again. "You seem *so* familiar to me... but I can't place it. My wife would say it's the brandy. The weather has me indulging."

I grab the cage and parcel. I turn toward the door, but he cuts off the path.

"I think I know you." He scratches his beard. "You have the shape and voice of..."

"Geneviève Gareau. Yes, I know. The famous opera singer. The princess's—excuse me, I mean, now, the queen's—favorite artist." The word *favorite* almost burns my tongue. The arcana hiss beneath my skin, ready to protect me. My eyes dart all around. "I get that a lot since I, sadly, copy a lot of the most popular beauty looks. I should probably be more creative."

The door snaps open behind the shopkeeper, startling him.

"I've been looking for you all over," Rémy says. He wears a garish hat that covers most of his head and cups his cheeks. "Please excuse my wife, she has a penchant for teacup pets." He slides his arm around my waist. Heat ripples out from his touch. "I can't let you out of my sight, it seems. You'll get us both fined for being out late, and this poor man will get a business infraction for keeping the shop open to cater to your whims."

I scowl at him, and he winks.

The man steps to the side and eyes Rémy with curiosity and suspicion.

"Have you spent our entire fortune and gotten everything you need?"

"Yes." I nod.

"Thank you for taking such good care of her." Rémy does a little bow and opens the shop door.

"Wait!" the shopkeeper yells behind us.

"Hurry up, wife," Rémy says with a sheepish grin.

A smile bursts across my face. He can't see it behind my mask, but I wish he could.

Rémy and I dash out of the shop and into the nearest alley. I suck in a deep breath and hold Maman's image in my head again. The arcana in my veins turn cold and piercing, worse than the gathering wind around us.

He lifts his mask, his eyes comb over my face as if searching for me.

"It's still me."

He shrugs, then peeks out at the street, noting the number of guards.

"Ready?" I say, taking his hand.

He nods.

We lock arms, ease back into the crowd and right past the guards, headed to the pier.

11

The sea looks almost black from the ship's portholes. The dark stretches out like a blanket. We could sail to the end of the God of the Sea's ocean and be in the caves of the dead before we knew any better. Edel and I huddle in our steerage-class seats paid for by three complexion-crèmes we'd stolen from the teahouse. We are desperately trying to hide inside our thick hoods to keep warm. Rémy stands close by, jaw clenched, watching every person who passes.

Edel moans in her sleep, the sea's rough current making her sick. I pull her hair back and stroke her sweaty neck. The five teacup dragons curl in my dress skirts, the heat of them like tiny coals. I wonder how Fantôme is faring, and I miss her presence. Her being so far away kicks up a thousand worries.

I add another pair of leeches beneath Edel's jaw, hoping it'll rebalance her levels and battle the seasickness.

"How long's the trip to the Silk Isles? I should get her something," I whisper to Rémy.

"It's the second port stop. Carondelet is about two more hour-glasses," he says. "We'll arrive as the sun rises."

I stand up, steadying myself against the low slanted ceiling.

"I'm coming with you," he replies.

"We can't leave her alone."

Edel swats at me, only semi-awake. "Go. I'll... be... fine...."

Rémy and I walk slowly through the narrow aisles, trying to hold ourselves straight as the ship rocks like a cradle caught on a stormy current. Cold air blasts me as we reach the top deck. I lift my mask, welcoming the air beneath its lace and velvet threads. It has kept me safe up until now, but it's starting to suffocate me. The deck spreads out long and flat. Carriage-shaped cabins sit in rows like jeweled plums along a center promenade. Rich courtiers sleep in comfortable beds or peer out of windows through eye-scopes at the ocean expanse or the stars above.

A midnight sky looms over us, full of warning and promise.

"Fresh barley water for seasickness," a vendor calls out.

"Sailor cakes straight from the hearth. Red bean, pork, and saltfish," another offers.

I buy a cup of barley water for Edel. The purse of leas given to us by Arabella is about empty. Twenty coins left. We'll run out of money by tomorrow. The Fashion Minister has to help us. We need a cushion. We can't only rely on the hope of selling more Belle products.

Very few people walk along the ship's promenade. We find a corner to stand in.

"Look," Rémy points out. "You can see the lantern-houses along the coast."

The tiny pinpricks of light glow like trapped stars in the distance.

"It's beautiful," he says.

"Nothing is beautiful anymore."

"She wins if you let her take everything. Even momentary happiness."

"I don't think I'll ever be happy again. I don't know if I want to be now that I know all these things." I shiver as a gust of wind hits us.

He steps closer. Warmth radiates from him like a heat-lantern. "There are people in this kingdom who have had to live with worse."

I scoff.

He leans closer; his voice drops an octave. "I'm not trying to be an ass, but think about what you read in the *Spider's Web*. Many have dealt with the ugliness of this world for a long time."

"You don't understand." A flare of anger erupts inside me.

"I will probably never fully understand, but I'm seeing new things, too. Parts of this kingdom that I never knew existed. I didn't know what life was really like for you, for Belles. They taught us you were here to serve—like us—but always made it seem like you weren't real. You were poppets and dolls to be used—not people. That we weren't the same."

I squeeze the nearest railing. The cold presses through my gloves.

"There are so many lies," he says.

I don't want to talk to him about this anymore. The teacup dragons stir in my pouch. "Maybe we should go back down to Edel. They seem cold," I say, trying to still the movements, but they clamber out of the pouch.

Rémy helps me secure them; gently tucking their small heads back into the waist-sash. The feel of his strong hands makes me want to lean into him, want to kiss him, want to erase all the worries and responsibilities—only for a moment.

His eyes find mine, the connection a thread thickening between us.

The dragons squirm again. I break eye contact and glance down. "No flying right now," I whisper hard.

Rémy tries to block me from the view of others on the ship's promenade.

Poivre wrestles from my grip and bolts over my head.

"Oh no," I say, trying to wave him back.

Rémy points up. "But look who it is."

Fantôme circles one of the ship's bows like a tiny cloud lost from the sky. Poivre chases her, a burst of red flame.

I whistle. Fantôme soars down to me and licks my face with her hot tongue. "Good girl. I've missed you, petite." A silver ribbon is tied around her neck like it's a bow and she's the present.

Rémy catches Poivre and slips him back into my waist-sash. He squeaks, and a hiccup of fire escapes his mouth, catching Rémy's finger. Rémy curses at him.

I attempt—unsuccessfully—to hold in a laugh.

Rémy's scowl melts into a grin.

I undo the ribbon around Fantôme's neck, and she dives into my waist-sash, reuniting with the rest of the teacup dragons, and the new one, Ryra. They nuzzle each other with recognition and start to tussle playfully.

I use some of Edel's barley water and sprinkle the post-balloon, so it's easier to see.

I rip open the back of it and fish out a note, a pair of half-dead sangsues, and a book.

A Belle-book.

It's inscribed with arabella flowers.

I hand it to Rémy, then fumble with the scrolled note, struggling to open it.

He reads over my shoulder.

Camille and Edel,

I understand why you needed a confirmation.

The answer to your questions:

1. My miroir métaphysique.

2. I fed one of your old sangsues to Ryra.

Watch the headlines in the morning. The early bird newsies will break the story that Sophia has taken Padma, Valerie, Hana, and Amber to her prison. But they aren't there. She brought them to the Royal Infirmary at the palace for a medical examination, but they were only here for five hourglasses' worth of time before she had them scattered all over Orléans again, reopening the teahouses secretly. Valerie is in the Silk Isles, Padma is at Maison Rouge, Hana in the Fire Isles, and Amber is in the Glass Isles. I don't know how long they'll stay there. Or if she'll continue to move them around like chess pieces.

She's creating a cat-and-mouse game to lead you into the trap. The longer you run, the more she believes the kingdom will turn in her favor. She envisions you arriving at the palace, trying to break into the Everlasting Rose, only to find your sisters are not there. She plans to record the incident and distribute the newsreels kingdom-wide, thinking this embarrassment will break you and the momentum you've gathered.

She's moving at a fevered pace—using my blood to create new Belles more quickly. But there's only so much that she can use on a daily basis without nearly killing me, and that will never be an option for her. I am the aether. One Belle in every generation has the strongest blood—additional proteins that allow for her to help grow the next generation. Du Barry called us the everlasting roses.

Camille, this is what I tried to tell you when I last saw you, but there wasn't enough time. You are your generation's aether. This is why Sophia has put a higher price on your head. She wants to use you, the way she's using me. She even intends to combine our blood, to see what that yields her. She thinks the strongest Belle ever made. The guards will not kill you if they capture you. She needs us to populate her garden because ultimately she wants to find a way to sell many of the Belles in Trianon Square and will bleed us dry to do so. I keep hearing her say, "One for every household."

I've sent along my Belle-book with more details on the matter. Commit it all to memory, then burn the book. No one other than Belles must ever know all the inner workings. This information cannot fall into the wrong hands.

You need to bring your sisters together, but be careful, Sophia has spies everywhere. More when I can.

—A.

I press the paper to my chest, the weight of her words holding my breath inside.

"What do you want to do?" Rémy asks.

The ship jerks. A baby pram being pushed by a woman crashes onto its side. Rémy races over to help her turn it upright and rescue the baby from the ground. The baby cries, the pitch of it searing through me, then blossoming an idea.

I tuck my hand into my pocket where the poison bottle always sits like a dangerous treasure. What if Belle babies could be born without their arcana? What if they could be healthy—and Sophia unable to use them?

I think of Valerie. She worked in the Belle-nursery, raising the new Belles with the nurses. She knows how we're born, how we develop. If those Belle babies are born without their arcana, maybe they can be healthy and like everyone else, and will be unable to be used and sold.

Valerie might know exactly how to stop that part of Sophia's plan. We could work together to determine how to use the precise amount of this poison in the right way to kill arcana—how to save those Belle babies from this fate.

I read the letter again. It doesn't feel real. Hate simmers inside me, sharp, hot, and prickling. Arabella's words are tinder for the fire inside me.

12

"Last port ahead." A bell rings and a man stalks through the ship's underbelly. "Half an hourglass until docking."

Edel yawns and stretches out her arms. The teacup dragons hiccup and startle with annoyance.

"Get up," I whisper to her. "We need to talk."

She's sluggish.

"How do you feel?" I ask.

"I'll be better when we get on land," she mutters.

"Arabella sent a message."

"Why didn't you wake me?"

"No time to argue." I hand her Arabella's letter.

She unfurls the paper. Her eyes grow bigger and bigger as she reads, the words soaking in. She whispers the words *aether* and *sold* and *everlasting rose*. "How can any of this be true?"

"It's all in her Belle-book." I show her the cover. "She's put in clippings from old Belle-manuals and detailed everything."

She runs her fingers over the book, their white tips purpled with cold.

"While we're here, I want to get Valerie, too. I need her help," I say.

"I don't understand *any* of this," she says.

"I don't know all the details, but Valerie must. Once we find her, she can explain."

"Carondelet! Prepare to disembark."

Outside the circular windows, the sun spills buttery-orange rays across the water, lightening the dark waves to blue.

I refasten the ribbon leashes around the teacup dragons' necks and feed them tiny squares of salted pork. Ryra sits atop my hood. Happy and full, the others climb onto my shoulders, hooking their talons into my traveling cloak. I adjust the royal emblem Arabella gave me back at the palace—a dragon with a chrysanthemum hooked around its tail—that announces me as a favored reptilian merchant to the queen.

"Ready?" Rémy asks, taking a deep breath and putting on his mask.

"I have to be." I gaze around, wondering if others will put on masks, if that's the fashion here. "Should we wear these? Or will they attract more attention?"

"I don't have a choice," he says.

"If you would let me change you—"

"We don't have time to argue," he replies as the crowd moves forward.

I look at Edel. Her cheeks are clammy with the sheen of seasickness. "Can you hold a glamour until we find out if masks are popular here?"

"I think so," she grumbles.

We hold hands, close our eyes, and call our arcana. My skin goes cold, the frost-laced wind now inside us as well as outside. Edel makes herself look like Du Barry—dark hair and a round face and beautiful full figure. I think of Maman again, assuming her outer appearance, but with deep black skin.

Rémy gawks like he did the first time I used a glamour.

"It's still me," I whisper.

"I know," he claims, though his eyes say otherwise. "I'm just getting used to it is all."

We walk onto the deck. Rich courtiers crowd the front with their servants at their sides toting children and boxes stacked like pastel patisserie treats.

"I wonder if there'll be more guards in Carondelet than Metairie," a wealthy woman says while adjusting her large hair-tower. A sleeping teacup koala shifts higher into her strands, snuggling in to avoid the growing wind.

"The whole world is under arrest right now," her companion responds.

"It's time for things to return to order. I can't last much longer without my beauty treatments. They're going to be opening more asylums than teahouses if our new queen doesn't get this all sorted soon," another adds.

"She's made a lot of promises."

"That's what children do."

"You shouldn't talk about Her Majesty like that," someone barks.

"One must figure out the Belle situation," a voice calls out.

I stiffen. Rémy's hand finds my waist. I hear Edel take a deep breath.

"I'm tired of all the Belles fuss. I'm ready for things to go back to the way they've always been."

A nearby woman shouts, "The Belles cater to one class. What about the rest of us who can't afford weekly or even monthly treatments?"

The woman with the hair-tower gasps, then cranes, looking for the speaker in the small crowd.

"They'll have to bring in more to meet the demand. It'll solve all this mess," a man in a top hat replies, triumphantly. "Like télétrope sales. When they're up, make more."

"Oh, hush up," a woman beside him says.

"Or we could get rid of all of them."

"Yeah, what about finding another way?"

"All of this talk is upsetting my teacup sloth," someone shouts.

A loud bell rings, stamping out the conversation.

A charged energy ripples over all of us. Rémy, Edel, and I make eye contact.

"Line up to disembark. Keep the queue tidy," a man directs. "No pushing."

The islands appear in the distance as the ship enters the Bay of Silk. Buildings boast sea-blue domes trimmed with a rose gold that glitters as the sunrise hits it. Swaths of land are covered in huge spiraled silkworm cocoons and orchards of mulberry trees. Men and women climb ladders to reach the stacked towers, armed with silk collection baskets.

Edel whispers, "Wow."

City-lanterns drift about like fallen stars, illuminating all of Carondelet's wonders—deep canals cut through the quartiers grasping ornate watercoaches that sit on the blue like glittering jewels expelled by the God of the Sea. Advertising banners flutter behind vendor boats as they stop at piers and hustle their ornate wares to customers. A kaleidoscope of shops stretch as far as I can see.

It's one thing to be in the lesson rooms at Maison Rouge standing before Du Barry's massive tapestry map of Orléans and another to actually see it for yourself. The world is vaster and more beautiful than she ever described. Each corner of it feels different and unique, part of a puzzle with disparate pieces that somehow fit together.

The ship docks. Newsies swarm the pier with the morning papers. Others hold poles displaying silkscreen banners of the Fashion Minister, Gustave du Polignac. We disembark.

"Early papers available!"

"Get the *Silk Post* here!"

"*Daily Orléansian* over this way!"

"*Sucré* and the *Beauty Tribune* fresh off the presses."

The sight of the Fashion Minister's face sends a temporary surge of relief into my bones. The silkscreens shift through images—his full lips break into a smile that lifts his freckled brown cheeks into a stoic and regal grimace. I almost lose hold of my glamour.

"Queen Sophia's new vivant dress line debuts today in preparation for the Coronation and Ascension. Come for a preview this afternoon with the Fashion Minister himself at the Silk Hall in Carondelet's square," a newsie hollers. "Look your best for our new queen."

"I've seen samples of the dresses. They'll sell out quickly. Place your orders early," another newsie shouts. "You don't want to be left behind."

"Doors open at noon on the dot," a third reminds. "Lines already forming along the mile."

"Let's go get Valerie," Edel says, marching ahead.

"Wait! Didn't you hear? People are already lining up to get in to see the Fashion Minister," I say. "We should see him first."

"We have two hours. That's too long to hold a glamour, especially after being sick. And we can't go in there with these tattered masks. We'll look out of place."

"But what if we don't get in, and they close the doors?" I protest.

"They want money. That won't happen," she replies, turning to Rémy. "What do you think?"

"You care?" he asks.

"No, but she does, so break the tie."

He sighs. "I think we should go assess the teahouse, see how many guards are stationed there and how we might get in."

I cross my arms over my chest. "Fine."

Edel pats Rémy's shoulder and he tenses. "We agree on something," she says and leads us to the line to board a small city boat.

"The teahouse will be near the square," Rémy whispers as we wait to board. "Nearest to the aristocratic Rose Quartier and the city's Imperial Mile." He points at the narrow canal to another prominent island. "All the cities are set up the same way."

"Silk Teahouse, please," Edel tells the watercoach driver.

"But it's closed, miss," he replies with a crooked grin.

"Doesn't matter. We have business there."

He shuffles away as we find tufted seats.

The watercoach driver takes us to a nearby island where the Silk Teahouse sits. We climb out onto the pier. Rémy tells him to wait for us.

Marble spirals cover the exterior of the teahouse, mimicking the pattern of the silkworm's cocoons. A sloped roof is crusted over with snow, and its pier is red like a tongue that's tasted too many strawberries. White sill-lanterns sit in the windows, dull and vacant.

Guards stand at attention in front of the doorway and along the pier. Dozens of them.

My heart beats too fast. How will we get past them?

There is a Receiving House just ahead that's a tiny replica of the teahouse and has a woman sitting inside it. A sign above her head reads SILK TEAHOUSE RECEPTION.

"I'll stand here to not draw as much attention," Rémy says. "But I'll keep watch."

"Ready?" I ask Edel.

I take a deep breath and make sure the glamour is strong. I grimace as the cold pain radiates inside me and my bones feel like they might just splinter into shards.

Edel nods. Rémy reaches out and gives my hand a squeeze before we go.

We approach the woman behind a glass pane. She thumbs through a gossip tattler and wears a simple lavender dress with a royal emblem around her neck. It bears a silkworm coiled around a chrysanthemum, identifying her as an important courtier from the merchant House of Silk. A fire-lantern bathes her white skin in reds and oranges. The circuit-phones swallow the walls behind her.

She doesn't look up. Edel huffs, then taps the glass. The woman flinches in shock and the tattler drops from her lap, the fall shifting the portraits and animated ink across the parchment. Her eyes flutter over us and she is, apparently, unimpressed. She pins a CLOSED sign to the glass, rescues her tattler, and resumes flipping the pages.

"Excuse me?" I say.

"Don't you see the sign?" she barks.

Edel punches the glass, which causes the soldiers nearest us to look up.

I cringe. "Edel."

The woman yanks open the window. "You could've broken it, you know that? The fine would be at least three hundred leas."

"You should've been courteous enough to open it," Edel replies.

"We're closed," she snaps. "Who are you?"

"Courtiers from the House of Rare Reptilians, and in need of emergency beauty work," I reply.

"Let me see your emblems." She stretches out her hand, waiting for me to untie the ribbon and place the heavy crest made of coral and ivory and gold in her palm.

"What for?" Edel asks.

"Not that I need to explain myself, but there have been forgeries floating around. I need to inspect them."

I gulp and remove the emblem. I hand it to her, hoping Arabella gave me a real one from the palace.

"Hmm . . ." She turns it around in her hand, gazes up at the dragon sitting on my shoulder, then takes out a set of scales and a monocle. She weighs it, then lifts the glass eyepiece. "This one passes inspection, but what about hers?" Her discerning gaze turns to Edel.

I almost sigh with relief, then say, "She's my assistant. Now, when will the teahouse be taking clients again?"

"When Madam Kristina Renault reopens—"

The circuit-phone closest to her rings. The cone-shaped receiver shakes left and right on top of its slender base. She lifts it to her ear and says, "Silk Teahouse reception, Mira speaking, we are closed until further notice. May I please take your message or appointment request?"

A loud voice shouts: "Additional vats needed to the palace port before sunrise by order of the queen."

The voice sends a jolt of lightning through me.

Elisabeth Du Barry.

Edel and I don't dare look at each other. Elisabeth survived the palace dungeons and is still working for Sophia. That truth swirls around inside me. I want to strangle her through the phone lines.

"Ensure Valerie is prepped for transport afterward," Elisabeth barks.

I squeeze Edel's arm and look up at the teahouse's windows. The sill-lanterns are unlit. No movement in or out. A space seemingly vacant. But my sister's in there. Only twenty paces away.

We have to get into that teahouse.

"Will do," the girl replies before cupping a hand over the receiver. "No one is at the teahouse. We've been sending people to Miel's Makeup Galleria on the Imperial Mile because they have a limited supply of Belle-products. Best to try there. Good day to you both." She slides the glass window shut again and points at the CLOSED sign.

The plan to get to Valerie bursts like a popped bubble.

We have to find another way in.

13

We settle into another shabby room in another boardinghouse to rest after using our glamours. We still have three hourglasses' worth of time before the doors open for the Fashion Minister's exhibition. Anxious flutters irritate my stomach, all the unknowns growing into a ball of nausea.

"How do we get to Valerie now?" I ask Edel.

She doesn't answer, her face buried in Arabella's letter, mumbling to herself about the aether and Sophia, trying to put the pieces together. Rémy stares out the window, his eyes surveying every passing body. The teacup dragons dance and play, chasing one another and the dusk-lanterns. Their scales glitter like beautiful gemstones. I watch them, thinking how nice it must be to be them, clueless, and without a worry. Their joyful movements remind me of how my sisters and I used to be as little girls.

I comb through Arabella's Belle-book to pass the anxious time.

Date: Day 3,428 at court

Sophia's Belle-growing apparatus was unveiled today. The clear vats will hold future Belles like wombs. Sophia called them cradles. She thought it made what she'd created sound better. Sweeter and softer.

I sneaked into the birthing chamber. The walls are filled with them now, stacked like eggs in a carton. I traced my fingers along gilded tubes that connected to massive arcana meters and tanks to be filled with my blood. Nurses used rolling ladders to tend to them.

The sight of the room was maddening. Du Barry hid the truth. She said we'd fallen from the sky like seeds to be planted. She said she rescued us from the dark forest and put us into the hands of our mothers. She said the Goddess of Beauty made each one of us in her image. The beautiful lie burned a pit in my heart.

I flip forward.

Date: Day 3,432 at court

The ministers have been holed up in the Royal Law Room of the Imperial Library for two days straight. Beds were brought in, and they were forced to work through the night on the new set of beauty laws to be passed after Sophia's Coronation and Ascension to the throne. I sneaked onto the balcony to listen to them argue. I caught some of the rules on the docket:

Citizens will be required to register their beauty work with the cabinet, including but not limited to installation of imperial cameos in every household for monitoring.

Beauty capital (an individual's ability to present themself) shall be measured with a rating rubric (scores given monthly from the Beauty Minister). High marks will be rewarded by the monarchy, for Orléans will be full of only beautiful things.

No woman shall be more beautiful than the sitting queen.

The debates over a new beauty price list was next on their agenda.

The new Minister of Belles, Georgiana Fabry, insisted the prices go up. Beauty lobbyists backed her desires, but other ministers disagreed, claiming it will create disenfranchisement.

The price list was now segmented by arcana.

MANNER:

    ALL PERSONALITY ADJUSTMENTS   1,750

    TALENT:

      TIER ONE   PHYSICAL PROWESS   3,750

      TIER TWO   ARTISTIC   4,270

      TIER THREE   SKILL   5,980

AURA:

    SURFACE MODIFICATIONS:

      HAIR COLOR   105

      HAIR TEXTURE   126

      EYE COLOR RESTORATION   50

      EYE SHAPE ADJUSTMENT   60

      SKIN COLOR RESTORATION   90

    DEEP MODIFICATIONS:

      FACE:

        CHEEKBONE SCULPTING   4,000

        MOUTH PLACEMENT AND SHAPE   3,000

        EAR PLACEMENT AND SHAPE   3,000

      BODY:

        LEG AND ARM SCULPTING   4,500

        STOMACH, BREASTS, TORSO SCULPTING   6,100

        HIPS AND REAR SHAPING   7,000

        NECK AND SHOULDER SMOOTHING   3,000

        HAND AND FEET ADJUSTMENT   2,000

AGE:

   SKIN TIGHTENING   125

   WRINKLE REMOVAL   200

I turn back to the beginning of the book.

Date: Day 2,198 at court

I feel terrible about what I did today. The nurses started taking more of my blood now, too much for it to just be to check my arcana levels. They wouldn't tell me why. Claimed it was to keep me healthy. When one of the nurses, Zaire, came into my bedroom with her cart of needles and vials, I restrained her and made her tell me what they were using my blood for.

She called me the aether, one of the everlasting roses. I thought back to when I was a little girl curled up in my maman's lap with one of the storybooks from the library at Maison Rouge. I can still see the cover—a rose with petals of every color and a gilded stem. Its pages told the tale of the Goddess of Beauty's gardens, and the rare everlasting roses, grown from aether seeds in order to birth the other roses.

I don't know what this means.

The late-morning headlines pour through the window and interrupt my reading.

"The *National*, second paper off the presses. Countess Madeleine Rembrant of House Glaston jailed by the queen for stealing Belle-products from Trianon's premier shop, Sugar Rose."

"Beauty pamphlets *Dulce* and *Sucré* both report that plum buns will most certainly sweep the Glass Isles—maybe the entire kingdom—after famed opera singer Geneviève Gareau sported a full derriere at her last concert. If only the teahouses were open."

"We should go line up," I say, wanting to get away from the headlines and this room. I tuck the teacup dragons in my pouch and add Arabella's Belle-book to my satchel. "We have an hour left."

Edel shrugs but pulls herself off the bed.

More headlines drift inside, like incessant waves threatening to swallow us.

"Just in from the *Orléansian Times*, Belles officially labeled property of the kingdom of Orléans, entrusted to its monarch. Hiding them is now considered treason against the crown with the penalty death by starvation box."

I flinch.

"Property?" Edel says, gritting her teeth.

"We've always been that," I reply, the truth hardening me from the inside out.

"The *Silk Post* learns that the queen is labeling any and all rumors of her sister's recovery as false press. She is still planning the funeral and memorial for her beloved sister. Her body is to be presented on the first day of the new year as planned."

Rémy pulls on his cloak.

"Papers," a voice hollers from the hall. The thud of the bundle hits the floor outside our door.

We can't escape the news.

Edel peeks into the hall and swipes them. Her eyes scan over the headlines. "Arabella was right. Here's the report about our sisters—'Favored Belles Padma, Hana, Valerie, and Amber locked in the Rose.'" She shows me the pictures. Amber grips the rose-shaped bars, shouting through them, her hair a wild storm around her head. We turn the page, quickly, sending the animated ink scurrying to settle. "But, Rémy..."

Rémy turns from the window. "What is it?"

"Your family," she stammers out.

He takes the paper from her and scans the pages. His eyes fill with anguish. "I have to go."

"What is it?" I rush to his side.

Animated pictures of Rémy's family fill the front page under the headlines:

THE FAM ILY OF THE TRAITOROUS IM P ERIAL

GU ARD—ACCOM P LICE TO FUGITIVE B ELLES—

IDENTI FIED AND TAKEN INTO CUSTODY

His three sisters, Adaliz, Mirabelle, and Odette, are chained and being carted off. His veiled mother follows behind with her head bowed. His father tussles with the imperial guards. The three girls sob, a storm of tears flooding their dark brown cheeks.

I remember the depth of their smiles and the sound of their voices and how they gazed at Rémy like he would be their hero forever.

Rémy immediately starts packing the few things he's amassed since being on the run.

"You can't leave without me changing you," I say.

"I don't like being changed and there's no time," he says.

"You have to. The guards will capture you the second you get to Trianon, if not sooner." I quickly prepare the bed for beauty work, pulling back the sheets and fluffing the pillows.

"And you need food," Edel adds. "I'll go buy some bread, nuts, and hard cheese. Things that should last you."

My heart is warmed by her willingness to put aside their rivalry and help him.

"No. I'll be fine," he replies. "All your money will be gone...."

Edel is already out the door.

"Your image will be plastered all over, and more prominent than the old Wanted posters, now," I say.

"I know," he says. "I'm leaving you and Edel my maps. I have them all committed to memory. They'll help you navigate every inch of Orléans. The ink updates as the master maps in Trianon are updated." He heads for the door.

I grab his arm. "You're not leaving here unless I change you."

Rémy stares me down, but I don't budge and finally, he sighs. "You know all of this is unnecessary, right? I know how to stay undercover. I have that hair powder to cover the stripe."

"I need to do this," I tell him. "I need to do what I can to keep you safe."

I light a fire in our tiny cookstove and fill a small, chipped teapot with water from our room basin. The noise of the hissing flames and the gurgle of bubbles smothers his protests. I take out the caisse Arabella packed for us and retrieve dried Belle-rose leaves to steep into the pot. My hands work fast setting out all the beauty instruments we have—a set of miniature skin-paste pots, metal rods, and charcoal pencils. I combine them with the items we pilfered from the Spice Teahouse. The small collection isn't even a fraction of the supplies we once had.

My eyes close and I remember the shelves upon shelves of beauty products at Maison Rouge and the Belle-apartments. The scent of pastilles and wax and candles fills my nose, and I'm almost back there.

But when I open my eyes again it's just this small room.

"Take off your clothes and lie down on the bed."

He grumbles but complies. The heavy thud of his boots hitting the floor sends a nervous shiver through me. We've been cooped up in small spaces together for all these days, and I've never seen his feet. Or any of him for that matter. He's only allowed me to use the hair powder to cover his silver stripe.

I turn around to give him privacy as he undresses but can still feel his each and every move. A tiny fire sparks in my stomach.

The bed squeaks as he climbs into it.

"Are you ready?" I bring over a cup of Belle-rose tea and set it on the nightstand.

"As much as I will be." He's tucked himself under the quilts, and his long dark arms lie on top of them.

I laugh.

His brow furrows. "What is it?"

"You're too far under the blankets. How am I supposed to work on you?"

"Oh."

"Just lie across the bed and drape the cover over...you know..."

"I know," he says quickly.

I wait.

"Are you going to turn around?"

"Shy, are we?" My cheeks flame.

He sighs.

I pivot my back to him. My heart flutters like the tiny candle inside the night-lantern between us.

"Done," he replies.

His long legs dangle over the edge of the bed like great brown trunks of muscle threaded with streaks of gray. But he's beautiful without his clothes on, even marbled with the sad color.

"What will you do?" he asks.

"What do you want me to do?"

"Nothing if I could help it, but I'm guessing you don't take no for an answer."

I touch the scar that hooks under his right eye. His skin is warm and soft.

"I'd like to keep that," he says.

I pull back quickly. "It's pretty distinguishable."

"It's been with me since I was born. Well, according to my mother. It was part of my natural template. It reminds me of her."

"All right."

"I like my skin color. The darker the better."

"Anything else?"

"Longer hair, maybe?" he says.

"I'll give you little girl ringlets."

The edges of his mouth curve into a reluctant smile.

I wink at him and coat him with bei powder. The white flakes cover him like sugar dust on a molasses tart. I smooth them across his limbs with a brush. He watches my every move, his stare intense and like he's trying to listen to my thoughts. My hands shake with nerves.

I close my eyes. The arcana awaken easily, rising to meet my call. A rush of heat lifts from my stomach, and it feels like it's both my gifts and something else. My blood races through me. Beads of sweat dot my forehead. The veins in my body pulse, and my heart picks up its rhythm. I pretend that I'm home in the safety of one of the Aura lesson rooms. I pretend that all that's happened never came to pass. I pretend that Rémy is a regular customer here to see me for a routine session. His form appears in the darkness of my mind.

I darken his hair to the color of midnight. I lengthen the tight curls into long coils, then knit them together like soft yarn until they fall over his shoulder in a thousand tiny ropes. I deepen the brown of his skin color.

I stare down at him and a smile erupts through me. I can still see him inside this new outer form. I didn't want to lose all the things I loved about the way he'd chosen to look.

He bites his bottom lip.

"I'm finished. Need tea for the pain?"

"It doesn't hurt," he replies.

"But you're scowling."

"That's not the reason." He sits up. The heavy sound of his breathing extends between us. My heart flutters like a trapped bird. He smells like ink, leather, and me. His breath hits my shoulder, sending a tickle down my spine. Thoughts of him jump around in my head like bubbles in a champagne glass: his hands around my waist, his nose buried in my hair, the feel of his lips, the taste of his mouth.

I shudder.

"What's wrong?" His gaze pins me in place, then slides around me, hugging all my edges. His eyes almost swallow me whole, moving from my face, down the lines of my neck, and slope of my chest where the mirror sits, awaiting all his questions.

"Nothing," I mutter.

"Use the mirror," he says.

I press a hand to my chest. "I already trust you."

"Just do it, so you'll never ever question it." He runs a finger along the path of the chain on my neck, his finger pressing into my skin, leaving behind a trail of heat.

I pull the mirror from beneath my dress, then prick my finger with a pushpin from my beauty caisse. He watches as I rub the blood in the mirror's handle. The grooves soak with it. The liquid climbs to the top, bathes the roses, and the glass fills with an image of his face—kind eyes, a perpetual half-smile, and a creased and serious brow. I can feel him—his strength and loyalty, his selfless-ness and protective instinct, his affection for me. The overwhelm-ing power of it surges through me.

"What do you see?" he asks, searching my face.

"I don't want you to go." My voice breaks. Silent and unruly tears breach the fragile wall holding them in.

I wipe them away.

He looks at me, then reaches his fingers to my face, his hands heavy yet gentle. I don't flinch. I don't move away from his touch. His thumb catches a tear beside my mouth. He doesn't stop wiping until they stop falling. The warmth of his hand seeps into my skin.

"You make me feel safe," I say.

He leans forward. "And you make me feel the same." His whis-per gets tangled in my hair. "But safety is never permanent. I sup-pose like beauty, it's unpredictable."

More tears well in my eyes. Different ones this time. I don't know what this wild feeling is. I want him to touch me again. I want him to kiss me. I want to know what that feels like. A seam inside me starts to rip, taunting me with all that could happen if I let him in.

"I have to go," he whispers. "You will be fine without—"

I touch his face, then press my mouth to his, shoving those words back in, and knowing that we can't be together, knowing he has to leave, knowing that our joke about being married was just that—a joke. Still, a blush blooms in my cheeks.

He freezes.

I pull back. My heart does a nervous tumble. His eyes gaze into mine.

A pocket of silence encapsulates us, the edges of it expanding and stretching throughout the room.

Neither of us moves.

I search his eyes for the answer to the kiss. Would he ever want me in that way? Have I crossed a line with him? Did I misinterpret what I saw in the mirror? Am I allowed to have these feelings?

I open my mouth to try to say something. The words *I'm sorry* tumble out.

He runs his hand along the curve of my neck and cups my face in his hands. I sink into him. He kisses me gentle and soft. All the worries about whether he wants me drift off like post-balloons.

We kiss until our lips tingle.

"I don't want you to go." My voice drowns with fear.

"I don't want to go either." His mouth softens and his eyes crinkle at the corners. "But I have to."

"What if it's a trap?" I ask.

"Then I'll work my way out of it."

"What if something happens to you?"

"I know the palace inside and out." He pushes back one of my frizzy curls. "You should find Charlotte, get your sisters, and meet me there. We can end this together."

I bite my bottom lip to keep it from quivering.

"You'll always know I'm safe." He fishes three leeches from the perforated jar and puts them along his forearm. "Send the gold dragon for me. She's my favorite." With his other arm, he removes a small sheathed dagger from his pocket, the handle white as bone and encrusted with pearls. "Keep this on you always. Even when asleep. Use it without hesitation." He puts the belt around my waist and buckles it. "And lastly, these." He takes his leather-bound maps from his pocket. "Carry these. They will reveal the details of each city you go to. They were developed by the Minister of War himself."

"Won't you need them?" I ask, removing the leeches as they tug and gorge on the blood in his thick veins.

I open the caisse of sangsues and remove a small empty jar. I use a tiny quill to label it with his name, put the leeches inside, then tuck it back into the compartment beside the leeches Arabella sent.

"I'm going to the palace. I know that place. Trust me."

I lean forward and rest my forehead against his.

We look at each other as if there's a rope suspended between us throbbing and pulsing, pulled tight by our shared circumstance. He flashes a smile so devastating and heartbreaking, one that tells me that this might be the last time we see each other.

I kiss him until we run out of breath.

14

Through the bedroom window, I watch Rémy disappear into the midday crowds. People shift around his broad shoulders and tall frame in an almost synchronized rhythm as if they know he's important. He strides forward through the world unafraid that there might be someone hunting him around every corner. He doesn't glance back even though I wish he would.

I need to see his face one more time. In case it's my last.

My worries congeal into a lump in my throat. I try to follow him with my eyes for as long as I can. The memory of his mouth buzzes along my lips until it's replaced by a terrible feeling like a too-tight hug. The desire for him to stay tugs at me. A tiny voice whispers: *Rémy leaving is a bad idea. This is what Sophia wants.*

But I know he can't stay. His duty is to his family. Without them, there'd be no him.

Edel bursts back in the room with a small parcel. "He left? And without his food?"

I burst. Tears stream down my cheeks. She sweeps me into her arms.

"He's going to be all right," she says, stroking my back until I calm down.

"How do you know?"

"He's Rémy."

I chuckle a little and pull away. I wipe at my face, trying to erase the emotion. Of course he'll be fine. He's smart and strong and calculating.

"Do you love him?" Her blond eyebrow lifts.

I try to form a lie, but I can't. "Yes." The word tumbles out, feeling too little to encompass all of these emotions.

"When this is all over, will you be together?"

"Is it going to be over?" I pull on my coat. "And what would that look like?"

"I don't know."

A bell rings outside. Vendors start shouting, trying to lure customers to their lunch carts.

"We've got to get to the exhibition. We're late," I say.

We pack all of our things and adopt glamours. I deepen the brown of my skin so it matches the chocolate pies being sold right outside our window. I pull my hood tight around my face and tuck my tiny beauty caisse, the teacup dragons, and the maps into my fur waist-sash.

Edel resembles our maman Iris—Amber's maman—with her hair thick, each strand a soft coil, and plaited in two fat twists that hit her waist like ropes of onyx. She packs our remaining Belle supplies into her pockets.

I use Rémy's maps to navigate us back to the aristocratic Rose Quartier. The crowd stretches out as far as I can see, loud and excited, reminding me of the night of our Beauté Carnaval. They swell like a tide on the massive staircase leading into the Silk Hall. My stomach flutters, the energy of it all finding its way inside me as we fold into the rest of the bodies and make our way out of the cold.

The building is a gift box made of glass panels trimmed with ribbons of gold. Silkscreens of the Fashion Minister's freckled face hang from the high ceiling interspersed with portraits of gowns displaying their various wonders. The room's windowed walls give a full view of Carondelet from every vantage point. The blue domed buildings glimmer like cream tarts frosted with blueberry glaze. Day-lanterns zip overhead carrying voice-boxes, and heat-lanterns glow like newborn stars.

"Gather around, everyone. The presentation will start in a quarter of an hourglass," a woman announces through the voice-boxes.

The crowd takes out ear-trumpets and eyescopes, anticipating the start of the show. Sweet-vendors slither through the masses wearing garments that display their treats. A woman dons a porcelain teapot-shaped hat and pours the steaming liquid through her spout into cups; another wears a dress that glows like an oven complete with spiced pies and bourbon tarts. A little boy pushes macarons from his top hat to be caught and consumed. A tall man has a billowing waistcoat from which he extracts peppermint bark, chocolate buttons, and caramel sticks. Peach post-balloons deliver glasses of champagne to eager, awaiting hands.

The teacup dragons squirm as the scents tickle their noses. I tighten my waist-sash, pulling them closer, hoping the warmth and heat of my body lulls them to sleep despite the chattering noises in the cavernous room.

The Fashion Minister's well-dressed team of dandies march

through side doors and yank thick red curtains along the walls and ceilings. The view of the city and the sky above disappears. Night-lanterns are extinguished, replaced by sparklers. Attendants ease the spectators away from the center of the room and form the crowd into a perfect circle.

"Gentleladies, gentlemen, and gentlefolk of the great Spice Isles, this is the first stop of this glorious world tour. Prepare yourself for the greatest Fashion Minister to ever serve the glorious kingdom of Orléans—the one and only Royal Minister Gustave du Polignac."

The room bursts into cheers. At the center of the circle the floor opens, and a platform soars, carrying with it Gustave. He waves at the onlookers, his false hand now gold and studded with emeralds as plump as ripe grapes. His hair sits in a spectacular cone above his head, full of diamonds. I'm flooded with memories of him, of his kindess toward me. My heart lifts with a flutter like it's taken off. He will help us. I know he will.

Beauty-lanterns rush throughout the room as cloaked bell jars descend from the ceiling.

He lifts a voice-trumpet to his smiling lips. "Are you ready?" he teases.

The crowd erupts.

"But are you?"

They clap and jump and whistle.

I gaze around wondering how they can all be so deliriously happy and unaffected by what's happening in the world outside this room.

The velvet cloaks drop away from the bell jars, and the dresses are revealed.

The crowd gasps.

"Behold, little darlings of the Silk Isles, my latest creations," Gustave announces.

The jars swivel and move like post-balloons without a precise destination.

"I'll tell you a little about my favorites. Well, I love them all, but there are a few that hold a deep place in my heart." One of the dresses shifts right over him. The bell jar pivots left and right to show off all angles of the gown. "This one is called the Phoenix. Didn't the story go that the God of Fortune's phoenix changed his feathers when the Goddess of Death lured him away every month?"

The crowd hollers in agreement.

"Pay close attention."

The feathered gown shimmers in oranges and reds, then the feathers change to molten gold, then midnight plums and blues.

Everyone cheers.

"Save some excitement," he replies, "for the Jeweled Worm."

Another dress moves overhead, cylindrical and writhing like a silkworm. Layers unfurl, first exposing a tier of white diamonds and glass pearls, then shifting to shades of crimson studded with rubies.

The crowd drums their feet.

"The Striped Sensation is next." The Fashion Minister bows as a three-piece suit appears in the nearest bell jar. The black and white stripes change to gold and silver, then plum and turquoise, while its matching top hat mirrors the colors.

"Bravo!" someone yells.

"Chic!" another hollers.

The Fashion Minister accepts the praise with a slight smile. "In collaboration with our new queen, Her Majesty Sophia Celeste the

Second, by the Grace of the Gods of the Kingdom of Orléans and Her Other Realms and Territories, Defender of Beauty and Borders, wants all citizens of this great world to feel deeply connected to her. By wearing these original dresses, you will indeed be closer to the queen and her brilliance."

His forced smile is unrecognizable to onlookers, but I've seen it before. He doesn't believe a word he's saying.

"My beautiful dandies will take care of you. Place your orders. Dress with purpose. Show the world who you are. May you always find beauty!" He flourishes his cape, then the platform lowers him back down and he disappears beneath the floor.

His dandies saunter through the eager masses with pen and parchment, noting orders and requests. One approaches us. "Care to put in an early order?"

"A very large order," Edel replies.

"How many?" he asks.

I clear my throat. His eyes flit over me. "One hundred of the the Phoenix, and fifty of the Jeweled Worm."

His delicately drawn eyebrows lift with curiosity. "Do you oversee a harem?"

I don't laugh. Sweat inches down my back as I try to hold on to the glamour, appear confident, and keep the teacup dragons still in my waist-sash.

"We run a very prestigious school," I say. "We want to meet with the Fashion Minister himself to tell him more of our needs."

"Many want to meet with him. He's quite a busy man," the dandy replies.

Panic wraps its fingers around my heart like a fist, squeezing so hard, it might burst. I take out our leas pouch, fish out the remaining coins, and press them into his hand. It's the last of our stash. It's not much. But hopefully garish enough to make him think there's more. "We know him very well."

Edel's eyes burn into my cheek, but I don't dare look at her for fear I'll lose my nerve. "Tell him his little doll has many leas to spend." I try to keep the desperation out of my voice.

He pockets the coins and motions for us to follow him. We zig-zag between groups of excited courtiers bidding on the displayed dresses and placing orders for additional ones.

"Why did you do that?" Edel whispers. "Now we have nothing." Her anger makes her glamour waver.

"He'll give it back to me, and more. I promise."

"But if he doesn't, we can't pay to stay at the boardinghouse tonight."

The gamble burns in my stomach.

"Then it's good we packed our things and brought them with us." I try to sound more confident than I feel. I try to maintain a haughty smile. I try to be the old me, who wasn't afraid to take any risk no matter the cost.

The Fashion Minister won't let me down.

The man taps his cane on the ground as he strides forward, the crowd parting for him, and he turns down one of the endless ornate hallways. Portraits dot the walls—depictions of royal families and famed courtiers enjoying all the Silk Isles have to offer. They sit in plantation carriages overseeing Gris workers or strolling through silk farms with lily-white parasols drifting over their heads like warm-season clouds.

He escorts us into a tea room. The walls soar in stripes of the Silk Isles' signature colors—ocean blue, cream, and gold.

Day-lanterns and beauty-lanterns chase each other overhead like celestial bodies. Servants push carts replete with teapots and sweets. The Fashion Minister sits on a raised chaise surrounded by people—courtiers, attendants.

"Wait here," the dandy orders.

My hands tremble. "Breathe. Hold it," I whisper to myself, and hope the words sink inside me because a quiver vibrates down my spine as it gets harder and harder to hold the glamour. A headache erupts in my temples. The silvery taste of blood coats my tongue. I'm moments from another nosebleed.

"Just a few more minutes," Edel says.

The dandy leans down and whispers into the Fashion Minister's ear. The Fashion Minister's eyebrows raise, and his gaze finds me.

"Clear the room," the Fashion Minister orders. "Everyone. Servants, too." His command bounces off the walls.

The room empties in less time than it takes for a single grain of sand to fall from one side of an hourglass to the other. As the door clicks shut, the Fashion Minister rushes over to us. I almost collapse into his arms from fatigue.

He holds me up. "Little doll?" His eyes scan over me.

I let the glamour drift away.

He leans back in awe as my skin returns to its regular shade of brown and my hair frizzes, each strand tightening into a curl. Blood streams from my nose.

He hands me a handkerchief, and I nod with gratitude.

"It is you." He wraps me up in his arms like I'm a lost child he's just found. The teacup dragons squeal, causing him to pull back. They peek their heads out of my waist-sash and glare at him, aiming tiny streams of fire at his face, which flame out before they can do harm.

"How adorable," he says, unperturbed.

Edel's glamour disappears.

"Ah, the troublemaking one that Madam Alieas always complained about."

"Alieas was the annoying one," Edel snaps. "And hello to you, too."

"Greetings, troublemaker." He puts a hand on his chest. "How were you able to disguise yourselves like that?"

"Our gifts," I reply with utter exhaustion. He takes my arm.

After settling us onto chaise lounges, he dashes to one of the drink carts and brings us two cups of hot tea. I sip eagerly, the warm liquid restoring strength in my muscles. I have never been so glad not to support my own weight. I let the teacup dragons roam around the room. Three pick at towers of macarons in search of something more savory, and the other three chase the day-lanterns through the cavernous space, tangling themselves in their silk ribbons.

The Fashion Minister stares up at them in awe. "There's a shortage of those. Our newest lady on the throne would be quite eager to get her hands on them."

"Soph—"

He puts his hand in the air, pointing at nearby beauty-lanterns. "Don't say her name. Similar to her blood jewelry, she's using enigmatics, fashioning them to resemble almost anything—fans, keys, royal emblems, even dresses themselves. Rumor has it, she's attached the tiny record-boxes to lanterns throughout the kingdom to be collected by her loyal followers. They target specific words and record gossip. Do you understand?"

We nod.

"Now that I've had a closer look at you both, I can tell you're run-down," he says.

"We need your help with two things—money, if you can spare it, and a way to get into the Silk Teahouse."

Without hesitation, he removes a leas pouch from his inner pocket and hands it to me. The weight of it is a comfort. "The teahouses are locked up tighter than a starvation box until *she* declares them open again. No one other than guards—and servants tending to the Belles—goes in or out."

"We know," Edel replies, then sips her tea. "That's why we're here."

"So, what's your plan?" he asks. "I mean, assuming the teahouse isn't your endgame."

Edel stops mid-sip, her strong gaze darting between me and the Fashion Minister. Her brow furrows with suspicion.

"If I wanted to capture you, you'd already be in chains and headed to that fancy cattle-pen prison," he snaps, before grabbing a macaron from a tiered tray and dipping it into his rose-pink teacup.

"But why should we trust you?" Edel says. "Why are you willing to help?"

He turns to me and blows me a kiss. "I've always had a soft spot for this one."

Edel's eyes blaze. "That doesn't mean you're not an ally of the monster who—"

"Be quiet!" His voice blasts through the room like a trumpet.

Edel blanches. My heart pounds.

"I am no friend of hers. She took my husband." His eyes sheen over with tears. "Under the guise of a job as a milliner, she is holding him against his will. Using him as a way to control me. I need her gone, too."

Edel opens and closes her mouth a few times, but nothing

comes out. I glare at her and will an apology to come from her mouth.

"I'm sorry," I reply.

He reaches for my hand and holds it with a squeeze. "It's fine, my poppet. I am used to being questioned like this. I can prove my mettle and worth." He cranes forward. "Our sleeping beauty is in the Gold Isles and is growing stronger, trying to get well before the ceremonies begin. I can't believe that's coming in four days' time."

My heart jumps. "How do you know?"

"I'm very close with our departed leader's beloved partner." He leans in, waiting for the lantern overhead to drift past, and whispers, "Lady Pelletier."

The pieces of this puzzle begin to shift into place. I glare at Edel, satisfied that this visit has paid off.

"Know our beauty is tucked away like a jewel deep in a mountain."

"Can you help us get to her?" Edel asks.

"And to our sister at the Silk Teahouse?" I add.

A knock pounds the door. "Royal Minister?" a voice calls.

"Yes, to both, but we have no more time for catch-up," he replies. "My duties call and anything that continues to deviate from them will garner curiosity and inspire reporting." He taps my nose. "You must rest overnight. Tomorrow, I'll get you where you need to go. But first, I must rescue your bodies and outfit you in something that won't raise such alarm. Come."

15

The mirrored walls around us fog with steam as we soak in natural hot-spring baths, the water heated from the very heart of the Goddess of Death's caves. We learned in our lessons that her bargain with the God of the Sea required her to allow for heat from her eternal fires to warm these waters.

Skylight windows reveal the midnight stars as they rise. Smooth white stone slopes along my back and bubbles remove the tension in my limbs. Edel only dangles her feet in as her eyes dart back and forth between me and the stone doors behind us.

"We shouldn't have stayed," she says. "We could've gotten Valerie tonight and set off for the Gold Isles. Now, we only have four days until the ceremony."

"Try to relax," I say.

"I still don't trust him," she replies.

"We're in his private chambers. He's sent all his servants and attendants away for the night. If he were going to trap us, he would have already had the guard take us away. It would probably make *her* love him more, and release his husband or make her imprison him. He's taking a risk to help us."

"You trust too easily," she replies. "They wrote about you in the papers, you know. You and her fiancé, Auguste."

A bleeding gash opens on my heart. "What?"

"There were reports in the tattlers about how she was angered by your daliance with him. Is it true?"

My relationship with Auguste replays in my head. His gaze heavy, his eyes with their ability to make me feel as if I were the only person in the room, the only person in the world. The sound of his name stirs painful memories I've worked hard to bury deep inside me, rattling and shaking them like snow in a flipped snowglobe.

"So, is it?" she presses.

"I made a grave error." The admission leaves behind an ache in my heart like the deep prick of a needle. All the secrets spilled between kisses; secrets that allowed his mother to discover sacred truths about the Belles and feed them to Sophia. I'm not ready to face that yet.

"You kissed him?"

"Yes."

"What was it like?" She eases deeper into the water.

"Fine."

She arches an eyebrow. "That's it?"

"I don't want to talk about him." I clamp my eyes shut, trying to erase Auguste, wishing I could remove all the memories of him that I carry.

"Did you love him?"

The question burns. She jostles my shoulder. My eyes snap open.

"What about Rémy? You said you loved him."

"I do. Like the way I love you." I grab her and pull her into the water. She relents.

"I saw the way you look at each other. That love must be different. What is that like?" she asks.

"Do you trust me?" I say, brushing away her question. She's always been a cold teapot, slow to warm.

"Yes."

"Good. The Fashion Minister will help us. In a few hours, we'll get Valerie and she will tell us what to do about the Belle babies and we will all go to the Gold Isles together."

"Don't want to talk about boys, huh?" She dunks her head in the steaming water.

She doesn't resurface for so long I begin to worry, then suddenly she comes up sputtering.

"Are you all right?"

Her skin is blush pink like a teacup pig, and water dribbles out of her mouth. "I will be once we leave here."

"We're getting closer." I grab her hand and squeeze it. "We will succeed. I know we will."

We soak until our skin prunes. Soft nightgowns hang from nearby hooks, awaiting our tired bodies. A side door leads into a small bedroom complete with a large four-post bed. A single night-lantern scrapes its head beneath the bed's canopy, and two carts sit at the foot—one with foods rich with arcana-resetting properties like salmon puffs, beef skewers, bacon-wrapped shrimp, and chocolate squares, and the other with jars of sangsues.

Edel stuffs her mouth with three salmon puffs. "I'm so tired I can barely chew," she grumbles, then climbs into bed and pushes the night-lantern out before pulling the curtains shut.

While Edel's light snores fill the room, I cover my arm with leeches and take out Arabella's Belle-book. Under the soft glow of a single night-lantern, I read through more entries.

Date: Day 3,510 at court

Sophia's beauty addiction has reached new heights. She changed her look for each of her morning activities—brunch with her ladies-of-honor, walking in the winter gardens, meeting her cabinet—and then, again, in the evening for her nightly card games and parties. Before one can join her, she's developed a vigorous beauty test for them. They must stand on a platform to be analyzed and scored. If found to be more beautiful, they are given two options—see me to immediately change themselves, or receive a fine and leave the palace. Most submit to this new routine because they are desperate to be in her presence.

I'm afraid of what's next for Sophia and her grandiose desires.

Date: Day 3,435 at court

Sophia brought in new cabinet members today during the assembly meeting. They filed into the Royal Law Room in the Imperial Library, all eager to be her puppets and do her bidding. I hid in the legal stacks while they met below.

Sophia revealed her imperial cameos—mirror-size and perfect for the walls or vanities—and the advertising campaign intended to sell them to the masses. She said the cameos will connect her to the people of her kingdom, when really they will connect everyone to her obsessive wall. The Royal Beauty Minister, Rose Bertain, challenged her in front of everyone, and the meeting ended early. Sadly, the minister will pay for that.

She's trying to have eyes everywhere. Next, she'll probably institute beauty checkpoints as she continues to turn the palace upside down. She receives a ledger of all visitors to her court now. The Minister of War has provided her with a thousand extra guards, pulling them from posts around the kingdom, despite his protests about the safety of the borders being at risk.

I take a deep breath, her words drumming up even more distress inside me.

A post-balloon putters into the room, sea blue and covered in silk threads. It knocks into the dying night-lantern over my head. I put Arabella's Belle-book to the side and grab the balloon's tail ribbons. It holds a rolled newspaper and a note marked with my name.

I open it:

My dearest owl,

I saw the night-lantern light in your room and figured you were still up. I wanted to tell you again how happy I am to see your face and have you with me. Here's a little something to read. Pay particular attention to the Letter from the Editor column. We can discuss in the morning.

Sleep well,

Gustave

I unfurl the newspaper. My heart squeezes.

The *Spider's Web*.

The white ink rises on the black parchment. A tiny ink spider trots along the border. Under the Night Edition header, headlines appear.

COURTSHIP OFF TO A ROCKY START: QUEEN'S
FIANCÉ STAYING AT SPRING PALACE IN GLASS
ISLES RATHER THAN THE IMPERIAL PALACE

MINISTER OF WAR'S FLEET MOVING THROUGH THE
WARM SEA IN SEARCH OF FUGITIVE BELLES

DANGERS OF BEING GRIS—MINISTER OF NEWS CIRCULATES
NEW PAMPHLETS DETAILING DANGERS AND WARNING

WILL THERE BE A WEDDING SOMETIME THIS
YEAR? QUEEN'S FIANCÉ DERAILS ALL TALKS
AND PLANS DURING PALACE MEETINGS

EYES EVERYWHERE! QUEEN'S NEW DRESS LINE
FOUND TO BE ANOTHER WAY TO CONTROL
AND MONITOR THE BEAUTY OF OTHERS

HOPE REMAINS AS THE FAVORITE BELLE
AND HER SISTER EVADE CAPTURE!

A tiny jolt makes me sit upright.

I find the Letter from the Editor column.

Dear Spiders,

A mandate to all followers!

In the past days, there has been debate about whether or not we, the Iron Ladies, support the Belles.

Despite how we feel about their place in society and their gifts, we back their endeavors. Belles Camille Beauregard and her sister Edel Beauregard remain at large, eluding the queen's efforts. As long as they successfully avoid capture, there's hope we can depose this queen and change Orléans once and for all. With her ego bruised and her attention set on revenge, she's vulnerable—distracted and unfocused on the pitter-patter of spiders' feet. Our sources say the palace has been locked down, with one sole checkpoint allowing entry in and out. Trianon is an occupied city, guards as plentiful as lanterns.

The Belles need our help.

Allies to our cause, we implore all followers to aid them if they come across your path. Share your food, shelter, or money. We pledge to replace all things lost in this noble endeavor and assist in any consequences administered if caught. I will honor them myself.

We are behind the Belles.

We stand in solidarity.

May our threads remain strong and our webs serve us well.

Lady Arane, Leader of the Iron Ladies

My breathing rushes out so loud it feels like words. A surge of adrenaline accelerates my heart.

They support us.

They support me.

I read it once more, tracing my finger over the white letters full of hope and promise and confidence.

I rush to the bed, yank open the bed-curtains, and jostle Edel. "Wake up," I whisper.

She grunts and rolls over.

My eyes cut to the door, and I wish Rémy were there, sitting in a chair beside it. It hasn't been a full day since he left, but the hole he's left behind is quickly becoming a gaping pit. I wish I could share this with him.

I gaze back down at the article, tracing my fingers over the white letters. I glance over Arabella's diary entry again.

The palace checkpoints. Does he know? I think of Rémy trying all the various ways inside the palace and being foiled at every turn. Did he even make it there? What if he's already been captured? I wish I could know if he was all right. I unpack one of the invisible post-balloons Rémy left for us. As the night-lantern light crests over me, the balloon's outline appears and disappears.

I take out parchment, my quill, and an inkpot. After three false starts, I finally quiet my nerves and write to him. It's not *too* early, I tell myself.

Rémy,
Sophia has closed all entrances and exits to the palace save one.
Be careful.

The quill falters before I finish. I think about how to close the letter. Writing the word *love* feels heavy and hard. What does it even mean? I know I care about him and don't want him to be hurt. What if it makes him feel uncomfortable? What if it's too strange a word and feeling to use now?

The hourglass on the table flips over, signaling another hour passed, inching closer to dawn. I scribble the word and fold the note before losing my nerve. I prepare the post-balloon with the charcoal. I pull one of the leeches I've just used from the porcelain jar and pin it inside the balloon.

"Or," I whisper into the dragons' cage. "Wake up, little girl." Her golden scales resemble leas coins. I ease her from the pile of sleeping teacup dragons, hoping not to wake them all. "I need you to find Rémy, petite. I need you to make sure he's safe."

I fetch a piece of bacon from the food carts, then pluck one of Rémy's leeches from my tiny set of labeled jars, and wrap it around the meat. She chomps it down, then coughs out a tiny tuft of fire.

"Not very tasty, I know, I know. Sorry." I tie a silvery ribbon around her neck like a collar, then open the single window in the room. A dusting of snow has fallen, and fog hugs the buildings. The lack of visibility should bode well for little Or. She'll look like nothing more than a fallen star, a tear of the God of the Sky, headed for the ground.

A good omen.

She flies off, and I watch her until she's a pinprick of light in the distance.

16

We wake three hours after the morning star has risen. Edel is in a panic, snatching at the bedsheets and clawing her way out of the massive bed.

"We slept too late," she complains.

I yawn and stretch.

"You needed your rest," a voice calls from the doorway. The Fashion Minister hovers in a leather travel cloak. "It's been so long since you've had such comforts, I thought I might as well let you enjoy them."

"We did," I reply, letting my legs linger in the softness of the sheets one moment longer.

"We don't have time!" Edel yells.

"Please settle down with the theatrics. We aren't in the Grand Opera House. That's been closed for a week, honey. I didn't wake you because I had things to put in place—to *help* you." He dangles another fat leas purse in the air, then sets it on the table beside the dragons' cage. "Get dressed and packed up, then meet me in the adjacent parlor for a late breakfast. You can't do anything on an empty stomach."

We bathe again, quickly this time, and dress in the new garments he's left for us, including thick cold-season veils.

I tuck the remaining teacup dragons, Fantôme, Poivre, Feuille, Ryra, and Eau, into my new waist-sash that is expertly tailored to hold them and even has peepholes for them to gaze out, compartments for each to nuzzle in, and a side pocket that allows me to slip food in and out. I smile. There's even a space for Rémy's maps, and my beauty caisse. I'll have to thank the Fashion Minister later.

"Where's Or?" Edel asks, tying her hair up and away from her face.

"I sent her out last night to deliver a message to Rémy." I fit the sangsues into new travel jars left for me by the Fashion Minister, and parcels of food into my satchel.

"Shouldn't you have consulted with me first?" She flattens the dragons' portable cage and puts it in her bag.

"You were snoring into your pillow," I reply. "I did try to wake you up, I'll have you know."

"You could've waited until the morning to send her." She swipes the second leas pouch from the table.

"And have that glittering little dragon flying about in daylight? No, I thought it better to do it at night."

"Fine. But I like to *know* things."

"Fine. Then I have something to show you." I hand her the *Spider's Web* paper. "I had to warn Rémy after reading it. The Letter from the Editor."

"Little dolls," the Fashion Minister calls from the adjoining room. "The food is growing cold."

I lead the way. Edel follows, her eyes scanning the page, and she crashes into the table.

Beside the Fashion Minister, breakfast carts sit as tall as the hair tower he sports today, laden with tiers of quiches, trays of steak skewers, stacks of honey crepes, and carafes of milk and snowmelon juice. My stomach growls at the sight of the decadent food, erasing the memory of mornings filled with lumpy porridge and hard biscuits at the various bordinghouses.

"I see you got the paper I sent you last night," he says.

"I couldn't sleep," I admit.

"Many throughout the kingdom struggle to as well. They lie awake, panicked with worry. I can't imagine many of us are getting the proper rest." He plucks a strawberry from a warm pile of sugar-dusted crepes.

"Only Soph—"

He tsk-tsks. "Shh, don't forget not to say her name."

I nod and take a caramel-drizzled waffle from the cart.

"And you'd be surprised. I don't think she's sleeping much either. It's hard to try to keep things together when all you have are fear and lies."

Edel gazes up from the paper. "They're tracking us?" she says to me.

"Indeed. Supporting you from afar," the Fashion Minister inserts.

"What will they want in return?" she asks him.

He sits back and narrows his eyes. "I'm not sure I understand what you mean?"

"There's always a price for help. No one does it for free," Edel says. "If they're a group that lives away from the rest of us, rejecting beauty work and tradition, then they can't *really* like us. We represent the things they hate."

"I didn't read it that way," I say.

"Because *you* have hope," she says with a snarl.

"And you have none," the Fashion Minister says. "But resistance comes in many forms and alliances take many shapes. Sometimes it's all fire and storms, cutting off the heads of important people. Other times, it's slow, a crack forming in glass, inching forward sliver by sliver, spreading out across the entire surface." He takes a bite of his strawberry; the juice dribbles down his lips like pale blood. "You don't always have to agree fully to work together. Our stars can align in various ways."

The boom of thunder shakes the room.

Edel and I flinch.

He gazes up at the skylight windows. "The weather's starting to turn. The papers said we'd have thundersnow. The God of the Sky is angry today. He's always a bit fussy as the new year approaches."

Edel stuffs a beignet into her mouth. "I'm ready."

"So, you now have money, and I'm going to take you to the Silk Teahouse. Once you have your sister, be sure to leave by the northwest door. That's the house's pier for deliveries and discreet visitors. A private boat will be waiting to take you to the city of Céline in the Gold Isles. You'll be headed up the Rean Mountains to see our sleeping beauty."

His plan laid out before us invites a calm to settle into me for the first time since I left the palace.

"Do you both agree?" he asks.

I look at Edel, who hesitates a moment, then nods.

I reach for the Fashion Minister's hand. He takes mine and

squeezes it. "Thank you," I say. I wish I could make him understand how much his help means to me, but there's no time.

He rises to his feet. "I have replaced your old travel cloaks, and you can use the veils I left for you. Masks aren't as in fashion here or the Gold Isles. The veils help block all the snow they're plagued with and with all the teahouses shut down, it hides fading beauty, so they've made it into a *thing*." He sighs.

We drape the dark veils over our heads. The Fashion Minister crisscrosses the ribbons along our necks and drapes my royal emblem on my forehead like the center jewel of a diadem.

The Fashion Minister opens the door and barks to an attendant standing outside the parlor room, "Ready my carriage."

"Yes, sir, Minister," the man replies and bows.

We follow the minister out a side door and into a luxurious imperial carriage the size of three put together. The goldenrod cushions and teakwood paneling enclose us in the front chamber, safe from a heavy snow that's started to fall. Chandelier lamps tinkle as the horses clip-clop over the cobblestones in the aristocratic Rose Quartier of Carondelet.

"She's spoiling me," he says, noticing my eyes taking in the carriage's luxurious interior. "Thinking it'll make me hate her less for taking my husband or somehow win me over. Stamp out my suspicions and doubts."

A servant hobbles around, attempting to serve tea. Instead it drips down her purple servant gown like streaks of mud.

"You should be better at this by now," the Fashion Minister snaps at her. "Steady yourself." He stands to demonstrate.

My stomach twists. I open the carriage drapes and gaze out. Ice coats the window with a delicate lace pattern, and snow scratches the sides of the carriage like sugar grains. Crowds still swell the entrance to the Great Hall as we pass. They're all huddled beneath snow umbrellas with heat-lanterns floating close. Eager faces bear toothy grins and hands clutch leas pouches, ready to admire the dress exhibition and place their orders.

I think about what we might find inside the teahouse. I think about seeing Valerie again, which calls back the pain of losing Amber.

"What's our plan?" Edel asks me.

"We'll go straight in and use our arcana to disarm anyone in our way."

She nods in agreement.

"Don't be so quick to be loud. Try being like a whisper first," the Fashion Minister advises. "Valerie will most likely be very weak."

"Why? What do you know?" Edel asks.

The carriage arrives at the pier before he can answer. Snow-lanterns dot its pathway to a series of lavish watercoaches, like beautiful jeweled swans ready to swim to the teahouse shore. Guards survey the pier, but not as many as when we first arrived. The woman still sits in the Silk Teahouse reception booth, a fire-lantern bobbing over her head and illuminating her face like a tiny sun.

"I've left instructions with my boatman to wait only an hour-glass," the minister whispers before tapping the glass with his cane.

The woman jumps, then slides open the window.

"Sir, Minister, what a great honor it is—"

"Prepare a watercoach. I need to see the house madam," he orders.

She bows her head. "But of course. Would you like me to call ahead so she can—"

"All I'd like you to do is prepare the coach."

"Yes, sir, Minister." She scrambles out and to the pier.

We follow. This time, she doesn't ask for identification. She barely even looks at us.

"I should call for a servant to assist with the pedaling. We are closed, so they're all inside."

"Yes, please. I do not want to arrive disheveled and out of breath," he says.

She scrambles with the circuit-phone and requests a servant to come to the pier. After hanging up, she gazes at him lovingly. "I adore the new dresses—"

He raises a hand in the air, swatting away her enthusiasm like an annoying fly.

The servant arrives in a watercoach. We step onto it and sit beneath an ornate canopy. Heat-lanterns orbit us like bayou birds.

The woman pedals. A wobbly bow-lantern is a beacon as the snow rushes down from the sky. The teahouse is even more beautiful up close. Porcelain replicas of silkworms are curved into spirals and move as the wind hits the building. I glance back at the pier we've left. The small receiving house is blanched by the snow. My stomach dips and knots itself. Will the woman call the house madam and alert her? Will Valerie be removed in the few minutes it took for us to arrive? Will the guards be waiting to arrest us?

The teacup dragons wiggle in my waist-sash. Maybe they can sense growing fear. Maybe they can feel the worries I've been trying too hard to hide.

Edel opens and closes her fists like she always does when she's mad or worried. The wind flaps the canopy, stretching its fabric with the threat of yanking it off, claiming it for its own.

The woman parks the boat and helps us out onto a small pier. Guards hug the teahouse, in perfect formation around its edges like petit plums bordering a sweet cake. Snow collects on their hats and shoulders yet they don't flinch.

I try to count them. Twelve. No, thirteen. No, it could be more. I can't see them all as the snow barrels down. It makes me wonder how many are inside. We would never be able to disarm them all. Are we walking into a trap? Should we have gone straight to the Gold Isles for Charlotte? Perhaps I was too rash in my planning.

The poison bottle in my pocket feels heavier now with the weight of what we are attempting to do.

The double doors of the teahouse open before we reach them. A woman greets us in a garish dress that reminds me of parrot feathers. A crown of black hair is braided on her head and interwoven with winter blossoms. "Sir, Minister, to what do I owe this great honor?"

"Madam Renault." He leans forward and kisses both of her cheeks.

"As you know, we are closed at the moment." She smiles and the rouge-stick on her mouth is painted to resemble a flower in bloom.

"Ah, yes, I was in the room when the very decree came down from our new majesty. However, I have an emergency." We enter the foyer and gaze up into the house. The open levels reveal a guard on each floor. "Let me introduce you to Lena"—the minister motions at Edel, who curtsies—"and Noelle of the House of Rare Reptilians."

I bow.

"They are dragon merchants and traders. I plan to present them to the queen as a surprise, but they need a quick beauty touch-up before going to visit with Her Majesty. It's so close to her Coronation and Ascension ceremony—three days and counting," he says, pressing his manicured hand to his chest. "I thought it was nothing you and your girls couldn't handle."

I pat my waist-sash and the teacup dragons peer out of it.

"How lovely," she replies, then bows her head. "Thank you, Gustave. However, I must see their faces. On the new queen's orders, anyone who enters this teahouse must be registered." She snaps her fingers at a nearby servant. "Bring the ledger."

I glance at Edel, catching the outline of her eyes. She nods.

"You would embarrass them by forcing them to show themselves looking not their best," he replies.

"It's fine," I say.

The arcana send a shiver over my skin. As I undo the veil, I feel my hair and face change. Edel mimics me.

The Fashion Minister nods when we reveal ourselves.

Madam Renault studies our faces. "Still quite pretty."

"But not perfect," I add. "And Her Majesty requires that."

She agrees.

I place the veil back on and let the glamour fade.

"So..." the Fashion Minster says.

"But we have no Belles here, Your Grace."

He takes her hand and strokes it. "You're not a very good liar. I know you must have one or two at the ready. They tell the cabinet members everything."

She leans close to him. "But I'm not supposed to."

"Darling, it'll be our little secret." He winks. "I'll be sure to send you over a dress from my new line. A vivant dress that captures the depth and breadth of your beauty. You have been maintaining it well. I have taken notice."

She blushes and her severe mouth softens. "I only have one Belle available. The other is, well, you know, indisposed."

"One will suffice." He removes an overstuffed coin purse from an inner pocket in his jacket. "For your trouble."

She accepts the money.

"Please note that they like having their treatments done together in the same room. I know you can accommodate. Your teahouse is rumored to be the best, even better than the Chrysanthemum."

She beams. "Those Du Barrys have been running the whole tradition into the ground. There's decorum and order that must be adhered to. No corners cut." She snaps at a nearby servant, "Prepare the large chamber on the fourth floor."

"You are most gracious, my lady. I won't forget this favor." The Fashion Minister grins, offering Madam Renault his arm. They saunter deeper into the foyer.

My heart drums as we follow behind. The Fashion Minister distracts her by telling her about the low silkworm harvest this season and how it's affected the production timeline for the queen's line of vivant dresses.

The teacup dragons in my waist-pouch squirm as if they're responding to the nerves cramping my stomach. I pat them, trying to calm their excitement, as I take in our surroundings. Where could Valerie be? Edel does the same, craning her neck to see down darkened corridors.

An attendant marches out with a young woman. A silver collar studded with diamonds loops around her neck, drops down her chest, and clasps her wrists together. A pillbox hat sits on her head and a short face veil masks her eyes, nose, and mouth with lacy silk. Her skin is the deep crimson of a recently bloomed Belle-rose, ready for plucking, and she has two mouths, a regular one and a small one beneath it.

Du Barry's words haunt me: *"There will be a favored set of Belles, and a secondary set to ensure that the needs of the kingdom are met. Basic supply and demand."*

"Why is she chained?" I ask.

The Fashion Minister eyes me.

"The queen's orders. She sent a new government-mandated Belle guide by official post-balloon last week. After those fugitive Belles left the palace." Her gaze is strong as she searches for eye contact.

The Fashion Minister loosens the purple cravat at his throat.

"What about the Belle from the favored generation? We would prefer her," Edel says.

The Fashion Minister's eyebrows raise with alarm.

Madam Renault pales. "There are no Belles from that generation here." She tugs the girl forward. "This one is very talented despite what her outward appearance might suggest."

The Fashion Minister stares at me, awaiting my response.

"The queen will be doing away with segregating Belles into favored classes and secondary classes. They will all occupy the same sphere regardless of how they turn out. The new Minister of Belles, Georgiana Fabry, will see to it," she adds.

Simply hearing that name—Auguste's last name—stings.

"Ada is very talented," Madam Renault repeats.

The girl steps forward. I fixate on the bright red of her skin tone and that tiny second mouth beneath her bottom lip as it opens and closes. I swallow down my burning desire to scream.

"I will oversee the session," the Fashion Minister replies. "I am consulting on their looks. Giving them a full makeover to please Her Majesty."

Madam Renault grins. "What lucky women." She walks forward, and we follow.

We are swept into a treatment room. The vaulted ceiling is frosted with gold and blue, wide arching windows overlook the water, and beauty-lanterns bathe shelves of beauty instruments and Belle-products. The walls are threaded with white-and-gold silk like a tapestry, and tiny perfume blimps cascade above us.

The memories of a life filled with beauty work and appointments rush back. The ledgers full, Bree helping me with clients, Ivy at my side, the moments with Auguste—and Rémy.

"The room must be cleared for privacy. Only the Belle and us," the Fashion Minister says to Madam Renault.

The servants freeze.

"But it isn't protocol," Ada replies, sounding just as we once did when clients wanted to break the rules.

"It will be today," I say.

"The servants must stay," Madam Renault replies. "House rules. I do hope you understand."

For the briefest moment, I think Madam Renault might be protecting Ada. I know what can happen when we're left alone with the wrong client. Prince Alfred's disgusting face invades my memory. I still wish I could see him stuffed into a starvation box for attacking me.

The Fashion Minister flashes her a weak smile, then looks at us with distress in his eyes.

"The least you can do is give us privacy while we prepare," the Fashion Minister states. "Go fetch us tea or something, and bring a food cart. I'm famished."

The room empties, doors closing behind Renault and the others. Edel starts to speak, but the Fashion Minister shakes his head and points to the doors. We spot the shadows of feet just outside of it. Then he raises a finger up to the ceiling.

Confusion mars Ada's face.

"Enigmatics," he whispers. "Ada, if you'd please prepare."

She nods and rushes around checking the details like Edel and I would: making sure adequate beauty-lanterns float about, setting out pots of Belle-rose tea on the table, adding pastilles to melt on chafing dishes to fill the room with a lavender scent, draping a large table with pillows and linens. As she works, I trace my fingers over the fleur-de-lis Belle-symbols etched onto each item in her sparkling beauty caisse and ponder how different our lives were only a month ago.

I remember the first time my sisters and I sneaked into the Belle-product storeroom. After the house had gotten quiet, we'd stolen night-lanterns and dragged them to the back of the house. The room's wonders had unfolded to us for hours: perfume atomizers and color crème-cakes and rouge-sticks and powders and kohl pencils and golden vinaigrettes and pastilles and potpourri and oils and sachets. The room smelled heady and sweet, and we'd fallen asleep there after powdering ourselves all night. Du Barry made us write one hundred lines each as punishment.

I search Ada's face for something, anything that resembles the connection I have with my sisters. Can we trust her? Will she be happy once we reveal ourselves? Or will she turn us in?

The risk churns in my stomach.

But we have no choice. We must tell her of our plan. But as the Fashion Minister has pointed out, Sophia could very well be listening. Why hadn't we planned for this? I don't even have a spare piece of parchment on which to scrawl out a message. Then I remember another treatment room, another moment I needed to communicate in silence.

"Undress," I say to Edel. "I have an idea."

I know there is confusion in Edel's glare as she stares from behind her veil, but she obliges. I wave Ada closer.

"I want to show you a technique that we both enjoy and would like you to use," I tell her.

Edel disrobes and climbs into the bed.

"Ready?" I ask.

"Just get on with it," Edel mumbles, the frustration stewing just under her words.

I grab a bei-powder bundle, then sprinkle it over Edel's back, coating it evenly with a makeup brush. My hand wobbles.

The door slides open and another servant slips in.

"We need hot towels," the Fashion Minister orders. "Bring them now."

The woman turns back around and scurries out.

I push my shoulders back and wave the brush in the air to get Ada's attention. In the bei powder along Edel's back, I write a message.

Where is Valerie?

I lift my veil and she sees my face.

Ada gasps and falls backward into a teacart. "The favorite," she whispers.

That word cuts across my skin. The Fashion Minister reaches down and puts a hand over her mouths.

"They're always listening," he reminds her.

"Don't say a word," I whisper. "I promise we're here to help. We need your assistance."

Ada nods and the Fashion Minister eases his hand off her mouths. She quickly wipes away my message and writes, *Near Madam.*

I snatch a rose from a nearby vase, then write: *Take us.*

Her eyes fill with fear, her hands trembling at her sides, but she nods.

17

"I'll stay here and distract the servants," the Fashion Minister tells us. "But be quick."

Edel throws her gown back on, and Ada leads us out through the servant entrance. The house is near silent. We tiptoe to a back staircase.

"This only goes to the sixth floor. The seventh is where *she* resides. We go up there when we've made a mistake and need a 'talking to,' as she calls it," Ada whispers. "It's Madam's office."

We follow behind her with our lightest footsteps. The upper floors are filled mostly with a maze of treatment salons and tea-rooms, but I spot a dining room and game parlor. Unlit lanterns litter the floors. I grip the rose stem so tightly the thorns push into my palm, but the pain is a tiny cut in comparison to the anger rushing through me.

"How old are you?" I ask Ada.

"I don't know."

"What happened to your face? Were you hurt?" Edel asks,

examining the deep red flush that lingers beneath her skin, and the tiny mouth beneath her bottom lip.

"No. It has always been this way."

I've lost track of which floor we're on when suddenly Ada's breathing quickens, and her pace slows. Ahead a man sits in front of a lift, head down reading a newspaper. We press our bodies against the walls, out of sight. His limbs are thin as the bayou reeds from our home island, and his pale skin mirrors the snow falling outside the windows. He whistles softly. The headlines jumble as he quickly turns the pages.

"Stay behind us," I tell Ada, then turn to Edel. "Let's trap him using this rose. We'll turn it into a cage."

Edel nods with a smile.

I close my eyes and the arcana wake inside me. My fingertips tingle. The rose blooms in my mind. I use the second arcana, Aura, to locate its life force; it's weak from being cut and put in a jar of water. Both Edel and I work together to push the rose to grow—the stem splitting into two and slithering along the floor like a pair of thorny snakes. The petals swell to match the man's size.

He shifts his paper down and jumps to his feet, but before he can move forward in our direction, the stem curls around his ankles and the petals swallow him in a red cocoon. His shouts are muffled and his attempts to run thwarted by the binding stems.

"How did you do that?" Ada asks.

"Just how you use the second arcana to grow a client's hair or stretch their muscle tissue," Edel replies.

Ada inspects the massive rose prison we've made as we file into the lift, clearly amazed. She jerks a lever forward. The gilded box sails upward.

"What do we do if she's up here?" Ada's eyes stretch with worry.

"The same thing we just did to him."

She smiles. "I want to learn how to do that."

"We will teach you," I reply.

The set of apartments is empty and dark aside from a single day-lantern hooked to the wall. Edel unties it.

"Now, where did you say our sister was?" I ask.

"Whenever I came up here to be scolded she'd take me to her parlor room. That's where I saw Valerie the first time. There's a bedroom." Ada leads us to a door crested with the Silk Isles' emblem— the silkworm entangled with a royal chrysanthemum.

I push the door open slowly. It's a cross between a tearoom and a small library. High ceilings hold glass windows that gaze down into the belly of the house, with each floor a decadent layer on an expensive cake. Tall ladders slide along mahogany shelves and sets of staircases spiral up to a balcony with more books. Velvet armchairs and tufted couches circle an enormous table littered with replicas of royal emblems sitting on a map of Orléans.

"What is this?" Edel asks Ada.

"She's always plotting and planning and tracking which important people live where. Which courtiers or merchants frequent which teahouses. I've heard her on the circuit-phones. She wants to run all the teahouses. That's her goal."

Beneath the subtle light, the emblems are luminescent and show who has the power in this world. It is only a handful of people.

"This way." Ada pushes through a plain, almost hidden door. Behind it, the room is small, its walls bare, and a bed consumes most of the space.

Its occupant is Valerie.

Edel and I rush to her side. Cerulean healing-lanterns leave strips of light over her face. Vases of flowers ring the bed. Her tawny-brown skin is tough and pruned.

"Valerie?" I whisper.

I touch the wrinkles along her skin. I want to smooth them for her, restore her face to what it once was. But I remember what Ivy said when I wanted to do the same for her—*It will damage your arcana*. I stare at the slope of her nose and the once rosebud shape of her lips and the chestnut of her hair. I can't help but touch her chin.

"What happened to her? What did that woman do?" Edel asks, her voice filling with rage.

"Overuse of the arcana. Ivy's skin looked like this, too," I reply.

"Can we fix it?"

"It's forbidden to work on other Belles," Ada says.

"It's forbidden to do a lot of things," I reply.

Valerie startles awake. "Camille? Edel?" her voice croaks.

My knees buckle, all the worry sliding off me.

Edel and I climb into her bed. The size of it almost swallows us.

"How do you feel?" Edel asks.

Her sluggish eyes brighten a little. "Terrible."

"We've come to take you with us," I say.

"How did you get here?" she asks.

"With a little help," Edel answers. "And we're going to go get Charlotte next and put an end to all of this."

"Where are our sisters?" she asks.

"They've been placed all over Orléans, according to the information I have. Padma is trapped at home, Hana is in the Fire Isles, and Amber is in the Glass Isles," I report.

"Are they all right?"

"We don't know," Edel answers, trying to sit her up, but Valerie's limbs flop every which way and she can barely hold her head straight. "Have you just done beauty work? Is that why you're so tired?"

"I haven't done anything." She fights to keep her eyes open, her lids falling like heavy curtains. "No beauty work in days."

"They're bleeding her. I see the vats of blood being taken to the dock every morning," Ada says.

"But why?" I ask. Valerie is not the aether, so her blood is not being used to grow other Belles.

"I don't know," Valerie says, almost out of breath.

More questions add to the storm brewing in my head. What is Sophia up to?

"We have to get you out of here, and get you well." I push back her once thick hair.

We try to lift her, but she flops back on the bed. I perch over her, wanting my strength to drift into her limbs. The bones in her shoulder push into my leg. A tide of worry rises inside me each time she moans.

"I can't," Valerie replies. "I need to rest for a minute."

"Ada, find some sangsues," Edel says.

I glance up at the hourglass in the room, the sand racing from one side to the other. We don't have much time left to get to the boat.

Edel grabs a cloth from the water basin on the side table and drapes it across Valerie's forehead. "Only for a few minutes, then we have to go."

"Valerie, I have a question." The poison in my pocket almost hums, full of power. "When you looked after the Belle babies, how were they grown? Did Du Barry let you see?"

"Why?" she says.

"Sophia is making more Belles, and I need to know how, so we can stop her."

"She kept two nurseries at home. One for the Gris babies born in the maternity rooms, and one for us." She coughs, then continues, "Sometimes she'd stay up all night, and I'd sneak into the Belle-nursery to see what she was doing. She'd bring a new crying baby inside after the evening star rose."

"Did you find out where they came from?"

Valerie nods. "She digs us up."

"What?" Edel and I say in unison.

"Well, some of us," she pants. "Out of the dark forest. I saw her from the nursery window."

"So much for falling from the sky," Edel snaps.

"No. That's true." Valerie takes a deep and labored breath. "But only one Belle falls. She plants the rest—the favored generation, at least, is grown that way." Her voice grows weaker. "I don't know how she makes the others."

I squeeze her hand and reach in my pocket to wrap my fingers around the poison bottle. "One last question before we try to move you again. Do you think Belle babies can be born without their gifts?"

Edel eyes me curiously.

"Why would you want that?" Valerie asks.

"Yes, why?" Edel adds.

"Sophia plans to sell Belles to the highest bidder," I tell her. Valerie's mouth goes slack with horror. "If we could save the next generation from this fate—"

"Then they could all live normal lives," Edel finishes, nodding in agreement with my line of thought.

I show them the poison bottle. "This might take away the arcana. But I wouldn't know how to administer it. Do you think you could help?"

Valerie's eyes bulge as she runs shaky fingers across the blue bottle. "I believe so. . . ." Valerie starts to drift off.

"Valerie! Valerie. Stay with us," Edel says, rubbing her shoulder.

"Should we try to move her again?" I ask, watching Valerie's eyes flutter.

"Let's check her levels. She's so weak, we might have to cover her in sangsues in order to get her strong enough to move." Edel turns to the side table and retrieves an arcana meter. She plucks needles from the base compartment of the machine and takes Valerie's arm; it's a pale brown branch draped across her lap. Valerie's blood barely fills three vials and slides into the arcana meter's slots.

I hold my breath as I watch Valerie's blood swirl through those chambers. The red liquid bubbles and churns. I wonder what her blood proteins look like now. I wish I could see them beneath Mr. Claiborne's optic-scope. My stomach flip-flops as the numbers begin to illuminate, and reveal her levels.

MANNER: One and a half.

AURA: One.

AGE: Zero.

A knot forms in my throat. She barely has any arcana proteins left in her blood. They are almost gone. This is what will happen to the Belle babies if the poison is successful. Can we survive without our gifts from the Goddess of Beauty? Will she be able to recover?

There's a crash downstairs. "Time to go," Edel says. "We have to move her."

Edel tries to lift Valerie again. I pocket the bottle and help hold up the right side of Valerie's body. She cries out with pain. Edel tries to wipe away a falling tear, but her fingers miss it.

"If she can't walk, we'll be caught," I reply, trying to hide the panic in my voice. "Ada, can you go get the Fashion Minister and bring him to us? We need him."

Fear consumes Ada's face.

I rush to her and take her hands. "He's on our side. He's going to help us."

"What about me?" she asks. "You can't just leave me here."

"We won't. I promise," I say. "Is anyone else here? More Belles?"

"Yes, they're chained on the fourth floor. If I'm not back in a quarter of an hourglass, then..."

"You won't have to worry about that. Just go."

Ada rushes out. We shift Valerie upright, her legs hanging off the bed.

"Good. Almost up," I say. "Just a little bit more."

The teacup dragons shift inside my waist-sash, peeking out, and the dagger at my hip shifts, a half-moon hooked at my side.

"What are those?" Valerie asks.

"Teacup dragons."

"I thought they didn't exist. Du Barry said..." Drool dribbles from her lips.

"Du Barry told us a lot of things," I reply, wiping her face. "They were given to me to help us."

She runs her fingers along their noses as they lick her, then she touches the dagger sheath Rémy gave me.

"All right, let's try to take a step." Edel hoists Valerie's arm around her neck.

"There's so much pain," she cries. "My whole body hurts. It feels like my bones are shattered."

Edel clears her throat and wipes away the tears brimming in her eyes before Valerie can see them. I'm not so quick, and a tear escapes my eye.

"Edel, Camille, I can't." Valerie squeezes my arm with all her strength. "I don't have anything left." Her gaze sears into mine, and her message crystallizes as her hand falls to the dagger at my waist. "Things will never be the same again." She grabs the dagger from its sheath and stabs it into the side of her neck. Her body jerks like a bayou fish caught in a net. She exhales. Her mouth goes soft.

Edel screams.

Not a single drop of blood oozes from Valerie's neck. The wound is dry.

She's empty.

I stumble backward and off the bed, hitting the floor with a thud.

She's gone.

18

"What happened here? I thought we'd embarked on a rescue mission?" the Fashion Minister says, marching into the room with Ada at his side.

"She...she..." The words won't form.

"She killed herself," Edel says with a sob.

The Fashion Minister perches over the bed. Valerie's body stares up at us—her eyes foggy, glazed like glass marbles. Edel drops to her knees. Tears are a storm of fat raindrops down her red cheeks.

The minister covers his mouth briefly, then says, "We have to go, now."

I can't move. I'm a statue sitting vigil at her side.

"We can't leave her like this!" Edel says.

"She's not *here* anymore."

"She needs a proper burial." Edel's eyes spill over. "So the Goddess of Beauty will receive her."

The Fashion Minister drapes a blanket over Valerie's face. Another sob escapes Edel's mouth. I am too stunned to cry.

"Hush or we'll all be caught. My head will be on a spike after an unpleasant tenure in a starvation box. It's way too beautiful to meet such a fate; I take such excellent care of it. And the two of you will be carted off to Sophia's prison to be milked for your blood—just like Valerie has been. My dandies will keep the body safe, transport it to Maison Rouge under the strictest of instructions. The corpse will be waiting for you to bury her. Now, we must go!"

"Don't forget about me," Ada pleads.

I turn to the Fashion Minister.

He sighs. "Another favor? I can see it all over your face."

"Can you help get Ada and the other Belles out?" I ask.

"And take them where?"

"Anywhere but here."

"More breaking of laws," he says.

"You've always done it one way or another," I remind him. "And when the Goddess of Death weighs your heart at the end of all things, she'll see what you did for us."

He leans forward and plants a kiss on my forehead. "If I keep my head long enough to get my husband back, I want to raise a child to have your spirit—and your looks."

I smile up at him. The thunder of footsteps rises from below and shouts rattle the house.

We scramble.

"I'll set her and her sisters free, but where they go is up to them," Gustave says. "My private schooner is waiting for you. It's not supposed to be out on the open waters, definitely more suited for short-distance travel and through canals and rivers, but we don't have a choice. My boatman is discreet, having served me for many years and having been privy to all of my dalliances. Just stay inside the cabin. He'll announce your arrival at the port, then he'll leave for half an hourglass to give you enough time to disembark in Céline before he returns to me."

"Thank you. I can't tell you—"

Madam Renault and her guards march into the room, choking the space and blocking all ways out. "What is going on here?" She paces in a circle, her little heels clicking along the floor. "I had a bad feeling about your visit, Gustave, but to find the favorite and her sister here? That's another thing entirely."

My heart sinks.

She gazes at Valerie's covered body. "What have you done to her?"

"What have *you* done to her?" Edel snaps, her rage loose and ready.

She laughs. "My duty. But, Gustave, it seems you're caught in something you shouldn't be. Something that might cause you to lose your pretty head."

"You won't touch him," I shout, shaking with anger. The teacup dragons peek out of my waist-sash, irritated and hiccuping fire. "Feuille, Fantôme, Poivre, Ryra, and Eau," I call out. "Burn everything."

I make a whooshing sound, and they mimic me. They bolt out and above our heads. Their tiny blasts of fire quickly ignite the tapestries.

"Arrest them all," Madam Renault orders. "And catch those little dragons."

The guards rush forward.

I pull Rémy's knife from Valerie's neck. The tiniest freckles of her blood mar the silver. The last of her. I prepare to use the dagger, though I don't know how. I think of Rémy. He'd say, *They don't know that you don't know how to use it.* I stab at the guards, pushing them back as the flames grow around us.

Madam Renault fusses with Ada, trying to pull her by the chain. Edel kicks and thrashes at the guards. The Fashion Minister throws anything he can reach in their direction. The teacup dragons' fire spreads through the room, igniting the bed canopy. It collapses, dropping fiery pieces on Valerie's blanket. The flames crawl along her body and catch her thick brown hair.

Madam Renault orders the guards to put out the fire.

My eyes blur from the smoke. The guards cough and choke. I can't see Valerie anymore. I can't see anything.

The Fashion Minister hollers out, "Run!"

I grab Edel and Ada by their hands and do as he says, stumbling from the room. The teacup dragons follow, still spreading their fire.

19

Soft beams of moonlight sweep along the ocean as the left eye of the God of the Sky rises. The Silk Isles' teahouse burns in the distance like a dying star. The edges of the imperial island glare as we sail along its coast—lantern-houses and piers and sill-lanterns in mansions that overlook the waves. The color is so different from the water that surrounds our home. I think of the terrifying stories we were told about the octopus living in the Rose Bayou. But we were never taught what lurked out here, what creatures inhabited the God of the Seas' vast domain.

"We won't get there any faster with you watching," Edel says. "And you're letting in a draft. The dragons are getting fussy."

"All the lighthouses are sending beams of light out. Don't you think that's strange?"

"No," she replies. "But it's freezing."

I close the drapes and turn back to the small but decadent cabin. The Fashion Minister's lavish watercoach feels like a palace apartment set afloat. Plush chaises and couches circle a long table

holding all the supplies we've amassed—Rémy's maps, a few stolen Belle-products we haven't had to sell, ink and parchment and a
quill, food for the teacup dragons, my beauty caisse full of labeled
sangsue bottles, the plump coin purses the Fashion Minister gave
us. Fire-lanterns hover throughout, lending their heat to the chilly
space. Cabinets boast all manner of treats—roasted nuts, cheese
blocks, baskets of macarons, casks of wine and ale. But I have no
appetite for any of it. We lost Valerie. We'll never see her again. I
can barely hold that truth in my head.

My throat burns, the taste of the fire still on my tongue. "What
if all our sisters are in pain like Valerie?"

"We can't lose another sister. We need to find a way to get to
them," she says.

"We lost Amber." It stings saying her name.

Edel's face is like stone. "I told you, she's changed."

My frustration, fueled by grief, bubbles over. "You weren't at
that dinner party with Claudine. You weren't at the palace. You
didn't see what Sophia did to us. She turned everything into a
game. She forced me to give a courtier a pig nose, she broke my
hand, she poisoned my food. I didn't get to talk to Amber about
all the things she'd made her do. Sophia is a monster. She bends
you into ugly shapes, and I regret every minute of her being able
to do that to me."

"I saw interviews with Amber bragging about being better than
us. Better than her sisters. More deserving of the title of favorite."
Edel's back stiffens, and her hands ball into fists as she readies herself for a fight. "You can't convince me that she always loved us."

"We all wanted to be the favorite. That means we had to be better than one another," I remind her. "She just wasn't nice about it."

"I never wanted any of that. I never wanted this life."

"Well, good for you for being above it all. But we're not all the same. We're sisters, but we're not the same."

"I don't want to talk about Amber anymore." Edel turns her back to me and reads a newspaper.

We sit in silence for a while, the worries stretching like dough between us. I take Arabella's Belle-book from my travel sack. I trace my fingers across the etched arabella flowers on the cover.

Date: Day 3,657 at court

I found the official Belle registry today. Every Belle who ever lived is accounted for. The favored ones and the non-favored ones. There were ledgers here going back thousands of years. Each generation laid out in family clusters. Names scrawled in parchment alongside their best arcana.

I wonder how many Belles there are now, how many Du Barry grew in my generation, and where they might be. The thought of trying to find them all and make sure they're safe becomes an overwhelming storm. I close Arabella's book to erase the thoughts.

The teacup dragons stir in their sleep just seconds before there's a tap on the window.

Startled, I pull back the drapes. Little golden Or perches on the tiny sill. I push the latch to let her in. She doesn't carry a post-balloon. Instead ribbons loop around her ankle, and she clutches a parchment scroll in her tiny talons.

"You found us, girl." My heart squeezes.

It's from Rémy.

Or lands on my lap. I untie the ribbons quickly and free her to reunite with her brothers and sisters.

Edel darts over to me, almost falling due to the rocky motion of the boat.

My fingers fumble with the note as I try to unroll it. His hand-writing is neat, each sentence perfectly placed on the page. I've never seen it before and the sight of it makes me smile. Edel tries to read over my shoulder, but I pull the letter close so only I can read it.

Camille,

All post-balloons are now subject to monitoring if they leave the city of Trianon. The air-postmen have been given strict surveillance orders. They collect them and transfer the messages into ledgers reviewed by the queen and her staff. If approved, the post-balloons can be released for travel. At night, they'll be using sky candles to illuminate the entire kingdom to watch for any alternate forms of communication.

The Minister of News has even developed weather balloons, which release rain down over cities and reveal invisible post-balloons, so don't risk using the ones we purchased. Send all messages with Or using her claw.

I'm still trying to find my way into the palace. Your note was extremely helpful, and I avoided making a huge mistake trying to use the old tunnel network.

My family is being held in apartments rather than dungeons. The Minister of War ensured that, and I am forever grateful. I'm going to break them out in three days' time, the same day as the coronation. I'm putting the pieces together.

Once I secure my family, I will come back into Trianon and wait for you. The festivities will have just begun, and it will be chaos—which is a good thing. Oftentimes, things are missed in a storm. Use the maps!

Be safe.

Rémy

"What does it say?" Edel tries to take the parchment from my hands. "Is it from Rémy?"

"Yes." I pull away. "It was for me. He told me that post-balloons are being monitored and not to send them in the direction of Trianon anymore. To send Or only." I tuck the parchment into my dress pocket, and it feels like a warm bayou rock through the fabric. His words run through my mind.

I will come back into Trianon and wait for you.

Be safe.

She frowns, her mouth pursed with confusion and irritation. "You're being strange."

"Fine." I take the letter out again and shove it at her.

She reads it. "I'm glad he's all right."

"You suddenly like him?"

"I don't *dislike* him." Her eyes burn into mine. "I don't love him like you do."

"He's been good to us. He was there for me at the palace, even when I didn't realize it," I admit. "He's important." The words *I love him* tuck themselves deep down inside me, afraid to be exposed to light and air once again.

The teacup dragons squeak.

"They need to be fed," she says.

"And we should write to Arabella about what happened with Valerie. She's probably heard about the Silk Teahouse burning already."

Edel feeds them salted pork, then hands me my quill, ink, and a small piece of parchment.

I scribble quickly.

Arabella,

Valerie is dead. The Silk Teahouse has burned down. But we've located who we were looking for, and are on our way there. We'll be with you, soon.

Love,

Camille

I read it out loud to Edel, and she grunts her approval. I put the dragons, except for Fantôme, in their cage and drag a cloth over its bars.

"You've got a journey tonight," I say.

Edel feeds her another cube of salted pork. I fish out one of Arabella's sangsues from our jars. Only two remain.

"Stay low." I kiss Fantôme's warm head and send her out the window.

Footsteps draw near to the door. A newspaper slides beneath it with a whoosh.

I grab it—the late-night edition of the *Herald*. The front page shows Sophia and Auguste at the Royal Opera under the headline: TROUBLE BEFORE MATRIMONY. She's all grins and her teacup monkey, Singe, hangs off her tall hair-tower like it's a low-hanging tree branch. Auguste grimaces, his long, tousled hair pulled back. He's grown a full beard and his eyes look sad.

I wonder if soon I won't think about him or remember him, if little moments like this will stop making the cut reopen, spilling fresh blood and pain. His picture stirs memories I'd worked hard to bury deep inside me, rattling and shaking them like sand in a flipped hourglass. How can I still feel this way about him when the thought of Rémy makes me smile?

I close my eyes and imagine arriving at the palace and facing Sophia. I see her surrounded by her pets—both human and animal—wielding her power, and him sitting on the throne beside her, slumped in the chair with a perpetual scowl on his face. I wonder what will happen to him when we stop Sophia from becoming queen. Has he grown to love her? Has he grown to support her?

The boat jerks.

"Drop your anchor," a voice commands.

I peek out from behind the drapes. A sleek black boat slides up beside our watercoach.

"Edel," I whisper hard.

She doesn't stir.

I jostle her arm.

She jumps.

"Someone is outside."

I whistle. All the teacup dragons wake up. I slip them into my pouch, where they curl back together and resume sleeping. I scramble to repack our things. My skin, my heart, my bones all thrum with panic.

There's a rumble as feet hit the ship's deck. Edel and I move to the center of the chamber, standing back-to-back, bracing for whoever comes through the door.

I place my hand on the knife Rémy gave me. Still spotted with Valerie's blood. My fingers buzz with the tingle of the arcana rising inside to protect me.

The door opens.

Three women enter wearing dark gowns edged in white, their faces covered with smiling iron masks. Etched spiders dot across their cheeks. Crowns of strange pink flowers twist around their heads.

"Don't touch us," Edel hollers.

One of the women laughs. "We don't plan on it." She pulls out two small thuribles. The metal burners explode with thick acrid smoke.

Edel coughs and clutches her stomach. The night-lanterns snuff out.

I wave my hands in front of my face as a dull ringing reverberates in my ears, but it's no use. My lungs fill with smoke, and the light disappears as I feel myself falling.

20

I fall in and out of a dream. Maman replaces Sophia. We're in the library at Maison Rouge. The space is dark and somber, furniture upholstered in deep maroons, crimson velvets, and rich golds, with heavy shaded lanterns sitting on each table. Tall bookshelves line the walls, the varnish giving them a bloody glow. Spines reveal legal titles—beauty and toilette laws, city decorum statutes, and royal family protocol—stretching back to the very beginning of Orléans. A large portrait series of Belle generations hangs from a mosaic ceiling by glittering strings. I'm small, skipping behind her from aisle to aisle, chasing her trailing nightgown.

"What are you looking for, Maman?" I ask.

She smiles back at me, her eyes alive with wonder and excitement. "A fairy tale that I want to tell you."

"I thought you knew all the stories." I catch her and slide my hand into hers; it's warm and strong. "You said you did."

"I do, but I need to get the details of this one just right. It's about the Beauty Trials and the everlasting rose. Did Madam Du Barry tell you about that?"

"No."

She smiles. "You'll see."

We sneak through more aisles until she pauses before a shelf of red-spined books. She runs her fingers across them, and I mimic her.

"Aren't they lovely?" she says, pulling out a thin volume.

"Yes," I say.

She cracks it open, sniffs the parchment, then puts it under my nose. "And they smell like..."

"Ink," I reply.

"Magic." She kisses my forehead. "Come, petite abeille." She leads me to one of the cushioned window nooks in the library. We look out over the Rose Bayou to the left—white trees holding their crimson petals and imperial boats navigating the waters to our canopied dock, and the forest behind our house to the right— all-consuming darkness as far as the eye can see.

She opens the book, traces her long white fingers over the calligraphy, and scans the page. "Before the Goddess of Beauty decided to return to her husband, she had to trust someone to take care of us."

"How did she do it?" I ask.

"If you listen, I will tell you." She pushes a finger against my nose. "So many questions before letting the story unfold. She established the Beauty Trials to draw out the right woman who could be trusted to take care of us."

"What's a trial?"

"A test." She points to pictures in the book of the Goddess

seated on a throne made of Belle-roses. "She wanted to make sure the woman would have the right qualities."

"Like what?"

She taps the picture of a line of women.

"Some of the same qualities that you have, little fox. Determination, strength, kindness, loyalty, fortitude, and most of all, selflessness."

My eyes soak in the pictures of various women standing before the Goddess. "What did they have to do?"

"See this chest here"—she traces her finger over the drawing—"it contains objects that start a divine series of challenges."

"Who won?"

"You don't remember the first queen of Orléans from your history lessons?"

I shake my head. She purses her lips.

"Don't tell Du Barry," I plead. "I don't want to have to write any lines."

"Madam Du Barry," she corrects.

I sigh.

"Never. Our secrets are ours." She winks at me. "Queen Marjorie. She was the first monarch of the House of Orléans. The Goddess also gave her an everlasting rose." She flips a page in the book and taps a picture of a black-and-red rose growing from blood-soaked soil.

"What's that, Maman?" I ask, circling my finger over the ink-drawn petals.

"A symbol that represents us," she replies.

My eyes widen. "Do you think she misses us? Do you think she'd ever visit?"

"I think if we needed her, she would come." She taps my nose. "But otherwise I think she's done with this world. She sent us. We are her everlasting roses. Our blood, *her* blood, is what has rescued this world and allows it to thrive."

"Can we call her on one of the circuit-phones? What if we really need help one day?"

She takes my hand in hers, knitting our fingers together like threads of white and brown yarn. "I don't think she'd send us here without being able to protect us if something went wrong."

The light from a single night-lantern is a shock, pulling me out of my dreams and back into this new and strange reality. My surroundings sharpen around me.

A dungeon.

A cage.

Metal bars lock us inside a cave. Long, pointed cylinders push through the stone ceiling like the spikes on a gigantic teacup porcupine.

My eyes are sore, burning with the memory of acidic smoke, but I spot Edel curled up on the floor a few feet away. A cold tremor jolts through my body as I begin to remember what happened. The metallic scent of stagnant water and steam tickle my nose. I lick my lips and wince. My lower lip is split at the corner and the taste of salt stings my tongue.

How long have we been asleep? How long have we been down here?

I touch my pocket. The poison bottle is still buried deep. I touch my stomach. The waist-sash is gone. The dragons gone. The dagger gone. The maps gone. The beauty caisse with the sangsues gone.

Terror drowns me.

"Edel." I touch her shoulder gently. "Wake up."

She groans and turns over, clutching her head. "What happened? Where are we?"

"I'm not sure." I struggle to get on my feet. My body sways as if we're still on the Fashion Minister's watercoach. My skull is light as a perfume blimp.

I stagger to the bars—curved, black, and containing no visible door.

"Who were those people?" she says, agitation sharpening her voice.

"I've seen those masks before, but I can't remember where." I strain to look through the bars. There's nothing but a great pit with water at the bottom of it. The view sends a wave of nausea through me. Sea-lanterns drift about, spreading tiny ovals of light over craggy rocks. The hiss of steam and the plunk of unknown objects falling into water sound in the near distance. A long stretch of black cables disappear into the darkness overhead.

"Hello!" I shout.

My voice bounces off every wall. Edel massages her temples. I shake the bars, and my own headache intensifies. I lean against the cool rock wall and breathe until it subsides.

Edel stumbles as she pushes herself up. She cradles her head. "I feel sick."

"This is exactly how I felt after Sophia tampered with my food."

Edel inspects the bars and tugs on them too. There's no give. Even if we could remove them, there would be no place to go, no ledge to help us escape. We'd fall more than a hundred paces into whatever lies below. That darkness. That water. Those craggy rocks.

"What would Rémy think of what we've gotten ourselves into?" I say.

"That we should've skipped seeing the Fashion Minister—or even Valerie. That we should've gone straight to Charlotte," she replies.

I can't argue with her. But we did need the money to get to Charlotte—not that we have any of it now.

A loud popping makes us jump. Edel and I move closer to each other.

A rickety carriage putters along the black suspension cable.

Edel and I hold hands.

The door opens to reveal a snug compartment covered in threadbare velvet and thick navy trim.

A face appears, shadowed by the soft night-lantern—a boy about our age with a crooked grin and a strange excitement lighting his eyes. He inches closer, trying to balance as he leans out, and pushes a slender basket through the bars.

"Where are we? And who are you?" Edel barks.

"That's not a nice way to greet someone who just brought you food," he challenges her. His hair is so dark it could be the night sky itself folded into waves.

Edel kicks the basket aside and its contents spill. "I'm not nice, and I don't have to be. You people are holding us against our will."

He smiles at her. "Well, it's nice to meet you, too. Would you like to know how the weather is?"

"I want to know where we are," she replies.

I gather up the food and inspect it, my stomach growling. A wedge of cheese and dried meat. I scarf down my half while Edel continues to spar with the boy. Her cheeks hold a flush and her hands are balled into fists at her sides. The way they go back and forth reminds me of how I used to talk to Auguste. The memory is a burning knot, and I swallow more food to bury it.

"You're at the mouth of the Goddess of Death's caves. We just call it the Grottos. I grew up on a nearby island—though no one even registers it on an official map of Orléans. If you live out here, you're considered unlucky. Not worth accounting for."

"Let us out." Edel tries to shake the bars again, but they don't budge.

"I'm afraid I can't do that. You're in the web now."

"He's right," a voice calls out.

We look up and spot a woman in an open-top dirigible, the words ORLÉANSIAN AIR-POST on it scratched out and replaced with THE SPIDERS. "Quentin!"

The boy jumps, almost falling. Edel reaches through the bars and grabs hold of him before he tumbles.

"See, I knew you could be nice," he says, earning a scowl from Edel.

"You weren't paid to chat, only to deliver food," the woman says. She's gray like a Gris, her eyes glowing embers with impossibly long eyelashes. Her curly black hair is pinned into an elegant knot, and beautiful. "Scurry along home now. I'd hate to have to tell Lady Arane about this. She'd dock your wages."

"Yes, my lady. May your threads be strong." He bows his head, she nods, then he cuts his eyes back at Edel. "See you around, hopefully." He shuts the carriage door, and it inches its way back down into the darkness.

Edel's eyes are fixed on the woman floating in front of us. I abandon the food and stand at Edel's side.

The woman studies us quietly. "I haven't seen a Belle up close in some time."

"It looks that way," Edel spits out.

"Your commentary doesn't bother me. I've quieted those instincts."

"Who are you?" I ask.

"I am an Iron Lady," she replies.

A glimmer of hope springs up inside me. "You're on our side."

"What?" Edel says to me.

"You support us." I press my face against the bars.

"We support *our* cause, and whatever will help us achieve it." She crosses her arms over her chest.

"And what is that? Locking us up? Why didn't you summon the guards?" Edel grips the bars. "Why torture us?"

"You call *this* torture?" She laughs and motions at the basket of food. "At this very moment, our future queen is finalizing her preparations to turn your favored generation into cows, to live in her farm prison where you shall be milked, your power bottled and shipped around the kingdom. The rest she will dole out to every household that can afford it."

Edel and I exchange glances.

"We are no friends to Sophia. I've read your papers. You know that," I say.

"But you've been used as instruments of power. We must ensure you aren't loyal to her in any way. Proximity to power can distort one's allegiances, can make you align with something that wishes to use you, just so you can be close to it."

"And why should we trust *you*?" Edel says. "You poisoned us and locked us up."

"Sleeping gas. It wasn't poison. Many nurseries use it to help babies fall asleep. You took a long nap. Only a few hours," she says. "We will determine if we can trust each other. You will join me on my dirigible, but once we get to the ground, you must wear these over your head." She holds up two sacks. "If you refuse, you can stay up here until you change your minds. Quentin will not be returning with more food, and hunger may coax you into making the right decision."

Edel and I make eye contact. She grits her teeth. But we have no time to argue.

"Yes," I reply for both of us. "We will come with you."

21

She uses a skeleton key to unlock the cell. Edel rushes forward like a storm cloud eager to burst with thunder and lightning and wind. I grab the back of her dress before she reaches the ledge and hold her close. The rage inside her almost seeps through her skin, a humming tuning fork sending ripples out.

We both gaze down into the darkness below, the expanse of it terrifying, a pit to swallow us whole. My mind fills with all the twisted and dangerous things that might await if we took that plunge.

"There's nowhere to run but straight into the Goddess of Death's teeth," the woman threatens.

Edel jerks back, knocking into me. I tighten my grip around her waist. "Calm down. We're going to get out of here," I whisper to her. "We will find our way."

"If you die down here, you become hers." The woman opens a small door and invites us to board her dirigible. "Ready? Or do you still want to run?"

Edel and I lock eyes, gaining strength from each other, then we ease on board and lower ourselves into two makeshift seats.

"Where are my teacup dragons?" I ask.

"Safe." The woman reaches up and closes the tiny fire hatch beneath the balloon. "For now."

"Is that a threat?" I ask.

"It's whatever you want it to be," she replies.

My stomach swoops as we sink deep into the darkness, the cold wetness turning warmer, the hiss of steam growing louder. When we were little girls, we were told that the Goddess of Beauty hated the Goddess of Death. They'd been sisters who'd fought and fussed over all things until they could no longer exist in this world side by side. Unpopular with the other gods for her unpredictable temper, Death was cast into the depths of the world to hide and deal with the bodies and souls of the dead. The grottos are the entrance to her lair.

We reach a small platform and step off the dirigible. Three masked women approach, gripping burlap sacks, their movements languid like spirits.

My stomach tightens.

"Why is this necessary? It's not like we can see anything down here," Edel snaps.

"Edel," I reply despite my fear. "We agreed."

"Listen to your sister," one of the women says, her voice raspy. "She is wise."

"No one is to know the way in and out of the spiders' lair," another says.

I drop my head forward, submitting to the sack. She pulls it over my head. "Good girl," she whispers.

The light is stamped out and my heart squeezes. Panic starts to overtake me but I try my best to fight it.

Another woman grabs my arm and shoves me forward. We walk along a rocky surface. The scent of water fills my nose, a mixture of the Rose Bayou from home and La Mer du Roi. The hiss of steam muffles our footsteps. *Where are they taking us?*

I take a deep breath and think of Rémy. He would say, "Pay attention. Be ready. You will be all right."

Small freckles of light push through the fabric.

The woman's grip tightens on my forearm, pinching the skin. "We agreed to go with you. No need to be so rough."

"Oh, Princess, I'm so sorry," she says sarcastically.

"We're not princesses," I hear Edel holler back.

"We've never been that," I add.

"Settle, or I'll break your arm," she says, her voice grating against my skin like rough parchment. "And I should for what you did."

My blood runs cold. What I did? How could I have done anything to offend this random person at the edge of the world? "Who are you?" I ask.

"You don't remember?" she purrs in my ear.

"I wouldn't be asking if I did."

"We're almost there," another voice says.

We trample down winding stone stairs. The air around me warms as we venture deeper, like we've stepped into an onsen. A thick, heavy sweat coats my skin.

The sound of applause is so sudden it startles me.

"Our dearest lady, we caught something interesting in our web." The woman elbows me forward, and I hit the warm stone ground with a thud. The sack is yanked off my head.

I look up.

A tall woman in an iron mask peers down at me. It hugs the contours of her face and neck, intricately etched with fine lines shaped into a severe expression. A ruby jewel nestles in the center like a terrifying and beautiful red-bodied spider. Gray robes kiss the tops of her bare feet.

I scramble up, struggling to lift myself upright with the cuffs around my wrists, and glance around. The massive cave is pocked with alcoves fashioned into homes with tiny doors and circular windows and ladders that lead down to long piers. Pavilions float on a blue-green lake, oscillating between small watercoaches. Oblong post-balloons zip around, changing from black to red and back again, their ribbons made of knitted silk to resemble spiders' webs.

A nested underground city. I've never seen anything like it. The strange beauty of it rattles all the things I thought I knew about what the edges and corners of Orléans might look like.

More women step forward, each wearing a mask with unique etchings.

"Who are you?" Edel shouts.

The women laugh, creating a sound ripple.

The tallest woman removes her mask—her skin is as gray as a teacup elephant, her eyes black as obsidian, and her hair white as snow. She almost resembles a wizened spider herself. "Edel Beauregard and favorite Camellia Beauregard, I am Lady Arane, leader of the Iron Ladies, editor of the *Spider's Web*."

Edel and I exchange a baffled look.

She's the most striking woman I've ever seen.

"We are the Iron Ladies, the Spiders, the Resistance. Welcome to the Grottos!" She spreads her arms wide.

"What do you want from us?" I ask.

"You can't hold us here," Edel says.

"You're free to go if you can navigate yourself out of the Goddess of Death's Grottos. Only a few know the way. Many have tried to leave, and we don't find them until they're reduced to bones. It is a web of tunnels, hence our name." She turns to the women flanking her. "How long would you wager they'd make it in the dark caves, my ladies?"

"Three hourglasses," one says.

"They're Belles, so I'd give them seven hourglasses," another replies.

"Too small and frail. Half an hourglass," a third yells.

Laughter fills the cave, the drone of it turning into a nauseating hum and stirring itself into my anger.

Lady Arane waves her hand to quiet them and smiles. "We don't plan on hurting you, unless you hurt us."

"You're too kind," I reply.

Her mouth flattens into a straight line. "You should be grateful to us. Lady Surielle saved you." The woman who steered the dirigible steps forward and bows before Lady Arane.

"We don't need rescuing," Edel says.

"Oh, but you did. Had your ostentatious watercoach sailed ten more leagues north, it would've run right into a new imperial guard checkpoint at Crescent Hook Lighthouse. They were alerting all fleets for an escaped ship."

Her words settle over me, and I remember the pattern of light hitting the water as we cruised along the edges of the imperial island.

"You would've fallen right into our newest queen's trap before we had the opportunity of meeting and possibly working together."

"Why would we want to work with you?" Edel says.

"Edel," I say through clenched teeth.

She cackles, setting off another cascade of laughter. "It seems you don't understand who we are."

"And your sister owes me." The woman who dragged me here steps forward and removes her mask.

It's Violetta. The servant from the palace. Claudine's lover. An anchor drops in my stomach.

"You killed someone who meant something to me."

The sweaty heat of nausea washes over me. The feelings of responsibility and regret. "I'm s-sorry," I stammer out.

Her face hardens as if we've both shifted back into that memory. Claudine's dead eyes and slack mouth are all I can see. I repeat my apology, but she crosses her arms over her chest.

"Not now, Violetta." Lady Arane nods at Violetta, who retreats, then turns back to us. "Many who resist the world's constraints live down here with us. We've found ways to combat the discomfort that comes with our natural templates. We've learned to harness the madness. We've learned to live without your kind." She paces in a circle around Edel and me.

The women smile at her and clap their hands, or stretch their arms in the air as she talks, waving them about with excitement.

"We are spiders," she calls out.

"Whom others can't see," the women chant back.

"But they will feel our bite."

"They will heed our lessons," they all reply in unison, then assume a tight formation, arms at their sides.

"And experience our venom," Lady Arane says with a smile. "We've been at this work for years, and both of you have just reluctantly woken up and discovered us. Lady Surielle?"

The woman from the dirigible steps forward and bows.

"Lady Surielle is my first disciple. The most agile. The one with the sharpest teeth." Surielle bows farther with Lady Arane's compliment. "Surielle, go and prepare my boat."

Surielle stands, her expression surprised. "Perhaps they need more time in the dungeons, my lady?"

Lady Arane pats Surielle's shoulder, while she holds my gaze. "I think after a tour of our humble abode, they may be ready. We'll dine on board. They will need further sustenance to ask all the questions they will need to have answered before they join our cause."

Surielle nods and leaves Violetta to watch over us, her gaze a hot poker fresh from tending a roaring fire.

I turn my back to her, unable to withstand her glare, and wish there was a way to explain what happened that night. Or better yet, a way to erase what happened.

"This is a bad idea," Edel whispers to me.

"What choice do we have?" I reply. "We must hear them out."

"What if they aren't who they say they are?" Her white cheeks hold a deep pink flush.

"Then we'll try our luck with the Goddess of Death's caves."

Edel holds my gaze. "We can do it."

"I know. We can do anything together." We nod at each other, then turn to watch as a sleek boat slices through the blue-green waters like a black fish. It reminds me of one of the Palace River canal boats but is large enough for a full staff.

"Come," Violetta orders.

We walk down the pier and step into the boat.

Under a dark canopy, modest cushions rim a decorated table.

Sea-lanterns and fire-lanterns knock into one another. A staff of women sets out plates of food—a rainbow medley of sliced vegetables and fresh fruit, a few wedges of cheese, and a small basket of steaming shrimp.

"How did you get all this food down here?" I ask.

"We have figured out ways to survive. With a little hard work things grow in the darkness and the fruit of the sea can be lured into these waters and caught in traps," Lady Arane replies. "With limited resources, the most interesting things can be born."

We all settle at a low table, sitting on plush cushions.

"If I remove the cuffs around your wrists, will you promise to behave?" Lady Arane asks. "I doubt you'd want one of my ladies to hand-feed you."

I nod.

"The question was mostly for the blond one," she says with a wink.

Edel grunts. "Fine!" Her face seems paler, her lips reddened from biting them with hunger and anxiety.

Lady Arane orders the cuffs to be removed. My wrists are grateful to be released. Bruises ring them, dark as the sangsues. Edel and I immediately start to eat.

The boat snakes along the cave river. The rock ceiling crests over us, boasting bright renderings of a night sky. The paintings of all the stars twinkle as if they're actually there. To the left and right, homes are carved into the sides of the grotto; tiny pinpricks of light escape small windows. Women wave and salute at our boat as we pass.

"Everyone who lives in the Grottos takes a vow of simplicity," Arane tells us, sitting back with a cup of tea. "No lavish clothes, shoes, or homes. No decadence, luxury, or excess. We only have what we need. We share most items as a community. We work hard to ensure all are taken care of."

"How long have you been here?" I ask.

"Since I was a young woman. I wanted to be the Minister of War, but was passed over for the position. I fell out of love with the world above and found this community—"

"So, you don't change yourself? Ever?" Edel interrupts.

"We have developed ways to cope. Eye drops to dull the redness. Powders to soften the hair so it's manageable and able to hold on to dye. But we remain gray and proud. We want to reset the world. Change how it deals with the realities."

I hear Maman's words: *The favorite shows the world what is beautiful. She reminds them of what is essential.*

"With Queen Sophia the usurper in power, we will never stand a chance at this. We're using the *Spider's Web* to influence popular opinion and seed the idea that we don't need to be so intent on escaping our natural forms."

The boat pauses at a pier.

"Come and see."

We leave the boat. Lady Arane leads us along a small incline. It empties at a set of dark curtains embroidered with spiders. She pulls them back to reveal a small room of silkscreens and strange, hulking apparatuses made of wood and brass and bolts.

"What is this?" I ask, gazing all around, my heart lifting with unexpected awe. House-lanterns sail about, illuminating all sorts of instruments—stamps, quills, calligraphy brushes, tiny letter blocks, wooden frames, and color vials. A wall of glass inkpots shimmers, the animated liquid glowing and clawing at their sides, desperate to escape.

"The heart of our web. Our printing press." Lady Arane enters with a flourish and runs her fingers over everything in her path. She points up. Above our heads hang drying newspapers with animated ink racing across the parchment. "This is where my ladies—and a few gentlemen—make our greatest weapon."

"How does it work?" I ask, following Edel as she examines the odd items in the space.

"Violetta," Lady Arane says.

She walks forward, mouth in a grimace. "We create our own parchment and animated ink, catching low-dwelling squids." She takes a piece of parchment from a stack and places it on a long table. "We write our articles and place it in our press." She points at the apparatus. "Just like the ones built by the Minister of News, these produce up to a hundred papers every turn of the hourglass. We've gotten many new followers and lots of support through the circulation of the papers."

Lady Arane touches one of the presses. "I plan to start releasing tattlers to get to those who avoid newspapers, so I can publish works that explore the greatest challenges facing us and make sure the people see the situation as it is, whether they want to or not. Real leaders tell their people the truth, setting the tone for their subjects. Without open leadership and a benevolent queen, Orléans will not survive."

"Princess Charlotte," I say.

"Yes, if she will listen to us, then there's a start. My healers have been visiting her. She's still weak but recovering slowly."

Her words send hope through me that we can remove Sophia from power. "That's such great news."

"You've seen her?" Edel asks.

"Yes, her and Lady Pelletier," Lady Arane answers.

"Where is she? If we can get Charlotte to the palace safely before Sophia's coronation, she can claim the throne and throw Sophia into the dungeon where she belongs," I say.

Lady Arane's mouth breaks into a smile and she nods. Our desires line up like two puzzle pieces locking into one another.

"Why haven't you done that already?" Edel says.

Lady Arane turns to her. "She's not well enough and we don't want to risk being caught before we had a chance to lay our trap. We thought you could help her with your arcana."

"The arcana can't heal," Edel replies.

"You woke her." Lady Arane turns to me.

"We cleaned her blood. Refreshed it, so to speak," I clarify.

"You could make her appear strong enough to face Sophia. She just has to make a legitimate claim to the throne. Sophia thinks she can lie to the world about her sister being dead. There's no telling who she killed and will put on display to get away with this. So, the question is... will you help us?"

"Can you also help us?" I ask.

"What do you want?"

"My sisters."

Lady Arane purses her lips. "Yes. We can assist with that. So, do we have a deal?"

"I need to talk to my sister in private first," I say.

Lady Arane nods. She motions for everyone to vacate the room. "We'll be outside."

Once the curtains drop, Edel rushes to me. "I don't think we should do it. Let's just find our sisters ourselves."

"But she knows where Charlotte is! And how will we get out of here if we refuse? I don't think they're going to let us march out and go on our way."

Edel drums her fingers on the table. "But what does she think is going to happen? The whole world will be all right with living the way they do? Gray and without beauty work? What if some people don't want to? They're all going to fight. We've seen how they act at the teahouses. What happens to us? Are we going to be free? Are they going to let us do whatever we want? Or let us do anything other than beauty work? There's no way they're going to just let us go."

I touch her, startling her out of the rant. "I don't know. All I do know is that we don't get rid of Sophia, we will be in chains. We will have to worry about the rest later."

Angry tears well in her eyes and she works hard to hide them from me.

"We will be all right. I promise."

"I don't believe in promises," she replies.

I slip my shaky hand in hers, reaching deep down to stir any bravery hidden there. "When we were little girls and you set off on your wild adventures—like swimming to the bottom of Rose Bayou to find the octopus creature or sneaking out into the dark forest behind our house—I always went with you. No one else would. I told you I would, and I did. Right?"

"Yes," she mumbles.

"I'm telling you right now that we will get out of here and we will get rid of Sophia, then we will get to work on the future. We won't return to the teahouses. We won't let that happen again—not to us, not to any of our sisters. But if we're going to succeed, we need the Iron Ladies' help."

Edel's brow furrows, and she shrugs. Her way of agreeing.

I go to the curtains and snatch them back.

"We're in agreement," I say to the crowd of waiting women.

Lady Arane smiles. She reaches her hand out. "May our threads remain strong and our webs serve us well."

We clasp hands.

The bargain is sealed.

22

Lady Arane's office glows like a sun trapped in a box. Night-lanterns and miniature sky candles warm the space amid the darkness of the caves. Tall bookshelves line three walls with frayed spines of old titles. Maps of the kingdom and its cities along with cameo portraits of Sophia's cabinet and other unfamiliar faces cover the table.

A dozen or more women stand when we enter. They're all various shades of gray, their straw-textured hair styled in different ways and full of multicolored powders, and their black eyes stare back at us with curiosity. They salute Lady Arane. Her presence sends a wave of serious energy through the space.

"Be at ease, everyone, and have a seat. Please welcome Camille and Edel," she directs.

The women nod.

"Belles, these are more of my disciples," she says to us.

The women introduce themselves in rapid succession, and I

can't hold on to all of their names. Two additional seats are brought for Edel and me.

Lady Arane removes her cloak, handing it to a nearby woman. A tiny gavel is placed in front of her. She taps it on a wooden pad. "I hereby call this official meeting in session. Thank you, loyal Iron Ladies. May your threads always remain strong," she says.

"And may your web serve you well," they chant back.

"First order of business is reviewing the modification boxes. Are they still on schedule to be distributed tonight?"

"Yes, Lady Arane," one replies. I think her name is Liara.

"Let me see them. Our trip above was fruitful in many ways." Lady Arane winks at me, then turns back to the woman. "I left more items to be given to all."

One woman stands and returns with stacks of hat boxes. She unhooks their closures and exposes their contents—toilette box items and rudimentary beauty products.

"I thought you all embraced a life without beauty," Edel sneers.

"These are for medicinal purposes. Choosing to live as a Gris person and embracing your natural template does have its challenges. We're not ignorant or untruthful about it. These items help our residents cope with the pain of it all." She lifts a vial. "This is eye serum." She shakes a tub of crème. "This softens the hair to prevent it from falling out." She closes the lid. "Get the point?"

Edel scowls and sits back in her chair.

Lady Arane returns her attention to her people. "Have the latest newspapers gone out?"

"Yes," one answers. "Just an hourglass ago. We sent the newsies and transports. The *Spider's Web* should reach major cities by the time the afternoon papers are distributed."

"Good." Lady Arane nods. "See, girls, what we're doing here?"

She turns to me, her dark eyes burning into mine. "Do you know what we really and truly want?"

"To get rid of Sophia," I reply.

"Yes." Lady Arane nods. "But I'm going to teach you three lessons while I have you. The first, when bargaining, never show your complete hand. Always keep the thing you want most tucked deep down." She drums her fingers on the table. "The ultimate goal is to force the House of Orléans to fall. To trigger another Beauty Trial."

"But I thought you wanted to teach the world of Orléans to embrace a life without beauty," I say. "Not another Beauty Trial. Is that ritual even real?"

The women fixate on me. The heat of their glares sends a nervous ripple down my spine.

"And wouldn't that be up to Princess Charlotte?" Edel adds.

"The people will have their say," she replies. "Even if we do succeed in removing Sophia and Charlotte takes the throne, her newly appointed cabinet won't solve the core issue—changing how beauty work affects this kingdom. We need an eradication of the old way, and new leadership as the first step."

"I assume you mean *you*. That's what this is about, isn't it? Your play for power," Edel challenges.

The women gasp.

"Edel," I say.

"How dare you! Her web is the strongest!" one says.

"She catches every fly—and even lions—in her threads," another barks.

"She is blessed," a third adds.

Lady Arane lifts a hand, silencing the angry women. "I want Charlotte on the throne so she can call for a new Beauty Trial. That is all. I have no delusions of grandeur about her actually dissolving the monarchy of her own volition or deciding that beauty work is killing the world and she should abolish it out of the goodness of her heart. Not all those who demand a change of leadership want to take on the task for themselves. I want a citizen of Orléans to prove that they have what it takes to lead. If we succeed and there's a Beauty Trial, let me enter and prove myself worthy. Let the gods choose me."

"You would make a wonderful leader for Orléans," one woman chimes in.

The others agree with applause.

Lady Arane taps the gavel. "Thank you for your support, but we all must be given a fair shot. The first step is to go see Princess Charlotte and petition her with our desires. See if she plans to challenge her sister's coronation and ascension. We will go see her immediately. There are only two days left until the official ceremonies begin and Sophia reveals that body."

"How will we get to Charlotte?" I ask.

"You will see." She turns to Violetta and Liara. "Prepare our transports."

Violetta and Liara rush out, and, after conferring with Surielle and giving some instructions, Lady Arane gestures at us to follow. We step outside and walk to the end of the pier, where eight wooden boxes sit in a row, their lids flapped open. Three are filled with all manner of goods. The others remain empty.

Edel speaks first. "Are those—"

"Coffins? Yes." Lady Arane gestures to one that is filled with Belle-products. "These are headed to Céline in the Gold Isles. My associates will take them to a warehouse near the pier."

"Why ship them in coffins?" I ask.

"Lesson number two, petite: Never do the expected," she says with a wink. "Port guards don't bother the dead. They're superstitious. Before Sophia began monitoring post-balloons, we'd send the coffins that way—anchor a hundred post-balloons to carry a coffin across the sea—shipping ourselves and our papers throughout the kingdom."

Three of her disciples climb into the coffins and place their masks over their faces. Edel and I exchange glances.

I take a deep breath. "How long is the journey?"

"Four hourglasses. Enough time to sleep, for the midnight star has just come and gone and it will be morning soon."

Edel's eyebrow lifts.

"Get in," Lady Arane orders.

"I'm not going anywhere without my teacup dragons and my knife." I cross my arms over my chest and plant my feet in place.

Lady Arane snaps her fingers.

A woman disappears and returns with a wooden cage. The dragons flit around inside, looking perfectly healthy. I poke my finger in, and they eagerly lick it.

"We did not harm them. They're quite beautiful and rare," Lady Arane says.

Another woman hands me my waist-sash. I quickly tie it. I open the cage. They climb all over me before settling into my waist-sash. Lady Surielle hands me my dagger. Rémy's dagger.

"What about the money that was taken from us?" Edel says.

"Give them back all of their belongings," Lady Arane orders.

Surielle tosses a purse in Edel's direction. It almost tumbles into the dark waters around us, but Edel catches it in time. I bend and rub my fingers across the plush pillows inside the coffin. Belle-products ring the perimeter. The familiar scent of perfumes and crème-cakes finds my nose.

I watch Edel climb into the coffin and the lid close over her. Cold flushes through me.

Lady Arane gestures at the box. "It won't bite. There are no spiders inside."

"How do you travel?" I ask, as all the other coffins are carried off to a boat and not one is left for her.

"I have my own way. Don't worry. You'll have Surielle, Liara, and Violetta, three of my most trusted. They know how to be in contact with me." She winks. "Meet you in Céline. The Gold Isles truly are beautiful. I was born in a small mountain town there. It'll be good to see it once more."

I climb inside the coffin and lie across the pillows. My back presses into them, and they easily take my shape. I barely have time to take one last breath before the lid closes over me and darkness descends.

23

Sweat soaks my back as my heartbeat picks up speed. I try to steady my breathing and calm the flutters in my stomach.

"You will be all right. You will be all right." I whisper the mantra over and over again. "Try to sleep."

The teacup dragons in my waist-sash squirm and adjust. I pat them until they settle. My brain is a tangle of worries: Did we make the right decision to trust them? Will they keep their word and help us find our sisters? What if they ship us straight to Sophia and collect their prize? What would Rémy think of what we're doing?

My vessel is lifted and carried. My stomach flips. I clench my muscles until I feel myself set down. Snippets of Lady Arane's instructions slip inside the box:

"Be gentle with these! We have first-timers."

"Take the southern exit out of the caves."

"Prepare my boat and I'll leave to the east. If we're being tracked, we'll split their attention."

After at least an hourglass's worth of time, the voices quiet and I recognize the oscillating motion of a boat. I feel like a toy caught in the choppy waves my sisters and I used to create in the onsen tubs at home as little girls. Servants would march us into the bathing chambers and tell us to wait at the edge of the largest, bubbling pool, but Edel would leap in first before getting permission and usually pull me in with her. Amber would scowl, then inch her way in, letting her naked body adjust slowly to the temperature. Padma and Valerie would gather the bathing toys and drop them in for us. Hana always entered last, after her request for more bubbles was denied.

I squeeze my eyes shut, trying not to remember those happier times, trying not to think about how we all won't be together again. The space feels bigger as I sink into the darkness of the coffin. I fall in and out of sweaty hallucinations and tumultuous dreams— Sophia's heckling me as we stand in front of her wall of cameos, the pained look on Auguste's face when his true intentions were revealed at that dinner, Rémy waiting for me in Trianon, the dead, glassy eyes of both Claudine and Valerie.

Finally, the lid of my coffin lifts and I feel the relief of a deep breath.

"Is everyone all right?" Surielle asks.

"I am now, thank you." My skin welcomes the cool air. She smiles down at me, her skin glistening like a gray pearl brought from the depths of the Cold Sea. I stretch and try to hold in a yawn. Sleep tugs at my eyelids.

"It's all cargo down here, so you can come out while we travel. It's about one hourglass until we reach Céline and the Gold Isles."

"Where's Edel?" I ask, just before her groan cuts through the space. I turn and find her open casket is behind mine. She's sitting up, her face an awful shade of green. I climb out of my box and rush over to her, scaling over crates and barrels. Surielle follows and together we try to get Edel up, but she cowers.

"I wish we had some barley water," I say, pushing Edel's hair from her forehead.

Surielle rifles through cargo boxes only to discover bottles of wart tonics, cases of wine, and all types of new télétropes.

"What is this? One of your ships?" I ask her.

"No. An overnight cargo vessel from the port of Nouvelle-Lerec."

I notice that Violetta and one other disciple are posted at the door, masks on and daggers in hand. I want to try to speak to Violetta about what happened with Claudine. I want to apologize and try to explain. But Edel moans again and burps up her sickness, and I can't leave her.

"Try to sleep," I tell Edel, helping her lie down again.

She rolls over, cradling her stomach. Surielle brings a cloak to prop her head up. I find a fan and flap a breeze over her until her eyes grow heavy and her breathing softens.

I find a place nearby to sit, a barrel nestled between two crates labeled BEAULIEU'S CHANDELIER-LANTERNS, and let the teacup dragons out of my pouch. They flutter about, stretching their wings while I keep a watch on Edel.

A silence settles over us, only interrupted by the squawk of a seabird or one of Edel's moans or the clomp of a footstep on the deck above.

Surielle steals glances at me, her black eyes combing over my hair and face.

"Have you always been part of this group?" I ask her.

"I ran away from home at thirteen and joined. My mother was terrible about beauty management. She made us change weekly to keep up with the trends. I hated it," she says. "I was in constant pain."

"How did you learn about the Iron Ladies' existence?"

"You have to know where to look. They leave clues. Spiderwebs and cleome flowers—"

"On buildings." I remember the cobwebs and flowers in the shop windows in Metairie. Makes me wonder how many small signs I missed. How much I hadn't been paying attention.

"What happened to you at the palace?" Surielle asks. "We've heard about this new queen for so long and read about some of her antics, but I don't know what is true and what isn't. I want to hear from someone who was there."

"So many things," I reply. "Sophia wants to be the most beautiful woman in the whole world and she will do anything to achieve it."

"But that is impossible. And frivolous."

"That is what she wants." The anger inside me ties itself into a heavy knot. "I thought she'd kill me with beauty work." I close my eyes for a moment. Sophia's wild gaze greets me, glaring. I shudder.

"She will be stopped," Surielle replies. "All of this nonsense will come to an end."

Her words sink down inside me, mingling with the rage simmering. "I know."

Our eyes meet and hold the same purpose.

"Surielle, Liara and I wish to speak with you," Violetta barks. Surielle joins the others at the door.

I take Arabella's Belle-book from my satchel and trace my fingers over the cover until my heart slows. It makes me miss

Maman's Belle-book. I open it and begin to read, hoping it'll make me sleepy enough to rest.

Date: Day 4,128 at court

Sophia carted me to her prison. The last wing is almost complete as she works the builders to the very edge.

Elisabeth Du Barry has been forced to live at the Everlasting Rose prison now. She tried to grow a dozen Belles and many of them were born too damaged to survive. Sophia gave her a guideline for the unfavored class of Belles. The only principle was that they needed to be suitable for beauty work but didn't have to be beautiful themselves. Many were born with too many eyes or without skin, and a few missing their faces.

So many of the babies haven't made it a full day.

My stomach swells with sickness, disgust sending bile up my throat.

"Camille," Surielle says.

I look up.

"Trouble."

She hands me a newspaper, the animated ink racing. An image of the Rose prison twirls like a carousel beneath the headline: CONSTRUCTION COMPLETE IN TIME FOR NEW CORONATION CEREMONY—AND ITS NEW GUESTS! The Fashion Minister's freckled face is pressed up against its pink bars, the iron warped into the shape of roses. His tears glisten as they fall down his cheeks.

My heart slams into my rib cage.

The portrait flickers.

Another face consumes the frame.

Dread fills my insides as the animated ink fills in.

The Beauty Minister. Rose Bertain. Her fingers curls around the bars, and she gives them a purposeless shake. My eyes race over the article below. The words trip over themselves as I read with desperation.

Gustave du Polignac, famed Fashion Minister, and Rose Bertain, the longest appointed Beauty Minister in Orléansian history, have been detained and are being held at the Rose until further notice. Regent Queen Sophia has announced that both individuals have failed her loyalty test and must be tried before her court to determine if they can remain in her cabinet for the coming year.

"Her Majesty will tolerate nothing but loyalty," the queen's most trusted advisor reported to newsies. "This quality will be the heartstone of her reign. A test of mettle will be administered often and without notice, including time spent in the Rose. These two ministers have been rumored to be disloyal to the crown, and we will get to the truth."

A list of the queen's grievances against the accused will be published after the Coronation and Ascension ceremonies as the queen institutes the building of her cabinet.

My insides are a riot of emotion—rage, sadness, horror, shock, and regret. All the things the Fashion Minister did to help us landed him in a torture chamber.

I did this.

I asked this of him.

And now, he won't get to be with his husband again, and he won't be alive if I don't get Charlotte back on the throne.

The sound of a port bell rings out above us.

"It's time." She shoos me back in the coffin.

Ceiling floorboards creak overhead.

Edel hiccups, then dry heaves. Spit dribbles down her chin. "We're almost there," I tell her. "Just hang on a little bit longer."

"I don't think I can," she moans. "All I can think about is vomiting. I shouldn't have eaten all of that food."

"Port of Céline ahead. Ready the anchors!" a man's voice drifts below deck.

Surielle and the two others rush back to their coffins. "Everyone in." She closes the lid over herself.

I secure Edel's lid, hoping it will muffle her moans and keep us from being discovered. The door cracks open and my pulse hitches. I whistle. The teacup dragons fly to me. I tuck them back inside my waist-sash, slip into my coffin, and slide the top over me. My rapid heartbeat makes my body tremble. Each time the teacup dragons squirm or burrow, it sends a nervous jolt through me.

The noise of footsteps and scraping pushes through the coffin's thin sides.

"Cargo unloaded first," a man shouts. "Start with the coffins."

I'm lifted in the air.

"I didn't realize dead bodies could be so heavy," someone complains.

"Hurry up! My maman said the heavier bodies carry their trapped souls."

I hear muffled stomping and grumbling and the call of early-morning vendors setting up their stalls for the day. I press my hands to the sides and hold my breath as I'm jostled off the ship. They set me on the ground. Sweat trickles across my forehead.

"We will be all right. We will get out of here." I whisper my mantra to the teacup dragons. "We will find Charlotte."

Outside, gulls caw. I can hear the lulling tempo of waves lapping the pier. Just as I'm feeling slightly calmer, a scream cuts through the air.

Edel.

24

I inch up the lid enough to see, but not enough to draw attention. The pier is a chaotic blur of bodies. Merchants toting their wares, lines of passengers headed to board ships and boats, the loading and unloading of parcels and people and boxes, and a network of fishmonger stalls. The energy of it all creates a nauseating hum of early-morning movement.

"Found a stowaway," a port guard says.

I watch as the men drag Edel from the coffin kicking and screaming. The small crowd slows to a stop to watch. Nearby newsies swarm, sending navy blue story-balloons overhead to capture it all—the first potential headline of the day.

I watch it unfold like a story on a télétrope reel, each picture clicking into its drum, spinning and whirling out of control, the scene growing more and more horrific.

Edel's arms thrash about. The guards struggle to hold on to her.

"Keep a grip on her!" one shouts.

She crashes to the ground and kicks at them. Her foot clobbers a guard in the head. He cowers, grabbing his eye. She tries to run.

Another one grabs her by the waist, yanking her like a rag doll.

"How much is the fine these days?" a port guard asks, taking out a ledger from his jacket pocket.

"Twenty-five leas per mile traveled, plus the port taxes. Ten days in the Céline jail if you can't pay," another adds.

A guard grips Edel's arm. "Why were you on this ship? Who are you?"

Edel vomits all over his clothes, then spits in his face. She's picked up and thrown over one of the guard's shoulders like she's nothing more than a sack of snowmelons. Her wails pierce the air. Each one hits me like an icy wave. She punches his back and more vomit spews from her mouth.

"I'm not paid enough for this," he complains. "It's too early. All these overnight ships are always trouble."

"Search all the coffins!" his cohort barks.

They turn and head straight for me. A punch hits my heart. I want to climb out and follow Edel. I try to keep my eye on her, but they're getting farther and farther away from my sight line. The men kick at the other coffins and bang their tops. They're almost to mine.

"Anyone in there?" one yells. "Might as well open up before we have to wrestle you out."

I close the lid and prepare myself. My hand falls to my dagger. My breath comes out rushed and in pants. The teacup dragons chirp with alarm. I unsheathe the dagger and hold it to my chest.

A series of bells rings out.

"Fire!" someone hollers. "The lighthouse."

"Get to the hoses!" the other one orders. "We'll finish the search after."

The men abandon the coffins and race away.

I push the lid off and it lands on the pier with a clatter. I can't see Edel anymore—only a crowd of bodies buzzing about and headed away from the pier. I gaze out and see the top of the lighthouse in flames.

One of the nearby coffins opens.

I spot Surielle. She motions for me to get back inside and presses her finger to her mouth in a shush, then closes herself inside again. The noise of approaching footsteps reaches my ears, but there's no way I'm getting back in that box. I have to go after my sister.

I duck and weave between the cargo on the pier, trying to find the men who took Edel. The chaos of bodies blurs. Jackets, dresses, top hats, heat-lanterns, snow parasols, winter veils.

A hand grabs the back of my cloak. "Where do you think you're going?"

I jerk around.

It's Lady Arane.

"You're supposed to be in your transport," she barks.

"They took Edel. We have to get her."

"We have to get to our safehouse."

"But—"

"I'll send one of my disciples out to track Edel. For now, hide. You're about to ruin everything." She points her fingers. "Look! More guards are headed this way. They won't just ignore the fact that a live woman was found in a coffin. They will complete their search. My fire diversion won't last long."

I spot a cluster of uniformed men and women running in our direction.

Reluctantly, I return to my coffin. Lady Arane closes the lid over me, and I lie flat. I rub my waist-sash to calm the agitated teacup dragons. Tears burn behind my eyes. I can't get Edel's screams out of my head. I can't believe this is happening again. I tremble with anger.

"I'm here to collect these," I hear Lady Arane state. "They're headed for the warehouse to await transport to the crematory."

My coffin is placed inside something that feels like a carriage. All the light is stamped out as more boxes are loaded up beside me. The teacup dragons free themselves from my waist-sash and spread across my limbs. Their nervous hiccups warm the too-small space, and I feel like we'll all run out of air. My chest is tight with worry.

The carriage moves forward, bumbling over cobblestones, making several turns. I'm jerked back and forth with each one.

I clobber my head on the side of the coffin. The teacup dragons protest as I knock into them. The Belle-product jars crack and spill all over. The perfume chokes us. My breath catches and burns like honey bees are trapped in my throat.

Hot tears soak the pillow beneath my head.

First, Amber.

Then, Valerie.

Now, Edel.

And who knows the fates of my other sisters, Padma and Hana. Or Ivy even.

It feels like hours have passed. My stomach twists with the reality that we're probably very far from the port now, and from Edel.

Maman's mirror bounces on my chest, its grooves sharp and piercing. I wish for her to come back. I wish for her to help me fix all of this. I wish for her strength to help me come out of it alive. All the things I'd planned feel like they've turned to wisps of smoke, each tendril headed in opposite directions.

The carriages stop.

I hear Lady Arane's voice again.

Boxes shift around me.

I am lifted and moved into a cavernous room filled with voices. I can tell how large it is by the way the voices echo. Boxes are set on top of mine. The thud of them makes the teacup dragons fuss.

I shush them and clench my eyes shut. How long will we have to stay in here? Where are they taking Edel? Will I be able to find her? A headache thuds in my temples. The box feels like it's vibrating and spinning beneath me.

I bang on the wooden sides. I can't stay cooped up in here any longer.

"Camille," I hear Surielle whisper.

I knock on the wood. "I'm over here."

I try to push the lid again, but it's too heavy.

Slowly, Surielle and Violetta remove the boxes above me, then yank open the lid. Several morning-lanterns float through the warehouse, scattering strips of light over battered boxes.

I sit up. The teacup dragons fly out, stretching their wings with glee. Stacks of coffins are lined up all around us. The air stinks of rotten flesh.

Surielle helps me out. My arms are shaky.

"Keep watch for our lady," she orders Violetta and the other woman. They pivot and go to the warehouse door.

"Where are we?" I ask.

"A warehouse for the dead," she reports.

"How far are we from the port? We have to go back for Edel," I say, but my voice breaks, and my legs buckle under me.

I'm alone now.

I've failed everyone.

She catches me before I hit the floor. "I got you," she whispers.

"We have to go back to the pier," I mutter, out of breath.

"It's too risky," she replies.

"I can't leave her."

"If you chase her, they will take you—and *us*—and this whole thing will be over. Sophia will win. Do you want that?"

Her words harden inside me.

"Lady Arane is just outside. We are to wait for her. That's the order."

"Edel would come for me. She wouldn't just sit back and let them take me." I collect the teacup dragons, tuck them into my waist-sash despite their protests, and drape my travel cloak and veil over me. "She wouldn't do *nothing*. I need her. I won't lose another sister."

Surielle steps in my path, blocking my attempt to leave. "You can't. I won't allow it." She snatches a dagger from a black sheath. "I'm in charge when Lady Arane isn't present."

Violetta leaves her post and rushes to Surielle's side. She reveals a matching blade. Both catch the light from the floating lanterns overhead. The steel twinkles and shines with the promise of drawing blood.

I put my hand on the knife Rémy gave me. A hot, seething ball of anger amasses in my stomach. The arcana awaken and linger beneath my skin.

Violetta flinches. "She's killed people with her arcana."

"And we've killed people with our daggers." Surielle's eyes blaze with intensity. "We have the authority to cuff you again if you don't cooperate. Bargain or no bargain. But I don't want to have to do that." She flicks her knife at me.

We don't move, each of us as still as a statue.

Newsies rush the streets outside the windows hollering about their midday papers.

My heart races alongside the shouting.

"Get them here. The *Glass Post*, just in. The *National*, arriving soon!" one shouts.

"The Regent Queen reopens the skies to receive coronation gifts. Read about the items she desires in the *Trianon Tribune*. We've got the official list. Be sure to address the post-balloons and set them to land on the Observatory Deck, says newly appointed Minister of Royal Gifts."

"Famed courtiers and kingdom celebrities already headed to the imperial island. Check out our limited edition column for a glimpse of the best dressed and best looks."

"Commemorative beauty-scopes to be sold during the coronation hosted by the *Orléansian Times*. Be sure to get one. They're going to be a collector's item."

The shouting subsides.

"Let me out of here," I almost growl.

The Iron Ladies don't move.

A blimp flies past the dirty window featuring the latest imperial headlines.

We all flinch.

NO M ORE SECRECY—WE'RE IN THIS
TOGETHER, SAYS NEW QUEEN!

THE ROSE PRISON TO REPLACE MAISON ROUGE AS
PRIMARY RESIDENCE FOR BELLES—TO ALLOW THE PUBLIC
TO SEE THE INNER WORKINGS OF BELLE TALENTS

LEARN HOW TO GROW YOUR OWN BELLE-GARDEN! YEP—
THEY'RE GROWN LIKE ROSES! READ ALL ABOUT IT

ROYAL WEDDING POST-BALLOON INVITES SENT OUT
TODAY IN TIME FOR AN AUSPICIOUS NEW YEAR!
HOPE YOU ARE LUCKY ENOUGH TO GET ONE!

TWO NEW TEAHOUSES BUILT IN SILK ISLES TO
REPLACE THE ONE LOST DUE TO FIRE

BEAUTY FOR ALL—QUEEN TO PASS OUT NEW PETIT-ROSE
BEAUTY TOKENS TO THOSE WHO EARN HER LOVE

"What's going on here?" a voice calls out from behind us.

We pivot and find Lady Arane standing at the back doorway.
She holds her mask in her hands, her gray skin severe in the light.

"She threatened to leave," Surielle reports without moving
her dagger.

"Surielle, stand down. All of you," she orders.

"But..."

Lady Arane puts a hand in the air. "I've sent two ladies to track
Edel. We should have more news soon."

"I'm going after her." My fingers have grown slippery around
Rémy's dagger, but I grip the handle more tightly.

Lady Arane's eyebrow lifts.

"We had a bargain," I seethe. "We help you, and you help
me. Now your ridiculous travel arrangements have gotten my
sister taken, and I'm supposed to wait patiently?" The teacup

dragons circle overhead hissing and hiccuping fire, mirroring my agitation.

She moves closer.

My arcana hum beneath my skin.

"Be careful, my lady," Violetta says. "I've seen what she can do."

"You should listen to her," I say, filling with rage.

"Lesson number three has come faster than I hoped—resisting has a price. And this is the cost. You lose people you love for the greater good of others."

"I need my sister. I've already lost two. I want Edel back."

"That's not true," she says. "You also want revenge. You want Sophia to pay. You want Sophia off the throne like the rest of us. You know that she's poison for this kingdom. You know many more will die if we don't remove her. Once we meet with Charlotte and challenge Sophia, this will all be over. We can free Amber. The guards will release Edel. We will get all of your remaining sisters. None of that can happen if we deviate right now. Some things must wait, however painful. My ladies will track her." She holds her hand up as if swearing an oath.

My promise to Edel drums inside me. That we would get out of this. That we would succeed.

This journey has made me into a liar.

Lady Arane takes another step toward me. My arm quivers, wanting to strike.

"We must go. The longer we delay, the more likely we will be tracked. Our guide awaits." She hands me an iron mask. "You're one of us now."

25

Mountains stretch as far as the eye can see, their snow-capped peaks disappearing into the clouds. They hold layers of gilded mansions, shops and pavilions pressed into their facades, and a bustling port at their feet, as if the God of the Ground poured golden liquid down the sides of these great summits, and it assembled itself into a vertical city. Carriages suspended on glittering cables lift into the air like gold blimps headed for the God of the Sky's lair. They empty beautiful passengers on promenades that circle the mountain like a set of rings stacked on a plump finger. Jewel-box-colored city-lanterns illuminate Céline's vertical quartiers.

The world is bigger and vaster than I could've ever imagined, bigger than Du Barry could've ever described, more wondrous than any depiction in any of the thousands of books in the library at Maison Rouge.

Snow trickles down on us, soft and light, stamping out the sun and collecting on the heat-lanterns drifting behind their owners.

Many of the people around us laugh and giggle and hold hands. My heart pinches thinking of my sisters. The memory of Edel's screams cuts through me. She rarely cried. She was never afraid. She was our troublemaker. She was always the strongest of us.

I swallow angry tears. I remember when Edel and I got scolded for going too far into the forest behind our home. Maman secretly called her the bat of our generation, always drawn to darkness and mischief. Edel had lost a bet, and the consequence was venturing beyond the graveyard's edge. I'd gone with her while our sisters watched from our shared seventh-floor balcony. The endless shadows swallowed us whole as we tiptoed beyond the thumb-shaped tombstones pushing from the dirt at its edge. Du Barry had told us a monster lived in that forest and protected it from unwanted visitors, especially children. We made it ten steps in before Du Barry came running after us like we were headed over a cliff. She toted us back by the elbows like buckets from a well, and we had to write five hundred lines each about why we would never go into the woods again.

"This way," Lady Arane orders.

I snake behind her, flanked by Surielle and Violetta, Liara bringing up the rear. Their faces are covered completely. The light catches glimpses of their masks, but an onlooker might confuse them for silver makeup or a new beauty trend.

Newsies race past us shouting the afternoon headlines:

DEAD PRINCESS CHARLOTTE'S BODY IN TRANSIT
TO TRIANON TO SIT IN MEMORIAM

TWO DAYS UNTIL CORONATION AND ASCENSION CEREMONY!
GET YOUR TICKETS TO IMPERIAL ISLAND, BOATS FILLING UP!

QUEEN'S COUSINS ANOUK AND ANASTASIA
UNINVITED TO CEREMONIES AND FINED FOR THEIR
BEAUTY WORK ... DEEMED TOO PRETTY!

TAUPE, MAUVE, AND PLUM TO BE QUEEN'S
CORONATION AND ASCENSION COLORS

We cut through the pier crowds and join snaking lines of people waiting to board carriages headed to the city layers. My limbs burn with nervous energy. My thoughts are an overfilled teacup, drowning its saucer. The piercing pitch of Edel's screams ruptures through me. The memory hits me over and over again, then begins to blend with Amber's shrieks from the boardinghouse.

"I will get them back," I whisper to myself.

"What was that?" Lady Arane asks.

"Nothing," I reply.

"Last car on the right," Lady Arane orders. "Get in and spread out. No eye contact."

A carriage porter corrals the line. "Seventh layer. Keep the line tidy. Have your leas ready or you can't board. I'll have no foolishness in my section. Follow directions or be left behind."

We shuffle into the plush carriage behind a couple who can't keep their hands off each other. The woman presses her cold brown cheeks against her companion, who retaliates by pressing his pale white fingers to the crook of her neck. Their infectious giggles fill the quiet space.

I find a seat and look for things to distract me from the chaos of thoughts in my head. Currant cushions and mahogany paneling enclose us, safe from a gathering wind. Heat-lanterns knock into one another over our heads.

"How do those who can't afford the lifts get up to the city?" I ask Surielle.

She doesn't answer, her gaze fixed ahead as if she doesn't know me.

The people around us clear their throats. Some laugh and hide judgmental smiles behind gloved hands.

"The winding path, of course," someone says.

Lady Arane shakes her head at me.

The lift pauses at the market quarter, where shoppers file out, eager to bargain and barter in the stores on this layer. More well-dressed passengers join us, toting hat boxes and lantern carriers and hand trollies bursting with parcels.

We climb higher, pausing at various piers to load and unload people. I stare out the window at the twinkling lights we've left behind, then at Lady Arane and her disciples, who sit like statues. I'm just wondering if we'll be taking the carriage to the very top of the mountain when Lady Arane rings a bell above her head.

"Garden Quartier," the porter announces, as the lift pauses at a level that glows pale green and gold from city-lanterns. Black railings hold winter flower boxes, each bloom wearing a tiny cape of snow.

"We're getting off," Lady Arane whispers.

Surielle waits for me to stand, then takes her place behind me.

We shuffle out and join a crowd on the promenade. Blimps soar in tandem with the crowd's movement, advertising new beauty products soon to be released and the Fashion Minister's vivant dresses. Some feature cameo portraits of Queen Sophia and her promises for new beauty laws. Her hair is all white and loosely curled like a snowstorm trapped around her shoulders. Diamonds dot along the new teardrop curve of her eyes, and she winks at onlookers every few seconds as the blimps circle.

It's almost as if she's watching me. My stomach lifts with panic. Guards patrol the crowds, studying people, but most of the shoppers slip in and out of shops, not paying them much attention.

I glance down at the pier where we began our journey. The lights are tiny pinpricks now, and I feel like we're so close to the sky I could steal a cloud.

I turn around looking for the stairs, but Lady Arane moves forward and I fall into step behind her.

We pass tightly packed shops squeezed next to each other like macarons in a pastry box. Lady Arane stops in front of a door marked CLEOME'S COLLECTION OF CURIOUS FLOWERS. The shop window boasts a miniature greenhouse bursting with colorful blooms.

It's empty of customers.

We enter. A chime sounds. The ladies survey the space. I walk along the edges of the room, running my fingers over a pot of what Maman used to call skeleton flowers in our greenhouse at La Maison Rouge. Her favorite. As a little girl, whenever we'd been tasked to water them, I'd watch in awe as their white petals turned translucent when the liquid hit them, every vein and fiber inside exposed to the light.

I pull one from the pot and put it in my pocket.

Lady Arane whistles.

A pretty clerk peeks from behind a curtain, spots Lady Arane, and nods. Lady Arane approaches a massive bell jar in the middle of the room. It holds a bright cleome flower. A plant-lantern oscillates above, sending down its tiny rays of sunshine.

Lady Arane admires the flower, then whistles again, this time letting the air from her mouth rush into the holes in the bell jar.

The teacup dragons wiggle in my waist-sash, eager to get out, as her whistle sharpens.

"What is she doing?" I ask Surielle.

"Using the key," she says, without taking her eyes off the flower.

The flower curves over and touches the glass. A nearby cabinet inches forward from the wall. Without uttering a word, the clerk hands Lady Arane a night-lantern and Surielle a heat-lantern. Lady Arane slips behind the cabinet, leading the way. Violetta and the other disciple nudge me to follow.

A long winding set of stairs descends down into the dark belly of the mountain. I can't see where they end.

"Welcome to the Spider's Path," Lady Arane announces.

The cabinet closes behind us.

"What is this place?" I ask.

"One of the largest palace fortresses ever built," Lady Arane tells me. "It was called the Yellow Sapphire, but was abandoned by superstitious Queen Jamila because it's believed to contain an entrance to the Goddess of Death's caves. But people say that about many places. Regardless, it's been sealed off and remained unused for decades."

We weave through sharp passageways. The skeletons of post-balloons and night-lanterns scatter the floor. Tapestries of cobwebs coat the walls. The Iron Ladies use their daggers to rip them down so we can continue to pass. We walk for what feels like three hour-glasses. I try to remember all the turns.

Five lefts, and six rights. If I have any hope of trying to make my way back, I have to memorize it.

Surielle hands me a pouch full of water. I gulp it down, then sprinkle some on my fingers, jamming my hand in my waist-sash for the teacup dragons. Their little tongues lick my fingertips thirstily.

Ahead, the silhouette of a man is outlined in the warm glow of a fire-lantern.

Lady Arane whistles again.

The man pivots and parrots her tune.

I freeze. The power of the arcana collects in my hands.

It's Auguste.

26

The sting of seeing him again pins me in place. My legs are weak under me. His hair is cut short and his skin too pale now, the color of eggshells.

Violetta pushes me from behind. "Move forward," she orders, but her words don't register.

My mouth is dry. I feel like all the blood inside me has drained out. I had worked on steeling my heart against this moment. I had trained it against the sound of his voice and let Rémy creep into the crevices left behind. I had thought my feelings for Rémy, combined with my anger, would stamp out any flicker of feeling left inside me.

But they haven't.

"May your threads be strong," he says to Lady Arane.

"And may your web serve you well," she replies.

The cadence of his voice slips beneath my skin.

"Your Grace," she says.

"Please don't call me that." He frowns.

My heart becomes a drum, each beat growing louder and louder, my pulse furious.

"Let me introduce you to my esteemed ladies. My first disciple, Lady Surielle. Second disciple, Lady Liara, and third disciple, Lady Violetta."

They each bow in turn.

The arcana linger right under my skin, reacting, joining the anger inside me. I fish out the skeleton flower in my pocket and sprinkle it with water drops from the water pouch. The petals lose their color and reveal their insides.

"And of course you already know our favorite Belle, Camille Beauregard," Lady Arane says.

I step forward into the night-lantern light.

His mouth drops open and his eyes comb over me. My gaze burns into his. My nerves tingle with revenge. The world around us dissolves. The mountain. The Iron Ladies. The pockmarked lanterns. The teacup dragons.

It's just him and me.

Memories of the night of Sophia's party hit me in waves—the secrets I'd shared with him spat back at me in front of everyone, my private words twisted into unrecognizable shapes and stretched out in the open and subjected to judgment, our closeness exposed to light and air and shriveling like rotting fruit.

His eyes telegraph a thousand apologies.

The teacup dragons gaze out of my waist-sash and cock their heads to the side.

"Camille." My name sounds like a firework when he says it. A loud, popping thing that echoes off the walls. It throws me out of our bubble and back into the long corridor with the Iron Ladies gawking at us.

"What is this about, Lady Arane?" I ask. "Is this some sort of trap?"

"What do you mean?"

"He's an enemy." I grit my teeth.

"Not to us."

"Camille, let me explain..." Auguste starts toward me with his hands out.

I stretch the petals of the flower in my hand until they're the size of the lift carriages we took up the mountainside. Lady Arane and her disciples jump back, shouting in alarm, but I pay them no mind. I cinch the petals around Auguste's waist, trapping him in place. "Don't come near me."

"What are you doing, Camille?" Lady Arane steps closer to me, but I am still as stone. "He's taking us to see Princess Charlotte."

"Step away or I'll snap him in half," I tell her, "and then do the same to you."

"Let us talk in private," he says, his breath ragged as I coil the stems tighter and tighter around his waist and rib cage.

"We had a bargain," she reminds me.

"Our bargain is on hold," I yell.

Anger flares in Lady Arane's black eyes as she glances from Auguste to me. Her jaw clenches and her cheeks vibrate with rage and helplessness. Finally, she nods and her disciples move farther into the passageway, but their daggers remain fixed on me, glinting in the night-lantern light. Ready to stab me at any moment.

Auguste and I stand face-to-face. I hold him pinned like a doll. His eyes gleam.

"Are you going to let me out of this *flower*?" he says.

I tighten it around his waist, thickening the fibers until they're like metal and have the capacity to crush his bones. "Should I?"

"I'm sorry," he stammers out through labored breaths.

"*Sorry?*" I laugh. That word is too small to wipe away the things he did to me. "That's it?"

"I admit it all. I was wrong. At first, my mother had me convinced that helping her was the right thing to do."

"You lied."

"I withheld information."

His expression is anguished, but I can still sense his smugness, like his lips would betray him at any moment and tip into a half-smile.

The memories become a tornado, the turning of a télétrope off-kilter.

The way we argued.

The laughter.

The way he slipped beyond my boundaries.

The sparring.

The way he touched me.

The secret post-balloons.

The way he kissed me.

Sophia's voice rings out between us: *"I've been told you think I'm a monster. That you called me that, in fact."*

"You told Sophia everything she needed to know to terrorize me and my sisters."

"I didn't know what I was doing."

"You made me love—" My voice breaks, and I clear my throat.

"I loved you," he says. "I still do."

The words are like poison darts to the chest. The betrayal twists into bitterness that feeds the anger.

"I tried to stop it all, but I was too late. The pieces were already in motion."

I don't believe him.

I can't.

"I was just a game token on a board to you."

"No, you were much more," he insists, struggling against his bonds. "I hated having to . . ."

His words become a vise tightening around my heart, so I force him to feel the pain, too. I tighten the petals around his core, and he lets out a piteous cry.

His words stumble out between gasps for air: "That's why I'm here. When I realized I couldn't stop what I'd started, I convinced Sophia to choose me as her king. I knew I was clever enough to get her to. Then, I could stay close and disrupt all her plans. I've been working with the Iron Ladies for the past month. Right, Lady Arane?"

Lady Arane steps out of the passageway, arms crossed, sweat shining on her gray forehead. "It's true. He's been our palace informant. Integral to keeping tabs on Charlotte and her condition."

"How?" I prod.

He slumps forward. Sweat pours down his face. "I can't feel my legs."

I loosen the petals' grip on his waist ever so slightly.

"After what happened with Claudine, I found Violetta and helped her leave the palace. We kept in touch. When she joined the spiders, I fed her information, and she got me a meeting," he tells me.

Lady Arane confirms his story with a nod.

"See?" he says, his eyes hooded and—I notice for the first time—ringed with bruises from lack of sleep. "I tried to fix what I'd done. I don't expect you to forgive me. What I did was a betrayal, and trust is a thread between people. Once broken it's hard to mend." He sighs. "I know what I did. I know I couldn't possibly make it up to you, or have a second chance."

"No," I spit.

"But I have your sister Padma with me. I hope you'll talk to her and confirm that I've treated her with nothing but the utmost respect."

I lose my concentration and the flower shrivels. Auguste falls forward, crashing to the stone ground with a thud.

"Padma? She's here?" My vision blurs.

"I convinced Sophia to let me take her with me, so I could maintain myself for the papers. But in reality, I wanted to help her find you. And I knew you'd be upset, and I'd feel that wrath." He rubs his rib cage. "Deservedly so."

"*Upset*," I say, my laugh sharpened by fury. "Take me to my sister."

27

Auguste traverses the tunnels swiftly and silently as if the path is ingrained in his muscle memory. The shape of him is the same, long and lanky, and his stride is confident, his steps pounding like he owns the very ground he walks on.

I ball my hands into fists, trying to quiet every roiling part of me that wants to reach out and hurt him the way he hurt me.

Our footsteps reverberate down the long, winding hall. The cold of the mountain feels caught in the stone all around us, as if the smooth rocks could release snow and wind at any moment. I clench my teeth to keep them from chattering. The Iron Ladies follow behind us, their whispers crescendoing as we snake along.

He steals glances at me.

I glare back.

There's no warmth for him left.

"Violetta first brought me here," he says, taking a left turn. "She showed me the tunnel network. We started working together right after Claudine's death."

The sound of her name still takes the breath out of me.

"I feel horrible about what we did to Claudine," I admit. I don't know how to make it right. I don't know if I can ever fix it.

"So do I," he replies. "I want to fix so many things that have happened."

"I should've stopped it. I should've refused to participate."

"You couldn't have. The rest of us in the room should've challenged Sophia. Stood together against her terrible game. We can't expect one person—or even two—to take the entire burden of resisting on their shoulders. We all have to stand up and say *no*."

I don't know if I ever want to stand with him. Even if he's done the right thing in our time apart. His betrayal is a wound—crusted over, perhaps, but infected and bruised.

"After you woke Charlotte, everything was in chaos. The queen's body needed the ritual treatments to begin its journey to the afterlife, rumors about Charlotte spread everywhere, Claudine's death became newsie fodder, and your escape hit the press like a storm. That, at least, provided the perfect distraction so that we could move Charlotte," he says.

"Well, aren't you a hero?" I snap, the anger inside me loose and ready to hit him once more.

"I'm not telling you this to make you feel differently about me. It's probably too late for that. I don't expect you to forgive me. I don't even know how to ask. But I wanted you to know what happened before you see Charlotte." He nibbles his bottom lip.

I find a pinprick of light ahead to fixate on. I won't look at him. I won't give him any indication of how I feel about any of this.

We turn right. The tunnels smell of metal and iron and rust. Mining-lanterns hang from strings on the ceiling, casting sickly flickering light on the walls.

"Sophia has turned the palace and Trianon into her playground. Installing beauty checkpoints alongside security ones, so she can control everyone."

The image of her shifting blood cameos comes to mind. Then, she was simply keeping tabs on her court. Now, she's found a way to watch everyone, the entire world.

"She tortures those who she deems more beautiful than she. If they don't comply, she locks them up until they relent. She's created new starvation boxes that allow her to watch as their beauty drifts away."

"Sounds like Sophia. She's been given everything she's ever wanted and now, she might be queen." A cold, slippery sensation trickles through my gut. "Who is doing her beauty work?"

"I don't know," Auguste replies.

I think of Ivy and Amber. Of Edel. The things she could be forcing them to do.

The narrow passage opens into a large courtyard before a once decadent palace carved from the belly of the mountain. Gold-and-silver filigree crawls over tall towers. Heat-lanterns and night-lanterns dance around each other, becoming tiny suns warming and lighting the darkness.

"All the passages are plugged with blockades except for this one," Auguste reports.

A set of guards acknowledge him with a nod. They step aside and allow us entry to climb the stairs behind them.

We mount the seemingly endless steps leading to the palace entrance far above. Gilded lifts sit in disrepair with rotten cables. I can imagine the once grand balconies overlooking lavish gardens of mountain flowers, the layers of luxurious private chambers, sumptuous feasts, and overflowing pitchers of champagne and wine, incandescent-lanterns made to capture the light of the outside.

At the top, Lady Arane and Auguste whistle a matching tune. It excites the teacup dragons. They escape my pouch, racing up to the cavernous ceiling and chasing one another like aggravated post-balloons.

I call their names. They dive toward me and tuck themselves back in my waist-sash.

"They're beautiful," Auguste says.

I don't acknowledge his compliment. I don't even look at him.

Eyes forward. Shoulders back. Mouth pressed into a frown.

He leads us to an entry flanked by guards. They nod and let us pass. Tunnels branch off in several directions. The remnants of decadent spaces are laid open: skeletal chair frames, broken tables, blankets of dust. I can imagine the cavernous halls filled with light and warmth and bodies and laughter.

We reach a set of doors, and a guard opens them. An old receiving room sprawls out before us. Gold-flecked walls soar to our left and right, touching at high ceilings and lofty peaks. The space is divided into sections—a bedroom, a workshop, and a parlor. Cerulean healing-lanterns leave blue-tinted streaks scattered about. A dark-haired woman hunches over a worktable mixing liquids into vials and pressing herbs along parchment paper. The massive fireplace roars with light beside a bed.

The woman looks up at me, her piercing eyes so pale and gray they shine like silver coins. Deep wrinkles ring her colorless mouth, and gray streaks her hair and lingers right beneath her skin.

Lady Zurie Pelletier. The dead queen's beloved.

"Camellia." She rushes to me, wrapping me in a hug. She smells of medicinal pastes. "What are you doing here?"

"Camellia is here to help," Lady Arane answers before I can.

Lady Pelletier pulls back and inspects me, cupping her warm hand beneath my chin. "We're so glad you're here."

Lady Arane removes her cloaks and orders her Iron Ladies to post at the doors with the other guards.

Lady Pelletier takes my hand. "You're the reason our Charlotte is awake. You must meet Her Majesty now that she can speak."

Hope springs to life inside me. I realize I didn't fully believe until now. She sweeps me forward to the bed and pulls the curtains back. A night-lantern escapes the bed's canopy. "My darling, we have an important visitor," Lady Pelletier says.

Charlotte glances up from reading a book. Her eyes are bright, yellowed by the lantern light and glistening with sickness. Thin brown curls spread over her frail shoulders, and the once bald patches on her head have started growing back in. Lady Pelletier leans down and kisses her forehead.

"Your Majesty," I say with a bow.

Charlotte's eyes drift over me, taking me in. The teacup dragons climb from my waist-sash and onto my shoulders. She marvels at them, and me.

"You look different from the pictures," she replies, her voice soft and so very different than Sophia's.

"Better or worse?" I ask.

A smile plays across her lips. "My sister has a way of making everyone look bad in the papers—and Wanted posters." She reaches out a hand to me. I slip mine into hers, and her bony fingers feel like a pile of twigs. "I owe you my life."

"How are you feeling?" I ask.

"Better but still weak," she responds.

Lady Pelletier stares down at her, stroking the top of her head. "We're doing whatever it takes to get her strong for the days ahead, for her to take her rightful place."

Charlotte takes a deep, labored breath, air rattling in her chest.

"We will get you well, petite." Lady Pelletier pats Charlotte's hand, then turns to me. "Your sister Padma has been using sangsues to draw the remaining poison out of her."

My heart flickers. "Where is she?"

"She's in the next room, resting. I'll show you." Lady Pelletier sweeps me from Charlotte's bedside.

I follow her into a bedroom reminiscent of our apartments at Maison Rouge. A large bed sits in the back corner beside an open window. Behind a silkscreen, Padma sleeps in a smaller bed, her black hair a mess over the pillows like a spilled ink jar.

I almost trip over my dresskirts as I run to her. "Padma!"

She wakes with a jump. Her sluggish eyes brighten. "Camille!"

I almost fall into her arms, enveloping myself in the scent of her—flowers and powders and home.

I hold my breath to keep from crying, then my words rush out in sputters. "Are you all right?"

She looks fine. Tired but fine. Nothing like the condition in which we found Valerie.

"Yes, I am well," she replies. "And you?"

"Better now!" I tell her. Trembles vibrate through my arms and legs, and I fight to hold on to her, to never be taken from her. A fissure rips inside me, all the worries and stress pouring out of me, all the anger and disappointment and frustration. She strokes my hand. I wish she would tell me everything will be all right like our mamans used to.

But she can't.

We sit in my tear-soaked happiness.

"I saw the news about Amber, then about Edel," she says, pulling back. Tears coat her eyes, which are the same color as mine. "Do you think they're all right?"

"I don't know." I wipe my wet cheeks. "They're being held in the Everlasting Rose. No telling if they're being tortured, if they're surviving whatever experiments Sophia is doing on them."

I open and close my mouth a few times, trying to find the words to tell her what happened to Valerie. But nothing comes out.

Lady Pelletier approaches. "Camille."

I look up from Padma.

"It's time for our nightly meeting. You both must come with me. We're going to put our plan into action."

28

The war room is like a decayed honeycomb. Faded paintings of the great battles in Orléansian history bleed along the walls. Weapons hold rust and cobwebs. Guards are stationed around the room beside every door and window.

The Iron Ladies, Auguste, and Lady Pelletier gaze at a map of Orléans spread across a wooden table along with small replicas of the kingdom's fleet. Newspapers sit in mounds. House emblems are organized under labels—SOPHIA SUPPORTERS or SOPHIA OPPOSERS. A variety of merchant and high houses straddle the line between the two categories.

"More and more pledge support every day." Lady Arane stands, pointing at the royal emblems. "We have two days to get Charlotte to the palace. I say we arrive at the Royal Square and make a spectacle. Our regent queen loves a show above all else."

"We could lure her out of the palace," adds Surielle.

Violetta claps in agreement with this statement.

"We cannot march into the Royal Square with an army," Lady Pelletier replies. "She will just take Charlotte."

"We have the numbers," Surielle says. "We can make a huge and impressive showing. Hundreds alone in Trianon await our call. We can move others in from the isles and cities."

"I agree with Lady Pelletier that this isn't the way," Auguste replies. "She's got her trap set. She's told the world that Charlotte is dead. She plans to present a body and she will. Not many have seen Charlotte since she fell into her unfortunate slumber. They will buy into her lies. They already are. She's used the news and the newsies to her advantage. The *Orléansian Times* ran a poll yesterday and many love her. They will believe that whatever body she trots out is Charlotte."

"But the moment Charlotte shows her face and allows inspection of her identification marker, the world will know the truth," Surielle says.

The table grows quiet.

"What is the *truth* in Orléans?" Lady Arane says, then turns to me. "You and your sisters spent your entire existence altering appearances, shifting reality, catering to the most shallow whims. This world was born out of a rotten, poisonous seed—and now, the framework is laced with it. Everyone spends all their time trying to look like something else. The masses will believe what is presented to them, as long as it's compelling and beautiful. Thanks to you, they no longer have any idea what's real—what's true."

Her words sting and rattle me, the truth of them pressing beneath my skin as I begin to understand exactly what she thinks of us. Padma squirms at my side. I attempt to get the conversation back on track.

"Sophia will expect us to make a big show," I state calmly. "She will have planned for it. She is most likely counting on it. I think we should be like a whisper." I use the Fashion Minister's words, the image of his smile cascading through my mind.

"I agree," Lady Pelletier replies, leaning across the table and pulling out the map of the palace grounds. "I've known this child my whole life. She craves spectacle and assumes everyone else thinks the same way she does."

"I've been told there's only one way into the palace now," I say, boldly repeating Arabella's warning about the main entrance.

"You've *heard* . . ." Lady Arane replies with suspicion.

"I have my own supply of information." I sit up a little straighter.

"Camille is right," Auguste says. "It's not known to the public, but the northern entrance to the palace serves as the checkpoint in and out. The other three gates have been closed citing 'repair' and are being closely monitored. She has plans to have them shut permanently once the construction on the Everlasting Rose is complete."

The mention of the prison sends a shudder through me. The images of the Fashion Minister and the Beauty Minister are ever present in my mind. I can't close my eyes without seeing the anguish in their eyes and the pain in their faces. So many people are suffering, and it's up to us to end it.

Lady Pelletier taps her finger on the table. "We should go in through the queen's tunnels and bypass the single checkpoint." She turns to me. "That is how Arabella smuggled you and Amber out after you woke Charlotte."

Lady Arane purses her lips and considers. "The element of surprise. . . . Hmmm . . ."

"Sophia has discovered those passageways," Auguste

interjects, sucking all the hope out of the room like air in a pierced post-balloon, sending it plummeting to the ground. "As Regent Queen, she was briefed on the tunnels, as is protocol."

"We don't have time to send someone to find the right way in and report back. Once the coronation happens, Orléansian law is clear. We will have to topple the entire cabinet," Lady Arane says.

"Maybe it needs to be erased and remade!" someone else shouts.

The group explodes with opinions. Their voices agitate the teacup dragons in my waist-sash. The various ideas swirl around me, none of them settling or feeling like the right thing to do.

I wish Rémy were here. His quiet determination. His ability to see all aspects of a problem. His ability to present his ideas and then listen to others patiently, without arguing. His ability to remain calm. My brain is a chaos of thoughts on how to get into the palace, growing louder over the arguing voices. Only one thing is clear—one or all of us will have to walk straight through the front doors of the palace. What kind of person would Sophia be unable to refuse? All the moments spent with her shift through my mind—her insatiable desire to be the most beautiful, to be feared and loved by all, and to have the most attention in every single room.

I let the irritable teacup dragons out to explore. They knock over the house crests, making a mixed-up mess of the Iron Ladies' chart—those they have identified as Sophia supporters and opposers.

The door slides open. A guard pushes Charlotte into the room in a wheeling chair.

"Your Majesty," Lady Arane says.

Everyone stands to greet her.

"So happy to have you join us." Lady Pelletier rushes to her side and places a hand on her cheek, then moves her to join us at the table.

"I could hear you down the hall. But this person you speak of . . ." Charlotte begins to say, her voice wobbly. "It doesn't sound like my sister. Not the one I knew. Sweet, always in pursuit of adventure, a lover of gifts and trinkets, and full of laughter. My mother used to tell us stories of our births. My sister loved hers. Maman said there were shooting stars the day she came, and she was destined to bring light. But all I've seen is darkness since I've woken."

"She is changed." Lady Pelletier takes the princess's hand.

"I've been reading about what has happened in Orléans since I've been asleep, none of it good." She sighs and leans back in her chair. "The world has twisted her. Warped her."

"More than just that," I say, but no one looks up, and they launch back into sharing their various plans. Their voices rise over one another, each trying to drown out the next, each thinking their idea is better, more sound.

"We can alter the course the world is on," Lady Arane says, striking the table with confidence. "We can make sure Charlotte is queen." She looks at the princess and steadies her voice. "The *rightful* queen."

"I need more time to recuperate. If Sophia is as bad as you say, I'll need all my strength to do what needs to be done," Charlotte replies.

"Queens don't rule alone. You will have counsel and support," Lady Pelletier assures her. "We will make sure you're ready. This is what your mother would want."

"Do I look like a queen?" she asks the table.

Her eyes gleam with sickness beneath the night-lantern light. A soft cloth swaddles her head and her hands fight stillness, tremors moving them without her control. The light brown of her skin fades, gray seeping in along the edges of her face.

"We thought bringing Camille here could help with that," Surielle interjects. "She will make sure you appear strong."

Everyone turns to face me.

"Yes. I will make our rightful queen appear healthy and formidable," I tell them.

"And then what?" Charlotte asks. "How are we to enter the palace?"

I close my eyes and see Sophia on the throne, her teacup pets racing around her as she tortures women standing on dress blocks. I see the Sophia from my dreams, laughing and sneering beside her imperial blood cameos. I see Rémy and Edel and Amber and Valerie. An idea surges through me, the hope of it blazing bright and revealing what I must do from the pits of my heart.

"I will be her wedding gift," I say, my voice slicing through the room, pouring out louder and sharper than I intended.

"What did you say?" Lady Arane demands.

"I will march through the front doors," I announce.

"Excuse me?" Surielle asks.

"Auguste, you will write to Sophia and tell her you're sending a dragon dealer to the palace in honor of the upcoming Coronation and Ascension. She needs teacup dragons for her menagerie. They're lucky and auspicious. She will be able to meet several and pick one."

"That doesn't solve the issue of how *we* will get inside the palace. One person can't topple an entire kingdom," Lady Arane fires back.

"But one person can start a fire," I reply. "Sophia loves nothing more than a beautiful gift. You just said so, Your Majesty." I gesture at Charlotte. "One of the newsies said Sophia is reopening the skies to receive offerings in celebration of her coronation. You are adept at moving cargo no matter the method of transport. So send your entire army in a set of gift boxes via post-balloon. They're being collected on the Observatory Deck, I believe. Someone get the latest papers."

Lady Arane lifts a suspicious eyebrow and looks at Auguste. "What do you know of this?"

"That it's brilliant," he replies.

I don't let his compliment make me smile, though his confidence in my plan strengthens it. I sit up a little taller and push my shoulders back.

"I remember going there as a child to look at the stars through the gigantic optic-scopes with my father," Charlotte says.

"Violetta, go get the papers," Lady Surielle orders.

Violetta nods and scurries out.

The table stares at me, waiting, anticipating. I will my thoughts to settle into coherent shapes. I take a deep breath and continue. "I will make sure the doors from the Observatory Deck to the inside of the palace are open so you can come down into the palace. And that whoever watches over the gifts . . . cannot effectively do so anymore." The words are thick on my tongue. My willingness to harm a stranger feels so easy and wrong, and not a choice.

"The Ascension Ball starts after the midmorning star in two days. It's an all-day affair according to the latest papers," Surielle says. "If we arrived that morning, we'd be able to infiltrate easily. The palace will be in the chaos of preparation."

"We will forge special masks for the occasion and join them

only to..." Lady Arane rubs her fingers under her gray chin, considering my proposal. "Yes, yes, I think I like this."

"But the question is..." Surielle perks up. "How will you just march into the palace without being recognized? Your face is plastered all over the kingdom."

I close my eyes.

The arcana are a small throbbing tendril under my skin, a reluctant thread buried deep that I pull to the surface with an angry tug. A cold prickle crawls up my spine.

I hold a portrait of Maman in my head.

My body changes.

Everyone gasps.

I hold a portrait of Lady Arane in my head.

My body changes.

I hold a portrait of Surielle in my head.

My body changes.

A headache pulses in my temples. Blood trickles down my nose.

"What...how...?" several voices say.

Padma stands, slipping her hand in mine. "How did you do that?"

I lose the glamour. She gazes at me, her eyes brimming with questions. "I'll teach you. Edel taught me."

I wipe my nose, then turn to the table. "I know Sophia. I have experienced her torture. I know what to do." I clasp my hands together. "Your Majesty, Padma and I will work together, if you feel well enough, to make sure you look strong and beautiful to face her and the people of Orléans."

"I will stay and help Charlotte travel," Padma offers.

A hush comes over the room. Lady Arane cups a hand over her mouth. Excitement thrums in their veins—I can feel it.

"Are we all in agreement?" I ask, the power of the bargain swelling around me.

"Yes." Auguste stands.

"Yes," Charlotte replies. "That is what we must do. We will plan to arrive by sundown before the ceremonies begin. We will meet you on the Observatory Deck."

"I'll leave in two hourglasses. Prepare a transport," I order.

"May our threads remain strong and our webs serve us well," Lady Arane says. "And may you, Camille, trap our enemy."

The treatment rooms in the subterranean palace resemble a painting plucked straight from the Belle history books in the Imperial Library. Grand pools stretch out in each direction, water ravines sloping through the mouths of massive fireplaces. A constellation of cracks decorate each empty hearth—mosaic images of the gods fractured. Candelabras clutch half-burnt candles bearded with rotten drippings.

Lady Pelletier pushes Charlotte into the first private chamber. She unties three night-lanterns from the back of Charlotte's wheeling chair, and sets them afloat. They drift about, their pleats of light revealing a long table covered in a blanket of dust. Moth-eaten pillows cling weakly to the remains of their intricate embroidery. Cabinets contain decayed Belle-products.

"Your Majesty," I say, and turn to her, "maybe we should do your beauty work in the receiving room where your bed lies."

"I couldn't bear to do it out in the open with all those people," she replies.

"We could clear the room," Lady Pelletier adds.

"No." Charlotte raises a weak hand. "I can handle a little dust."

Lady Pelletier starts clearing the table. She coughs as dust clouds explode around her. One of her attendants helps Charlotte from her chair. She wobbles before taking her first step toward the bed.

"Should we lift you, Your Majesty?" the woman asks.

"No." Charlotte straightens her back and takes a second step.

Padma and I exchange glances.

How will she be ready to face Sophia?

How will the kingdom support her claim to the throne?

I take a deep breath and point to the cabinets. "There's probably nothing we can use here."

Lady Pelletier produces a few of the Belle-products Edel, Rémy, and I had stolen from the Spice Teahouse.

"Glad to see those haven't gone missing," I reply.

"We don't like these circulating in our dwellings for fear of triggering old habits and stoking old impulses from our followers."

Padma takes them from Surielle. She sets out the few Belle-rose elixir vials, four miniature skin-paste pots, and one small bei-powder bundle. "It'll have to do."

We unbutton the thin gown Charlotte wears. Gray rises from beneath the brown of her skin, swallowing it. Her bones protrude, and I resist the urge to count her ribs.

Padma and I nod at each other. She coats the princess in white bei powder.

Lady Pelletier tips the vial of Belle-rose elixir to Charlotte's mouth, easing the liquid down her throat.

"Do you have a desired look?" I ask her.

"Make me look the way my mother would want me to."

Her request tightens my throat.

"I'll focus on her hair and face," Padma says. "And you her skin and body."

I nod. "We must go slow. One thing at a time." I remember my first beauty session with Princess Sabine and all the treatments I tried to complete all at once, almost killing her. I hear Ivy's words and feel the pinch of missing her too. Hopefully I will see her and all my sisters soon.

Padma and I stand on opposite sides of the table. We reach across it and hold hands. Padma's arms quiver with nerves. I squeeze her fingers tighter and close my eyes.

Princess Charlotte's body appears in my head—frail, almost gray.

The arcana hisses through my veins with warmth and familiarity.

"You first," I whisper. "Hair."

A patchwork of frizzy brown curls sprout from Charlotte's scalp; the scars left behind from Sophia's poisoned comb zigzag across the soft flesh, barely healed, but the new growth of hair covers them.

"You next," Padma says.

"Your Majesty, are you all right?" I gaze down at her.

She nods.

I run my fingers over her skin, deepening the brown so she matches her beautiful mother, Celeste.

Padma fattens her cheeks, the outline of her skull no longer visible. I do the same to her body, thickening her muscles and plumping her frame, fortifying her bones, and giving her the shape of an hourglass.

Sweat soaks through my clothes.

Charlotte starts to resemble the young woman I saw in portraits before she fell into the long, poison-induced sleep.

The doors snap open.

"Camellia!" Lady Arane says. "I'm sorry to interrupt." She clutches a newspaper. "You must go right now."

She holds the paper out. The headlines scatter. The words *torture* and *guard* and *Rémy Chevalier* scramble.

Chains crisscross over his bare chest. Blood drips down his dark arms, gashes oozing and pulsating.

I rush to her and grab the pages from her hands. The headline reads:

CAMELLIA BEAUREGARD'S TRUSTED GUARD CAPTURED
AT PALACE—TO BE EXECUTED IN THE ROYAL SQUARE

29

I fall back on the bed, all the air rushing out of me. White spots stamp out my vision. Worry and anxiety drum through me.

"Camille, what is it?" Padma asks.

She helps me up, the grip of her brown hands comforting but not enough. I think of Rémy, of his strength, of the fact that he needs me, and I pull myself together to stand up straight.

"She's right. I have to go."

"But we aren't finished—"

"I will send word when I'm safe." I kiss her cheek, and she pulls me into a hug. "I love you."

"I love you, too," she whispers.

I swallow down tears. Being with her made me feel a little less alone, a little more confident that everything would be all right. But I will see her again. I have to believe that.

In a nearby chamber, I dress quickly, pack my belongings, and gather the teacup dragons. I walk out expecting Lady Arane only to find Auguste leaning against the wall.

"What are you doing here?" I snap.

"I've arranged for one of my boats to take you to Trianon. The imperial fleet will grant you safe passage if you sail under my flag. I've sent word ahead of my travel plans, and the gift I'm sending to my fiancée—a dragon dealer named Corrine Sauveterre."

The words *thank you* can't form in my mouth.

I nod.

"I've already started having the gift boxes made to fit each one of the Iron Ladies," he adds. "They'll be beautiful on the outside and—"

"I don't need to know the details—just that they're being sent. I need to go."

"Yes, of course." Auguste leads me back through the winding network of tunnels. The teacup dragons fly above us, their scales catching the light from the single night-lantern he carries. The melody of their flapping wings and the pounding of our footsteps are the only conversation between us. I constrict like a corkscrew, knots coiling tighter and tighter as the unspoken words are a set of knives twisting inside me.

The throbbing gashes on Rémy's body appear over and over in my mind, thoughts of him being tortured drowning me.

Auguste's eyes search for mine in the subtle darkness.

I march forward, picking up my pace. The tunnels grow colder as we snake through them, the outside close. The scent of snow and ice replaces the stench of stagnant water and rust.

He whispers my name.

I ignore it.

He touches my arm.

"Don't!" I snatch it away.

"I'm sorry."

"You think that word can fix it?" My teeth clench. "Do you know how small that word is? Too tiny to fix what you did. Too easy to try to sweep away all the things you set in motion."

"What can I say? What can I do?"

"Nothing. It's impossible for you to erase this. It would be like asking for the sun to leave the lair of the God of the Sky. Or asking the ocean not to rush the shore." I run ahead, hoping it's the right direction. "I don't have time for this. I have to get to the palace."

"I know there's nothing I can ever do to make you trust me again," he shouts out behind me. "But I've been trying to do *something*—*anything* in my power to right this wrong."

I stop and whip around to face him. "You gave her exactly what she needed to destroy me! Me *and* my sisters!"

My voice booms off the cavernous walls. I don't care who hears me. My anger transforms into something that could live outside of me, a windstorm bursting from my chest made of thunder and lightning and furious rain.

"I didn't know." His hands shake at his sides.

"That answer will never be enough. It will never be all right." My glare burns into him. I wish it would reduce him to nothing, show him how I felt after I discovered what he did to me. "Valerie is dead. Amber and Edel and Hana are under Sophia's control. Who knows what she's doing to them?"

"We will stop her," he says. "I can fix this."

"*I* will stop her. *I* will fix this. I will end this," I say through clenched teeth.

We lock eyes. The deep brown of his irises is rimmed with red like chocolate malt candies dipped in cherry glaze.

"Are you done?" I shout.

I harden into stone as his shoulders shrug forward. "You're

still the most beautiful girl I've ever met, and even more so when you're mad."

His compliment stirs into the fire inside me. "And you're still an ass who thinks charm and compliments are bandages."

"No, just sharing the truth." His voice breaks. "If I have to... and if something happens, if things don't go as planned...I will make sure no harm comes to you, and that...she doesn't survive as queen. Neither you nor your sisters will ever suffer again. I'll do whatever I can to make this right. You have my word."

"And it's worth a grain of sand."

"I know, but you have it nonetheless." He tries to take my hand.

I pull it away from him. "Just make sure you hold up your side of the deal. Make sure Padma and Charlotte and the Iron Ladies get to the palace safely. That's all I want from you. I will take care of Sophia. I will take care of the rest."

"Understood."

We start walking again. He makes a left at a fork in the tunnels. Nothing is left between us.

Auguste's boat, the *Lynx*, skims the top of the ocean like the dragonflies that soared across the Rose Bayou back home. I wander around his private chambers. Sea-lanterns hang from hooks, and his desk is tucked into a corner. Maps cover the walls between the porthole windows. The scent of him lingers everywhere. The teacup dragons all nuzzle on a large horseshoe-shaped couch in the center.

I remember when I first met Auguste outside the palace, and he smugly reported that this was his boat. The memory is a hard lump in my stomach. I want it to burn a hole straight through and take with it all the memories of him.

The darkness outside the windows suddenly lights up, the sky filling with sparklers and star-shaped wish-lanterns as the God of the Sky and the Goddess of Beauty receive the kingdom's desires. It must be midnight. A new year has arrived.

"Happy days to come." The new year's blessing drifts down into the office from the deck above.

"The Year of the Goddess of Love always brings something sweet."

I hear the clink of glasses and more cheers.

I plop down on the couch with the dragons. They tuck themselves into the folds of my skirt and release tiny snores. I close my eyes and think back to this time last year. I spent the whole day making candy houses with my sisters. We lit tea candles and sat them inside our little creations, then placed them at the windows of Maison Rouge to call forth blessings from the God of the Ground. He'd find sweetness in this house and leave behind his goodwill and a fortune box for each sister. At midnight, our mamans had given each of us a wish-lantern and a slip of parchment to write down our heart's desires. I'd scrawled along mine: *I want to be the favorite.*

That wish is now a nightmare. So much has changed in just a few months. All those little girl hopes evaporating—wish-lanterns destroyed by winds. If only I'd known what my life would become.

I jam my eyes shut to prevent angry tears from falling. The smooth rocking of the ship lulls me to sleep, my body sinking deeper into the softness of the couch. But soon I am snatched into violent dreams.

I'm falling through the sky. Cold air catches every fold and layer of my dress, ballooning it like a pavilion bell. My limbs flap around me, unable to help me slow down. I fight to open my eyes, the wind pushing tears down my cheeks.

I look ahead and spot a shock of red hair like the crimson tail ribbons of a festive kite.

Maman.

I scream her name, but the syllables are lost in the howl of the gale.

We tumble forward, the speed of our bodies accelerating.

I try to catch her. I try to stretch out my fingers to grab the end of her dress. But she's just out of reach.

The dark tangle of the forest behind Maison Rouge lies ahead, the thick branches ready to engulf us, every naked skewer primed to stab through our insides. I scream and thrash about as Maman crashes into the boughs, their black fingers piercing her flesh.

"My lady," a voice whispers.

My eyes snap open. I leap to my feet, hand on Rémy's dagger.

Auguste's guard thrusts a pale orchid fortune box at me. "For you. Sweet days to come and good fortune."

"Thank you," I say, a little embarrassed.

I take it, the paper soft and supple, almost like skin, and slip it into a secret compartment in my waist-sash. It will be the only fortune box I'll receive tonight.

"Who is it from?" I ask.

"Mr. Fabry," he replies.

I suddenly want to shove it back into his hands, but he smiles at me like he's so happy to deliver this pretty box. I don't want to offend him.

"We'll be docking in Trianon in less than an hourglass. Prepare to disembark." He bows, then exits.

I tuck each one of the sleeping teacup dragons into my waist-sash. They fit like small jewels in their favorite compartments. I ruffle the long layers of my travel dress, pull on my cloak, and affix a veil over my face.

I call the arcana, letting the three gifts rush to my fingertips.

Just in case.

The city of Trianon appears in the distance, its outline glittering and the city-lanterns tiny pinpricks of light like stars in a dark swath of sky.

I will burn it all, if I have to.

30

"Take Lady Corrine to the address as instructed," Auguste's guard orders a carriage driver.

The royal pier sits away from the busy port. The remnants of wish-lanterns scatter along the cobblestoned streets and skim the harbor waters like debris coughed up by the God of the Sea. Ivory streaks scar the early-evening night sky as the fireworks taper off and those celebrating the coming of the new year have most likely had their fill of sweetbread and champagne and chocolate coins.

A gale freezes my cheeks, joining the deep chill shooting through me as I hold a glamour. The port guards don't even flinch as I climb into the carriage. Eyes straight ahead, arms at their sides, bodies frozen in place.

Strange.

"May your threads be strong," Auguste's guard whispers to me. I don't have time to ask questions before he closes the carriage door, and the horse clip-clops forward.

The space is cold and empty, the fireplace absent of wood and the small servants' quarters vacant. I cover myself with a veil, let my glamour disappear, and wipe the small trickle of blood from my nose. Carefully, I inch back the drapes covering one of the carriage windows.

The pier market is desolate, blue-lanterns snuffed out, stalls boarded up, and the twisting lanes empty. Wooden booths sit at the market entrance marked CHECKPOINT. A guard shouts through a voice-trumpet: "Invite-only into the imperial city of Trianon. Have your papers ready!"

The carriage slows, and a pair of guards approach. Their shiny black uniforms and the gray stripe down the middle of their hair make me think of Rémy.

I hold my breath and close the curtain.

I hear low gravelly voices.

An anxious hum ruptures through me—the wonder of how long it will take me to find him and what condition he might be in and if he's all right...and still alive. I brush that thought away.

The carriage moves forward again. They didn't even inspect it. Auguste's word holds such a great deal of power. Even though I would have preferred to live my entire life without seeing him again, I must admit that Lady Arane made a wise choice in taking his help.

We enter the Garden Quartier, where shops sit like stacked pastry and hat boxes, one after another, so high they disappear into snow-swollen clouds. Gold blimps circle overhead like fat, sun-kissed raindrops. Animated ink whips along their middles with a message—*Smile! Look Your Best for the New Queen Because She Is Always Watching!* Light-boxes drop from their bellies and flash beams of light every few seconds.

Sophia has eyes everywhere now.

The carriage pauses at another checkpoint, then moves forward. The driver taps the wall, and I flinch as he slides back a panel. "Prepare for arrival, my lady."

"Thank you," I whisper, adjusting the veil over my face and taking a deep breath.

It all begins now.

Finally, the carriage stops before a closed shop called Larbalestier's Bawdy, Bodacious Bowlers, Bonnets, and Mischievous Millinery. Post-balloons float behind the windowpanes carrying all manner of hats—bowlers, pillboxes, ferronnières, miniver caps, toppers, bonnets. The oscillating movement oddly soothes the rapid beat of my heart.

I enter. A bell chimes. The foyer smells familiar—roses, charcoal, and sugar.

Home.

I spot bundles of Belle-rose flowers tucked into the brims of many of the display hats.

"Hello?" I call out.

Tables are littered with supplies. Shelves hold proud hats that resemble jewels in the subtle darkness. An abacus sits on a ledge; the red and white beads catch the lantern light. The cashier table is spread over with newspapers.

Their headlines shimmer:

ORLÉANS CABINET PASSES ONE LAW BEFORE NEW
YEAR'S—SET TO REMOVE THE WAIST SIZE RESTRICTIONS

LADY RUTH CARLON, HOUSE EUGENE, ACCUSED
OF BEAUTY MIMICRY AND FINED 20,000 LEAS

Gossip tattlers glow, drawing my eye to the *Parlour of Titillating Tidbits* and *Speculations of the Foulest Kind*, their reports teasing onlookers:

SOPHIA TO TAKE A MISTRESS AFTER MARRIAGE;
LONG-TERM LOVE DUCHESS ANGELIQUE DE
BASSOMPIERRE OF HOUSE REIMS SEEN MOVING INTO
SPECIAL PALACE APARTMENTS YESTERDAY

RUMORED LOVE CHILD OF KING FRANCIS SLATED
TO BRING A CASE BEFORE THE MINISTER OF
JUSTICE TO OBTAIN A TITLE AT COURT

QUEEN'S BETROTHED WON'T BE AFFECTIONATE
WITH HER; OVERHEARD WHILE INEBRIATED TELLING
A COURTIER HE'S IN LOVE WITH ANOTHER

Auguste.

A woman marches out of the back of the store. She has a large hourglass shape, her curves fitting beautifully into a robin's egg–blue dress cinched at the waist with a golden sash, and her hair is pulled so tightly into a bun at first I don't notice its curly texture and streaks of gray. "You're right on time."

"I am Corrine—"

"I know who you are. You can get rid of your veil. We have much work to do. You are to meet our future queen in less than an hourglass's worth of time."

"And you're Justine, I'm guessing?"

"Never guess. And no, Justine is not here. She's off chasing materials for her latest hat. But you don't have to hide any longer. Or attempt to run."

265

A shiver prickles up my back. The familiarity of her voice seeps beneath my skin.

"You are Camellia Beauregard. You were seven stones when you were born," she says.

Her words startle me. "My name is Corinne Sauveterre from the House of—"

"It's me, Madam Du Barry," she says, reaching out her arms.

I stumble backward. "No."

"Camille, I could never get you to follow rules, you always wanted to do the opposite of what I asked—always in the name of curiosity." She pulls down the sweetheart collar of her dress and reveals her imperial identification mark, the cursive letters of her name—*Ana Maria Lange Du Barry*—spelled out in permanent ink.

My mouth drops open.

"It's really you," I say, reaching out to touch her, and she grabs my hand, squeezes it, and pulls me into a hug.

I crumple in her arms. Even though I spent most of my life fearing this woman and the past few months uncovering all the lies she told us, her scent wraps around me like a cozy blanket. The comfort of her quiets the anger. I'm a little girl again.

The teacup dragons inch their way out of my waist-sash and start to whiz around, spraying their tiny coughs of fire at the bigger one in the hearth.

"What happened to you? Where did you go?" My eyes search her body and face, her outside so different and foreign from the shape of her I've always known. But her eyes—they always keep the same eyes. I can see her in there.

She leads me to chairs in front of the fireplace. "We don't have much time. But while your bath is being prepared, I will tell you what I can. When the queen's death was imminent and Sophia's behavior ever more unpredictable, I'd caught wind that she was planning to replace me and topple our traditions. There was a rumor that they planned to hold me in the dungeons, so I tried to take Elisabeth and leave the palace right after you did, but they'd already taken her. So I had to go on my own. It is something I've regretted ever since that day."

"She was in the prisons with us for a while. How is she faring at the palace?" I ask, remembering the sound of her voice on the other end of the circuit-phone at the Silk Teahouse. My anger toward Du Barry cools slightly, seeming so silly now after all that's happened.

"She's been sending me information when she can. Sophia won't let her go. She threatens to put my daughter in one of her new starvation boxes—allow the whole kingdom to see her nude body and watch it turn gray." Her voice quavers, but she quickly coughs, pours tea, and hands it to me.

"Thank you." The heat warms my hands.

"Elisabeth sends me letters every week if she can," she says, pulling a wad of parchment out of her pocket, and handing it to me. "She helps me track information and inform the Iron Ladies."

I purse my lips. "How did you meet them? And why? You are a guardian. We were a business to you. And it was profitable."

"It was our way of life."

"But you lied to us. You kept so many secrets from us," I say.

"And I'm sorry for that. I truly am. But I know that apology might be too little and too late." Her eyes gleam with tears in the firelight.

"I spent most of my life being angry with you."

"And I'm sorry."

That word again. It means nothing.

"You weren't children for very long, but I should've done things differently than my maman. I mimicked what was in the Belle-manuals, what my maman and grand-mère had done." She puts a hand on her face. "Camille, you have to understand . . . this was the way it was always done. Since the beginning of time. It wouldn't even have occurred to me to do anything differently than what *my* maman had trained me to do. But then, I saw the way Sophia treated Amber, and then you . . . It was clear something had to change. Perhaps the Iron Ladies' way is the better way. I met them while evading Sophia's network of guards.

"I know you've seen Sophia's pods. I never appropriately explained the other Belles that you discovered at the Chrysanthemum Teahouse. I should've told all of you about how you were born. I regret not being forthright. Adhering to the guide, I foolishly didn't realize that you having knowledge would keep you safe if things were to ever go wrong." She knits her hands in her lap. "I should have shown you how it worked."

The memory of Sophia's glass contraption slides into my head. "Were we all born from those pods?"

"The favored generation isn't." Her voice cracks.

"Why not? How did we grow?"

"From the goddess."

"Is she even real?" Anger chokes in my voice.

"That story has some truth. The Goddess of Beauty used to send Belles down from the sky like rain, and they'd burrow into the ground as seeds and grow under the protection of the dark forest behind Maison Rouge. They were beautiful bulbs. When I was a little girl I'd go out there with my mother to tend to the Belles. I used to think the bulbs were diamonds—their outer shells glittered in the darkness. We'd make sure they were covered by the rich soil and pour the blood of the previous generation over the them for nourishment."

My heart races alongside her story. It sounds like madness.

"Guardians were tasked to tend to that forest. Protect it. Keep it holy. Keep it hidden."

"The one you forbade us to enter."

"But the one you were always drawn to. You thought I didn't know when you and your sisters would sneak out there." She stares off into the fire. "Over many weeks, thick stems would push out from the soil, holding the babies in petal-like cases covered with thorns."

I open and close my eyes. The images her words etch in my mind are like scenes plucked out of dreams and nightmares.

"Once you were born, we'd pair you with one of the Belles who returned from court. To help raise you and prepare you for your duties. Over the centuries, fewer Belles dropped from the sky, and the guardians had to adopt radical methods to keep up with the growth in Orléansian population."

Du Barry purses her lips.

"What did you do? What did the guardians do?" I ask.

"I'm ashamed to tell you these guardian secrets. Saying them out loud solidifies just how wrong they've been all these years," she says without looking up.

"I want to know. I deserve to know." My anger is a teapot boiling over.

DuBarry takes a deep breath and lets it out slowly, staring into the fire. "My great-great-great-grand-mère figured out a way to extract some of your blood, parts of your tissue, and replicate the growing process in controlled pods. But this created greed and more demand." She reaches out to touch my shoulder. "To be honest, I don't think she really knew what she was doing. She thought she was solving a problem, but she only created more."

I clench my jaw and say nothing. What was there to say?

"What she discovered, over time, is that there is one Belle in each generation whose blood is stronger than the rest," she continues.

"Me," I say, and she blinks, surprised. "Arabella."

"Yes. You are the aether, as the guardians call it. Or as I thought of it as a child, the everlasting rose."

Sophia's cruelty in naming her prison after us burns afresh. "That's not how the story goes."

"It never is."

She pauses and leans closer to the crackling fire in the hearth. Her eyes gaze at the wild flames.

"This world doesn't deserve Belles," I yell, standing up and pacing around the room.

"You are right to be angry."

She stands and reaches out a hand, but I avoid her touch.

"Angry? That word is too small to describe how I feel." My muscles tense and my fists ball. I want to knock every hat from every perch and punch every post-balloon until they crash to the ground. "Sophia has Amber and Edel and Ivy and all the other Belles you lied to us about, like Delphine. And Valerie is dead."

Du Barry flinches, clutching her heart and stumbling backward into her seat. "What?"

"You heard me. She's gone. Sophia bled her to death, and she couldn't handle it any longer."

Du Barry holds her head in her hands. "I'm so very sorry."

"I don't understand why this all happened—how the world

could treat us like this. How could you lie to us over and over again?"

"You need to understand the value of beauty and how it creates deficiencies in the world. Deficiency is weakness. Beauty is power. It creates need and desire and want. Not having it creates a market." Du Barry looks up at me, her eyes watery and her cheeks tear-stained. "I can never be sorry enough."

"I've heard too many sorrys and none of them change anything."

An hourglass on the mantel flips. A long silence seeps between us. It seems there is nothing more to be said. Eventually, Du Barry clears her throat.

"Your imperial carriage will be back to get you and take you to her," she says, all business. It is a tone I recognize. "It's time to get ready."

Time to face Sophia.

31

"This arrived moments before you did. Lady Arane had it made,"
Du Barry says, holding a small box in one hand as I stand before
a mirror. "I don't know how they got it into this tiny thing. It's not
bigger than a hatbox."

She hands it to me and I open it, removing a card on top of the
soft paper wrapping. It reads: *Pull the ribbon and wait for the dress
to reveal itself.*

"Where did the Lady order this from?" I ask.

"The shop next door—Lili's Marchande de Modes. Very popular on this street."

I peel back the paper covering to reveal a thick red velvet ribbon. I pull it. The box flattens and I jump back, startled.

Bolts of turquoise-and-gold fabric unfurl, tumbling out like an
ocean wave. Glittering sequins coat the fabric like scales. It starts
to assemble itself upright. A row of black-and-white bows dot the
center of the fitted bodice. The neckline dips into a sweetheart
with champagne beadwork and a graceful train. The skirt ruffles

alternate colors, and tiny golden cages push through. Finally, an oversize matching hat appears atop the box.

I gasp, circle it, and touch its edges. "It's perfect! Sophia will be intrigued."

The teacup dragons fly around the dress.

"There's a compartment in the bustle where you can store your things so you can travel lightly. Any luggage you might bring would be inspected, and your identity quickly uncovered." She shows me the small space almost the size of my satchel.

Du Barry's attendant whistles to get the dragons' attention and lures them into a low basin to wash the fireplace soot from their scales.

"Do you want their collars back on?" she asks me.

"No, thank you," I reply.

"Prepare her veil as well, Mia," Du Barry orders.

"I don't need one," I say with confidence, stretching upright.

"She will recognize you."

"No, she won't," I reply. I can't tell her about the glamours. Edel would never forgive me for divulging her discovery to the woman who lied to us our entire lives. "Please trust me."

"You must take it just to be safe. It's a new style called lace-skin." She holds up a tract of lace, shaped with the contours of a face, and rubs it against my skin. The thin black material spreads around my cheeks and down my neck like the intricate frosting on a cake. "All the ladies at court wear this now, to shield themselves from Sophia's gaze and hide their beauty for as long as they can."

Du Barry's attendant gingerly places each teacup dragon into its cage on my dress. They gnaw at the bars, hiccup fire, and stamp their talons in protest.

A bell chimes.

"It's time." Her eyes take me in and she touches my cheek. "You look extraordinary. If we never see each other again, I want you to know how much I do love you." Her voice cracks, and she clears it. "Don't lose sight of the *real* enemy."

"What's that supposed to mean?" I ask.

"Sophia is an enemy because she hurt you, hurt all of us. But the *real* enemy is inside every Orléans citizen. Cutting off Sophia's head—and trust me, I'd love to see it displayed in all its glory in Trianon's Royal Square—will do nothing, because another head will replace it. Stick to your plan. You must be a whisper in a field that turns to a roar right before she can sense it." She kisses my forehead like she did when we were little and earned high marks. The warmth of her mouth is the same. "I hope to see you again."

She presses the official imperial invitation into my hand, the paper thick with promise and danger.

The palace is awash with light, and the sky above it filled with snowflakes and pretty post-balloons headed to the Observatory Deck carrying gifts for the new queen. I smile for the first time in weeks, thinking about the Iron Ladies and Charlotte headed this way soon.

Courtiers spill out of gilded carriages pausing at the palace checkpoint. Revelers stumble with excitement and clutch the remnants of candy houses and empty champagne flutes. They sing traditional blessings and wish each other well. They shout their names, the syllables stretched with slurs and excitement.

I join the crowd. A set of imperial guards collects invitations and checks a parchment scroll. They let some courtiers in and reject others.

I walk up and hand the guard my paper. "Corrine Sauveterre."

"There's a star beside her name," one guard says.

"The queen has been waiting for her most of the night," the other replies. "We must rush her in before the others and send word ahead."

A golden post-balloon bursts from the checkpoint building. Its ribbons snap and flicker in the wind. I wonder what the note inside says. If she believed Auguste's offer of a gift. If she is excited to meet Corrine Sauveterre, premier dragon merchant, here to let her have her pick of dragons for her upcoming coronation.

My heart shivers under my rib cage. The teacup dragons protest in their new cages, their wings batting against the bars, irritated at being jostled around.

The guards lead me onto the palace grounds. The topiary maze is now a garden of flowers fashioned from jewels—roses with ruby petals and emerald stems. Perfume blimps making spritzing sounds skate over the fake flowers. Black gossip post-balloons stalk the gardens as if they've been calibrated to find information and sniff out stories in dark corners. The palace rivers are chockfull of newsie boats. They send fleets of story post-balloons up to the entrance like a storm of navy birds. A newsblimp weaves in and out of the palace turrets holding banners of new year's wishes.

All I want to do is take out Rémy's maps and let the ink reveal where the dungeons are. All I want to do is ensure his safety, then, first thing in the morning, I'll go to the Observatory Deck to make sure the Iron Ladies and Charlotte can arrive undetected. All I want to do is execute this plan without any problem.

I walk into the receiving room, and it has been transformed into a menagerie. Gilded cages descend from the high ceiling, made of fine porcelain edged in gold, holding every teacup pet one could imagine. A unicorn sports a tie. A pack of wolves wear tiny hair bows. A wall-length aquarium holds teacup fish, where a small narwhal chases a teacup shark. A family of teacup penguins shuffle an egg back and forth.

A flood of memories follows me into the foyer of the main entrance, and I am transported back to the night Amber was declared the favorite. High-backed chairs flank the long carpet. Onlookers sport monocles and press eyescopes to their faces and lift up ear-trumpets. Light pushes through the ceiling glass; threads of it stitch across my path, creating a tapestry of orange and gold.

We enter the throne room and I'm stunned in place, feet heavy and leaden.

Sophia is just ahead, perched on her throne, singing at the top of her lungs out of tune, her blond hair tower full of teacup swans. Her ladies-of-honor surround her. They look the same as they did weeks ago when I was here. Gabrielle, closest to her, with beautiful dark brown skin, rich and coated with glitter, then a new girl with hair the color of black soil who has replaced Claudine fawns over a teacup sloth, and little Henrietta-Marie with her nose in a book.

The sight of them fills me with rage. The arcana wake inside me, each skill a small, throbbing curl melding with my simmering ire. I'm not sure I can keep it contained. Sweat dots my brow and dampens the lace-skin Du Barry put over my face. With each breath I take, the anger bubbles up, clawing at my throat and eager to escape my mouth.

Sophia's new royal emblem banner hangs proudly from the ceiling. Her ladies-of-honor perch on pillows at her feet, watching and goading her on. Courtiers shout blessings and sweet nothings at her, desperate for her attention.

The room is chaos. I focus my attention ahead, not removing

my eyes from Sophia, wishing each glance could leave burns across her porcelain-white skin.

I move forward. Each footstep I take, I use my arcana to create a glamour. The cold pain claws up my spine. I deepen the brown color of my skin, stretch myself a touch to be taller, and darken my hair.

The taste of blood coats my tongue, slivery, metallic, and sharp. I hope I can hold off a nosebleed.

The attendant removes a voice-trumpet from his jacket. "May I introduce Lady Corinne Sauveterre, daughter of Alexandra and Guillaume Sauveterre of the House of Rare Reptilians in the Gold Isles," the attendant announces. "She has brought you gifts from your fiancé, Auguste Fabry of House Rouen."

The teacup dragons hiccup fire from my dress. Sophia notices and squeals. I reach the throne platform, my anger threatening to consume me as I get closer and closer to her.

Sophia races down the stairs, her favored teacup pets nipping at her heels.

"Your Majesty," I say, deepening my voice and bowing as she approaches.

"Welcome to my court," Sophia says, then turns to her ladies-of-honor. "Ladies, this is our new guest. She's brought me dragons."

I bow to her ladies as well.

"This is Gabrielle, Lady of All Things, a princess du sang and my very best friend," she says.

"This is Rachelle, my new Lady of the Dresses to replace the unfortunate loss of my friend Claudine de Bissay."

They all bow their heads in mock sympathy.

"And my little Henrietta-Marie, Lady of the Jewels," she adds.

Henrietta-Marie doesn't look up from her book.

"Pleasure to meet you all," I reply.

Gabrielle eyes me with discerning interest.

"Just look at these dragons!" Sophia gushes, reaching into one of the cages to try to pet my little golden Or, but she evades Sophia's fingers. Sophia's elephant, Zo, kicks her feet up at me and pushes her tiny trunk at my skirt. She squeals with delight.

I panic. Mr. Claiborne's warning pulses through me: *There's a natural perfume you have. Different than ours.* What if Zo or her teacup monkey, Singe, recognizes my scent?

"Let me see you," Sophia demands, facing me.

"Of course, Your Majesty. As you wish." I remove the lace-skin Du Barry gave from my face.

My heart beats against my sides as her gaze combs over me, her odd rainbow-colored eyes full of curiosity like a teacup cat nosing around a room in search of a mouse. Who is doing her beauty work now, and how absurd has it become?

"Do we know each other?" she asks.

"No, Your Majesty. I haven't had the pleasure to come to court before today." I bow.

"You are a beauty," she says.

The crowd claps.

"Though never as beautiful as you," I add, earning a smile from her.

She blushes. "Of course."

Zo trumpets at my feet, and I try not to flinch.

"Oh, Zo's very friendly," Sophia says, looking at the tiny elephant lovingly. "And it seems she likes you already." Her eyes drift all the way up me, inspecting each and every inch. "This bodes well for our potential working relationship."

Singe does a lap around me but keeps his distance.

"You will give me all of those glorious teacup dragons, correct? That's what Auguste said. My fiancé knows me so well." Her gaze fixates on them. "You saw the horrifying news about the loss of my other ones? Happened a week or so ago."

"I did. It was most unfortunate," I say with mock sympathy.

"Indeed. Most unfortunate. Once the perpetrator is caught, I will make them wish they'd never been born." She pauses to look out over the crowd of courtiers. "Even though Pearl, Sapphire, and Jet will always be remembered, I must replace them. The Goddess of Love was rumored to keep dragons, so I must have them all, and any others you're currently tending."

"That's not quite how it works," I say, steadying my voice.

Her court gasps.

"What does that mean?" Her pale blond eyebrow lifts with surprise.

"If you aren't present for their birth, my breed of teacup dragons must choose their owners. They must deem the person worthy. You see, they're very noble creatures. Exceedingly rare. All dragons are said to have come from the womb of the Goddess of Love. Their affection, loyalty, and disposition mirror exactly what love should be."

The crowd oohs.

Sophia scowls. "I am a queen. I was born deserving and worthy. My lineage and bloodline make it so."

"Of course," I say, and add a little bow to keep her from seeing me seethe. "But the dragons will have their say."

My words sizzle and crackle in the silent room.

Her rainbow-colored eyes burn into the top of my head. Sweat rises from my skin, cold and clammy. Maybe I pushed too hard, said too much. I swallow and try to hold on to the glamour. A headache blossoms in my temples. The taste of salt fills my mouth. The nosebleed will come any second.

"I enjoy a challenge," she snaps, reaching for Or's golden tail. Or lets herself be caressed, then curls back into a corner in the cage. "I always win."

"You are blessed by the God of Luck, and we will see which dragon chooses you."

Her mouth parts, but she closes it and grins. "Until then, you shall remain here as my honored guest." She waves a nearby attendant over. "Prepare the guest apartments in the east wing."

"Pardon me, Your Majesty, I don't mean to question your hospitality, but I must be in chambers nearest you. My breed of teacup dragons must acclimate to your scent. Bond, if you will. So that one or two may connect." I let a clever smile play upon my lips, hoping she takes the bait and puts me in Charlotte's chambers.

Her eyes widen. "I want them all to love me. So, yes, whatever is necessary shall be. I'm prepared to give you all the leas you could ever want, and spintria, too, if you prefer it." She turns to another attendant. "Give her my darling and dearly departed sister's room."

Courtiers flap their fans wildly as if a flash of warm-season heat stormed through the room.

"I couldn't possibly stay in Princess Charlotte's apartments. I am not of noble birth. Would it not be inappropriate?"

"She has passed on." The lie tumbles from her pink lips without effort. "At sunset tomorrow, I will present her body and we will mourn her officially. I cannot be queen until she is sent to the afterlife properly to be with my maman." She presses two fingers together and taps her heart, a sign of respect for the dead. The entire room mimics her. "I'm having a pavilion built in her honor on the palace grounds. It is my desire that you and the teacup dragons are as close as can be. I make the rules and I can break them."

I nod and bow. "As you wish."

"I do. I do." She takes my hands; hers are sticky and shaky. I try not to flinch or pull away. The rosewater scent of her sends a tangle of revulsion and rage through me, making it hard to hold on to my glamour.

"Your nose is starting to bleed." She hands me her own personal handkerchief embroidered with her initials and the House of Orléans emblem.

I quickly wipe my nose, the beads of blood soaking through the expensive fabric. "The cold season and travel have exhausted me."

"You must rest. The Coronation and Ascension Ball starts the day after tomorrow, and you must attend as my honored guest. You can wear one of my latest vivant gowns." She whips around to another attendant. "See that she's settled properly and all her needs are met."

"You are most gracious," I reply.

"And you are most welcome to my court."

I bow.

An attendant rushes forward with a sealed letter. "Your Majesty, this just arrived."

Sophia snatches it.

I stand up and see the words *Gold* and *Charlotte* and *spotted* before she rips up the note.

"I have to excuse myself," Sophia says, rushing off.

My heart pounds in my throat.

I must warn them.

32

Sophia's attendant walks me down a familiar hall to Charlotte's former apartments. The glitter of the night-lanterns and the scent of fresh cold-season flowers and the sounds of nearby laughter hurtle me back into the past. Memories of the night we left slice in like nightmares with each step I take. Rémy carrying Amber. Arabella's trunk and dragon eggs. It feels like both a lifetime ago and just yesterday—all spinning in my head to the beat of panic.

I need to find Rémy. I need to find Arabella. I need to figure out how to get to the Observatory Deck first thing in the morning. Trembles of exhaustion quiver through me, and the pain of holding the glamour sends more blood trickling out of my nose. I wipe it away as best I can, but it streaks the front of my gown.

The attendant pauses before a set of apartment doors. Charlotte's royal emblem is now absent, the wood naked, her presence erased. Mourning balloons carry cameo portraits of the "deceased" princess and her royal emblem. They carry tiny sound-boxes hissing out wails and cries every few minutes.

"Are you all right, my lady?" the attendant asks.

"Just tired."

"Time to rest."

I am ushered into the foyer, where a kneeling servant awaits.

"Lady Corrine, I leave you here to become acquainted with your chambers and your appointed help while staying with us." She turns on her heel before I can reply and leaves the room.

"Good evening," the servant says while standing. "May your new year be sweet!"

Her voice sends a shiver across my skin and stirs up thoughts of Bree buried deep down inside. It feels like shaking a snow globe. "And also yours," I reply. "What is your name?"

Her ponytail is a ribbon of honey down her back. I start to ask her if we've met before, but this is supposed to be my first time at court.

She looks up. Her eyes large and stretched, her skin dotted with star-shaped freckles. She looks like a doll from a shop window in Trianon.

She sets down a tray. A teapot, cup, and plate of sweets sits on top of a spread of newspapers and magazines. "I thought you might want something to read . . . and there's a note." Her voice drops an octave.

My heart knocks around in my chest.

"The queen's rooms are nearby. Hopefully, close enough for the teacup dragons to familiarize themselves with her scent." She launches into a detailed explanation of all the things I will find in these lavish apartments and shows me down familiar corridors. I don't care about any of it anymore.

I nod at the eager woman, trying to pretend I care, trying to keep from running straight out of here to find Rémy. The scent of

Charlotte lingers despite the perfume blimps drifting about. Just days ago, the ceiling was filled with cerulean healing-lanterns and a large four-poster bed containing her sleeping body.

"The bathing onsen is down the left corridor." She points. "And a small library to the right."

I gaze into the darkness of those halls, thinking of Rémy and Arabella, both tucked away somewhere in this expansive palace. Close yet so far away.

"Her Majesty has—"

Another trickle of blood escapes my nose. "Thank you. I must lie down and put my teacup dragons to bed," I say, cutting her off.

"Oh, yes, of course. I'm sorry." She bows. "Do you need additional help?"

"No," I reply, more clipped than I intend. "I'm just so tired from the journey."

"Understood." She nods and slips out.

I let the glamour fade and unhook the teacup dragons' cages from the dress. They eagerly stretch their wings, inspect the room, then settle on the perch of the bed canopy. Fantôme and Eau quickly fall asleep.

I push my hand into the dress pocket and remove the poison bottle, which I set on the vanity before removing the cumbersome dress. I unpack Arabella's Belle-book, Rémy's maps, the bottles of sangsues, and the case of eye-films.

Despite exhaustion, I rush to the room's desk and find parchment and ink.

I write to Padma:

P,

She knows that Charlotte is alive. She has been spotted in the Gold Isles.

Get in the air as soon as possible.
Love,
C

I whistle to Poivre and feed him one of Padma's leeches. "Find her. You're the fastest." I open a window and look out on the palace grounds. The Golden Palace River is filled with newsie boats and jovial courtiers singing and laughing and guzzling champagne.

I nudge the red teacup dragon out.

He disappears into the mass of wish-lanterns and post-balloons floating up to the sky. I turn to Rémy's maps. They almost hiss as I flip the pages and wait for the ink to settle. I trace my fingers along the drawings as they reveal each wing and its various chambers. My eyes droop with sleepiness, but I try to focus and search for the Observatory Deck and the dungeons, my heart torn about what to do first. I need to figure out the best way to get to the deck tomorrow so I can make sure Charlotte and the others can enter through it. If my plan doesn't work, there's no way in. But Rémy is somewhere in this palace being tortured.

I pace around. My hands shake at my sides. The indecision is a landquake inside me. If I find Rémy first, he can help me make sure that the Iron Ladies can enter.

My heart squeezes, giving me the answer to my question.

I have to find him, then I'll go to the deck.

I flip through the maps until the dungeons are shown beneath the receiving room.

I stir Or from her perch. "I need your help." She yawns but perks up. I take the last of Rémy's leeches and hold the writhing creature between my fingers. This is my last connection to locating him. "We need to find him, little friend. Don't let this gamble be a waste."

I pull on my cloak and the lace-skin again, and grab a night-lantern by the tails. I listen for the noise of servants before exiting the chambers. Adrenaline propels me, or maybe it's delirium from exhaustion.

Or flies in a circle above my head.

"This way, girl."

The teacup dragon hesitates.

"This way out."

Her big eyes grow large as glass marbles.

"Why are you confused? I will get us to the dungeons, and then, you take it from there." I whistle. She finally obeys, diving into the corridor.

I take out the map and navigate my way from the palace apartments to the receiving room. Jeweled chandelier lanterns hold frosted candles. Animated frescoes shift through the portraits of queens and kings, goddesses and gods. I used to love everything about this place—the bustling, beautiful bodies headed to the game rooms and tea salons, the scent of sweets escaping the golden carts of the royal vendors, lavish furniture spilling from every room.

But now, I see it for what it really is—a beautiful shell masking rottenness.

I skulk through the halls, hiding as guards patrol and courtiers stumble about looking for the exits to the Palace River piers or the carriage-house. Or drifts ahead, sometimes circling back as if she wants to return from where we came. I direct her to move forward.

Cold-season chrysanthemum trees grow up from the belly of the palace wing, their branches almost finding me as I race over the gilded walkways from one side of the palace to another. Empty chariots glide along the lattice cables. I race down a massive set of stairs and make a left at the entry fountain. Gleaming leas coins litter the bottom like drowned stars. It would almost be peaceful and settle the erratic beat of my heart, if I wasn't so terrified.

Footsteps invade the quiet. The doors of the receiving room swing open as I pass by.

I panic and find a dark corner to hide.

Servants carry a palanquin with a sleeping Sophia sprawled over the cushions. Her hair hangs in a tangled nest; her rouge-stick is smudged all around her mouth. Her teacup monkey, Singe, rubs her cheek. The heady scents of too much champagne and perfume linger as she passes.

Zo trots behind the small procession, trying to catch up with the palanquin. The miniature animal pauses, spots me, and cranes her neck. I duck deeper into my hiding place, but she trundles over and puts her little feet up on my nightdress. She wears a tiny jeweled crown that matches Sophia's. Her toenails are painted a bright mulberry. She sniffs my dress with her tiny gray trunk. I feel her fluttering heartbeat on my leg as she tries to climb it.

I try to shove her away. "Go on, now."

Or hisses at Zo, but she doesn't back off. Instead, she traces her slimy trunk along my wrist, sniffing the perfume ointment wiped there.

I push her away and lose the tail ribbons of my night-lantern. It drifts off.

One of the imperial guards yells, "Who is there?"

I turn back to the map and dart down the nearest corridor. Zo marches behind me making a tiny trumpet noise like an alert.

The guards pause, Sophia's palanquin perched on their shoulders.

This is it. I'll be caught, and all because of Sophia's ridiculous pet obsession.

"Shh. Go."

Zo's trumpeting grows louder, threatening to bring the entire imperial guard my way.

"Fetch me my beloved," Sophia shouts, her voice thick and heavy with champagne. "Do it *now*!"

I glance back down the hall. Sophia slaps the nearest guard across the face, then spits on top of his head. Revulsion pools in my stomach. The desire to hurt Sophia bursts inside me. Her evil, sadistic face flashes in my head like a télétrope reel.

Her laugh.

Her smile.

Her voice.

I think about squeezing her skull until it collapses, her hand until it breaks, her heart until it stops.

I see nothing but her.

I hear nothing but her laugh.

I feel nothing but the pain of her breaking my hand.

Rage churns in my heart.

Angry tears storm down my cheeks.

My vision blurs. My skin warms. My body prepares to use the arcana. I can't make it stop. I fumble with Rémy's maps, my tears soaking the parchment as I try to see the ink-drawn diagrams. I scramble to find one of the entries into the dungeons as I dart ahead.

Zo runs at my heels, chasing me like this is a game.

Sophia's high-pitched shouts hit me in waves as she barks at the guards. Zo's tiny heartbeat fills my ears like the flutter of a hummingbird's wings, followed by the noise of the blood rushing through her small body. I sink to the floor at the dungeon's entrance. The heat in my hands, the drum of my heart, and the movement of my blood create chaos in my stomach.

Zo climbs into my lap.

"Go away. Go away. I beg you." My refrain coils around me like a vise. I clamp my eyes shut. A headache throbs in my temples. My cheeks burn.

I slow Zo's heart.

I can't stop. I collapse forward, out of breath.

Zo lies on her back, eyes open, heart still.

A hand jostles my shoulder. The servant from earlier gazes down at me. "My lady ..." A pair of familiar eyes stare back, but I still can't place them.

The woman removes the tiny elephant from my lap and places her aside, then helps me to my feet. "What are you doing here? I came to your chambers to make sure you didn't need anything before bed. I followed you."

"It was an accident," I pant. The truth tumbles out: "I was looking for my friend and the elephant—"

"The queen doesn't keep her most important possessions in the dungeons. Too easy to be plucked."

I search her eyes. "Who are you?"

"Trust your dragon. He's been moved." She lifts Zo's tiny lifeless body, tucks it under her arm, and leaves me where I stand.

33

I watch Or as she flutters overhead, dodging coral and butterscotch coronation post-balloons. We head back in the direction we came—to the royal apartments. I run behind her, my hand on Rémy's dagger, the arcana hissing just beneath my skin, and my nerves ready to help me do whatever it takes to find him. What did she mean when she said he would be too easy to pluck from the dungeon? Is it really so simple to get into this fortress? If he's not there, then where is he?

The questions pound inside me, in time with my footsteps.

Blood trickles from my nose, and I wipe it away without stopping to pause. My arcana prickle inside my veins, achy and like nothing I've ever felt before. Maybe a sign of trouble. We dart back up the stairs and over the gilded walkways. But as we reenter the royal wing, Or turns left, away from the apartments and down another long corridor.

"Why are we going this way?" I ask her, wishing she could answer me.

Worries drum inside me, piling one on top of the other. Have the sangsues gone to waste? Is she confused? Why is she leading me this way?

My exhaustion makes it impossible to think and another nose-bleed starts. I know I need to rest and to reset the arcana. I've done too much.

Or pauses out front of Sophia's workshop. The House of Inventors emblem of cogs and gears and chrysanthemums glows in the darkness.

I take a breath and open the door. A sleeping guard is slumped over snoring, two empty bottles of champagne at his feet and new year's sweets smeared down his chest. I tiptoe past him.

The room holds even more items than it did the last time I was here. Moonlight escapes the glass ceiling, its beams leaving an eerie glow over the space. Beauty-boards perch on easels and litter the floor at the foot of the treatment table. Every wall displays a collection of blood cameos now. The portraits shift and morph alongside the noise of blood whooshing through brass piping.

Or zips ahead, hovering over a closet door.

I untie the single night-lantern from its hook.

Or leaves tiny scratch marks in the wood.

I open it.

My heart does a flip at the sight of him. Rémy is tied up, arms suspended in ropes, head slumped forward. His shirtless body is covered with lashes and brands—the wounds oozing with blood, swelling with infection, and smelling of burnt flesh. The deep brown of his skin is split open. A cut in his lip drips with blood, and his skull is now bald and covered in wounds.

I rush to him. "Rémy," I whisper, and cradle his head.

He jerks back. One of his puffy eyes opens as wide as it can.

"It's me." I pull off my lace-skin mask. "It's Camille."

"You here to rescue me?" he croaks out.

"Yes." I wrap him in a hug, all of my relief with it.

He grunts but lets his head rest in the crook of my neck.

"We've got to get you out of here." I pull away, take out the dagger he gave me, and cut the ropes. His body slumps forward, almost crashing to the floor, but I catch him.

"I can't leave my family here," he mumbles.

"We won't. I promise." I try to keep my voice from breaking. A pinch in my stomach grows hotter. The pain of seeing him like this threatens to consume me.

I muster all my strength and help him stand.

We hobble out of the closet. I take some dress-making fabric from a nearby table and wrap it around his body. "The guard is asleep."

Rémy drags himself ahead. "Where are you staying?"

"They gave me Charlotte's old apartments."

"Then we should take the—"

"You're not in charge this time," I tell him. Keeping him on his feet is taking all the strength I have. I reach down and grab one of the bottles at the guard's feet. "You're a drunk courtier who lost his clothes in the game rooms, all right?"

A painful half-laugh escapes his lips.

Or circles overhead. He tries to look up at her.

"I should've trusted her," I mutter. "I would've found you sooner."

Rémy and I ease past the snoring guard and amble into the hallway. I hold his weight on one side and pretend to fuss at him about drinking too much.

The hall is empty aside from a few servants who have just gotten the opportunity to celebrate tonight.

We turn left and right.

His legs grow weaker and his breathing more labored.

"We're almost there," I tell him.

The sound of footsteps ahead stops me.

I pull him into one of the salon rooms. He slumps against the wall. I watch as three male guards pass, chasing after three courtier women. Their kissy noises echo, then fade.

I stare at him. Rémy Chevalier, son of Christophe Chevalier, decorated—and now disgraced—soldier from the Minister of War's First Guard.

"Can you make it? We're just outside the doors," I whisper.

He grunts a yes back.

I grip his waist and drag him into Charlotte's apartments. I lay him across the bed and use the water in the basin to clean the burns on his chest—Sophia's emblems carved into him. The sight of them flares my anger. He winces each time I touch him.

"What did they do to you?" I ask.

"Everything."

I rest my hand on his cheek.

He takes it and kisses it. "Don't worry about me."

"You're covered in blood and burns and you're telling me not to worry." I put pressure on a cut on his shoulder.

"I've been trained to withstand it." He turns his head to avoid the wet cloth. "What's happened since I left you? Did you find Charlotte?"

I hold his head still and continue to wipe away his blood. "Yes. Remember those newspapers you got for us—the *Spider's Web*?"

He nods.

"We found the Iron Ladies. Well, they found us." I choose to leave out the part about the capture. "They have been helping to keep Charlotte safe. They're on their way here."

"How will they get inside?"

"The Observatory Deck," I say with pride. "Via post-balloon."

He struggles to smile. "Your idea?"

"Yes."

"But I need to go find the route to the Observatory Deck, so I can get there easily before the midmorning star and make sure the door from the deck to the interior is unlocked and unobstructed. They'll arrive and wait until everyone is at the Ascension Ball to attack."

He remains silent. I try to search his eyes for what he thinks about my plan. "What do you think?"

"It's smart—and unexpected."

His encouragement fills up the tiny holes of doubt inside me. He tries to sit up but leans back against the pillows again.

"Here. Stay still."

"How did you get here without her knowing?" he asks.

"Auguste sent me and the teacup dragons as a wedding gift." He stiffens.

A silence crackles between us, the noise of the fire in the hearth heightening it.

"You've seen him?" Rémy's swollen mouth purses.

My stomach becomes a tangle of nerves.

"He's been working with the Iron Ladies. Supplying them with information and help."

"You forgave him?" he asks.

"I took his help. Now, rest."

"Go open that door," he says, then traces a shaky finger along the edge of my face. "I missed you."

"And I you." I nuzzle my face into his shoulder and try to hold back the storm of tears wanting to break loose from my chest.

I lie there until his breathing slows and he drifts off to sleep and I know that he's going to be all right. But before I head back out again to find the route to the Observatory Deck, the bedroom door eases open.

34

"Camille," a voice whispers from behind.

I leap up from the bed at the sound of my name. It's the servant from earlier. The one who took Zo's dead body.

"It's me."

And just like that, I finally recognize her voice.

"It's Bree."

I race to her and wrap my arms around her. "I knew it," I whisper into her hair. "I knew when you were trying to show me around the apartments. Your eyes. I felt it. But I had to keep my disguise."

"I couldn't tell you at first. I didn't want to alert anyone and didn't think I'd be able to keep it all together," she says. "But after what happened with Zo ... I wanted to get rid of the body first and make sure it was safe."

I squeeze her tighter. "What happened to you?" I comb over her, touching her cheeks and arms. "Are you all right? I was so worried. They told me they put you in a starvation box."

"They did, but then when you disappeared from the palace, Elisabeth Du Barry came and got me out."

"She did?" I say, shock rattling me. Elisabeth Du Barry did something that didn't benefit herself?

Rémy coughs.

"Who is there?" she asks.

"Rémy."

Fear flashes in her eyes. "She will know."

I squeeze her hand.

"She has the guards lash him every few hours. If they find him gone, they will search the entire palace for him."

"That's why we have to work fast," I say. "Do you know where I can find Arabella? I need to see her, then get to the Observatory Deck."

Bree looks startled by the question. "Well...yes. She's right next door."

"What?" I gasp. I glance into a slit in the bed-curtains at Rémy. His mouth is slack with sleep, and the blood on his bandages is drying. His wounds no longer leak fresh blood.

"He will be fine here," Bree replies. "We'll close the bed-curtains. Any servants who come in will assume it's you. I'll make sure he remains hidden. Give strict orders to the other servants— as I'm a premier servant now—not to disturb you."

I nod, trusting her.

Knots of pressure and panic tighten throughout my body as I place the lace-skin mask Du Barry gave me back on my face. The anticipation of seeing Arabella again—of having help—is almost too great.

"Let's go. The apartments are connected."

We slip through a network of servant corridors. I hold my

breath until Bree stops walking. What if Arabella is ill like Valerie? What if she is unable to help?

"Ready to go in?" Bree waves me forward.

My stomach knots. "Where are we?"

"One of Sophia's tea salons."

"This is where she keeps her?"

Bree nods.

I imagine a sleeping Sophia passed out, smelling of champagne and macarons and flowers, and Arabella being forced to tend to her beauty work. Bree fumbles with her keys until she finds the right one. She jams it in and turns. The door opens. A chill drifts down my spine.

The room is tiny and dark with a single night-lantern whizzing about and a low fire in the hearth.

"Arabella?" I whisper.

Bree closes the door behind us. "We have to be quick. One of Her Majesty's favorite and most loyal servants oversees her."

I nod and tiptoe closer to the bed.

"Arabella?"

No answer.

I inch back the bed-curtains. Arabella lies there, propped up on the pillow. Her arms and neck are covered with sangsues, the little leeches pulsing black, then flushing red as they fill with her blood and share their proteins. The skin on her face is creased like parchment and so thin and pale that all the veins are visible beneath her skin. Her brown pigment has lost its depth and richness. My heart aches at the sight of her. It's even worse than I feared.

I reach out to touch her, my hand hesitating and pulling back like she's a stove too hot to touch.

"Arabella," I say a little louder.

She stirs and her eyes pop open. She presses back into the pillows.

"It's me, Camille."

She wipes her eyes. "I've been waiting for you. I tried to get to you earlier when I heard the announcement that Corinne Sauveterre, famous dragon merchant from the Gold Isles, had come to see the soon-to-be new queen. But they never let me leave these chambers, no matter what I do or say."

"What has she been doing to you?" I ask, as Bree brings over a tumbler of fresh water.

"Draining me of blood to send to the Everlasting Rose . . ." Arabella says.

The cruelty of the name still twists like a knife inside me. Arabella sips at the cup, and water dribbles out the corner of her mouth.

"To grow more Belles." She sighs and leans back into the bedding, waving the water away. Bree takes it, shooting me a nervous glance, and I squeeze her free hand.

"She did the same to Valerie until she had nothing left. And now she's dead."

Arabella shrugs, as if this news doesn't surprise or bother her. "She's been experimenting," she says. "She brought your other sisters back to the prison after the Silk Teahouse burned down. All except Amber."

"What do you mean? Where is she?" My heart rises in my chest threatening to bubble up.

"She's here," Arabella says.

I gasp. "At the palace? How? Why?"

"I don't know. But I heard her voice the other day. I thought, at first, that it was a recording or something for the newsreels

Sophia has been orchestrating, but it's been more frequent. I can't do Sophia's beauty work anymore—and she won't allow any of the other Belles from the unfavored generation to work on her—so I knew it would be just a matter of time."

My eyes dart around the room as if Amber were hiding beneath a beautiful piece of furniture.

"She has my focus on the few Belle babies here as she tries to find out how the favored generation is born. Her scientists have made so many mistakes. So many Belle babies have already died." She gathers her strength, sits up, and reaches for me. "Let me show you the favored Belle-pods."

I turn to Bree. "Watch the door, please."

She nods and takes up watch at the front of the room, clutching her hands nervously.

Arabella's entire body quakes as I help her slide open the door to the next chamber. The night-lantern follows us, illuminating hundreds of glass cradles etched with tiny golden roses. In each, a brown baby floats. Small hourglasses affixed to each pod are marked with animated ink that snaps across the glass with the labels *first cycle*, *second cycle*, and *third cycle*.

I run my fingers over the glass and peer in. Tiny feet and legs and hands and tight curls suspended in liquid and time.

I gasp. "They look like me."

"And me," Arabella adds. "Eventually, she wants to sell them to the highest bidder. Enable Belles to be kept like teacup pets and also use our blood to make beauty products."

"We can't let this happen," I say. Arabella takes my hand and squeezes it. The skin of her fingers is so thin, and her bones feel like sticks. "I can take care of these babies and ensure no more will be made."

I take my hand from hers and drop it into my pocket where the poison sits.

"What is that?" She takes it from me, fingering it, her watery eyes tracing its details.

"It takes away the arcana."

Her mouth falls open as her eyes find mine. "How?"

"It hardens the arcana proteins. But the amount has to be right, otherwise it could cause death." I watch her examine it as if its secrets lie on the edges of the bottle. "What if we both drank a bit of it, so that neither of our blood could be used to make more Belles?"

The heat of the question radiates between us. Arabella uncorks the bottle to sniff it. My heart skips.

"Be careful," I say, remembering the rapid destruction of the blood cells in Claiborne's optic-scope. "I believe I could also make sure that the aether of the next generation couldn't be used either."

She puts a drop of the poison on her finger and tries to inspect it.

"Arabella..."

She takes a gulp.

"No!" I grab the empty bottle from her.

Arabella's eyes bulge. She coughs—a gurgling, ragged sound. Her skin wrinkles in a blink, line by line covering her forehead to her cheeks to her throat, the brown shriveling like dried-out clay.

"Arabella!" I scream.

Her body hits the floor.

35

I can't hear the screams being ripped from my mouth. My ears clog and spots stamp out my vision. But the piercing rawness of my throat is real.

Bree claps her hand over my mouth and her other arm around my waist. "We have to go. Someone has probably already heard you." She tugs me away from Arabella. "Sophia will discover you're here."

"But I can't leave her." The sight of her body—another dead Belle body—sends another scream reverberating inside me. She is me. I am her. The aether. And now she's dead and the poison—my only chance to save us all—gone. The empty poison bottle falls from my hand. The glass shatters, each jagged shard a realization of how careless and reckless this whole thing has become.

"You have to. Someone is going to come check on her soon if they haven't been alerted by your screams already. You can't be here when they do." She pries me away, almost having to carry me, my limbs heavy with regret and anger and sadness and frustration and most of all, exhaustion.

Hope sputters out of me like the air of a dying post-balloon. First, it was Valerie, and now, Arabella.

How can I ever fix this?

How can I ever make things right?

She hustles me into the apartments. Rémy's gentle snores alternate with the hiss of the fireplace.

"Sleep," Bree whispers.

"How can I possibly sleep now?" My breath catches in my throat and my heart races. I put my hands on my head, trying to make everything slow down. I'm caught in a whirlpool. Even too tired to cry. "How could she do that? What was she thinking? I needed her help."

Bree tries to console me with tea.

I shove the pot away but burn my hand. The pain sears and I ball my fist and bite back another scream.

"You need to sit, Camille. So you can focus." She forces me into the chair beside the fireplace. "Let me look at your hand."

"It will—"

"Let me see it," she urges.

I flash her my palm.

"It will need a little ointment."

"It's fine," I say, even as it throbs.

"You will have to dance tomorrow at Sophia's ball." She goes to a recently delivered service tray and begins mixing honey with ice. "The invitation balloon is on the door hook."

I look over and spot it bobbing—its golden edges glittering in the subtle darkness. The sight of the pretty bauble, after what I've just witnessed, is absurd.

"I need to get to the Observatory Deck. I should've already gone. They will be arriving in the morning."

Bree kneels before me and gently coats my palm with her poultice. "You will. You will," she replies, her voice softening to barely a whisper. "I'll be sure to wake you, and help you get there. I promise."

Her vow is a temporary comfort. "Is it true that Amber is here at the palace? Can you get a message to her that I'm here?"

Bree's face twists. She tears a bit of fabric from a bedsheet and wraps it around my hand. "You rest first."

"What's wrong?" I ask. "Have you seen my sister?"

"Nothing is wrong." Bree stands and backs up.

"Please just tell me. Is she all right? I can't bear to lose another person I love." My heart lodges in my throat. "I need to see her."

"I'll find out where she's being held and get her a message," Bree assures me. "But only if you go to bed."

There's no way I can possibly sleep. I open my mouth to argue. Her eyebrows lift.

I stand. My skin buzzes, but the pain in my hand is already beginning to calm. I climb into the bed beside Rémy and lay my head on the pillow next to him without hesitation. The perfume of his skin has seeped into the fabric.

Bree ties a night-lantern to the bedpost hook and draws the curtains around us. "See you in the morning. I'll be in the servants' quarters just near the apartment's tea salon. I'll keep watch."

I nod at her, then turn my attention to Rémy. I study him in the soft dark. I run my fingers over his bandages and check them for blood. His cuts are crusting over.

He grunts and lifts his hand to touch mine. "Stop fussing over me. I'll be all right."

"Those wounds were deep."

"I know. I feel the bruises down to my bones," he says with a grimace as he tries to turn to his side.

"Don't move."

"You're very pushy."

"Yes, and you must listen to me."

He smiles weakly, then takes my hand, letting the pad of his thumb trace my palm. "I'm already feeling stronger. I promise." He stares at me. "What's wrong?"

"Nothing." I want to tell him everything, but it's too much, and I don't want to burden him. Not while he's still weak.

"I thought we established that you can't hide the things on your face." His brown eyes are full of concern.

"Please sleep. I'll tell you when you wake."

His eyelids flutter, heavy with sickness and pain. He out-stretches his arm, offering me his shoulder to lie on. I nestle against him and find a spot on the bed canopy to stare at, knowing I won't sleep much tonight.

36

Bells chime through the belly of the palace, snatching us awake. My head pounds after getting only tiny bits of troubled sleep. A voice-box on the side table announces, "Palace on heighted alert! All apartments, chambers, rooms, and persons will be searched before the ceremonies commence. Security measures in place!"

The teacup dragons bolt from the bed canopy, spraying agitated fire. I call their names and try to get them to calm down. Rémy moans as he tries to sit up. The bedroom door bursts open.

Bree dashes in out of breath. "She knows Rémy's missing, and they found Arabella's body." She almost collapses forward. "She's on a rampage looking for her teacup elephant Zo, too."

An anchor drops in my stomach. I glance back at Rémy on the bed. I put a hand on Bree's back. "Are there more guards inside the palace?" I ask. "Do you think they suspect me?"

"No more guards than usual," she says. "But they're watching and checking everyone. They will be going through every single apartment, including this one."

"I have to hide him," I tell her. "I have to get to the Observatory Deck before the midmorning star. How much time do I have?"

She pulls an hourglass from her pocket. "One hour," Bree says, "and the ball starts right after it, so you must get ready. She will be expecting you, and if you don't arrive on time, she'll suspect something. Your dress is here, too."

As if on cue, a gold-and-cream post-balloon ambles through the door. Its sides glow with Sophia's soon-to-be official emblem. At midnight tonight, she will be queen according to Orléansian law. The court will celebrate all day in anticipation.

If we don't stop her.

The post-balloon's tail ribbons haul a polka-dotted dress box with a note. The teacup dragons attack the balloon until it crashes to the ground.

I fetch the note.

Corinne,

Ten a.m. sharp.

Imperial Ballroom. We shall celebrate the start of my Coronation and Ascension ceremony and say a final farewell to my beloved sister. Hoping you bring your teacup dragons. They deserve to join us.

—Sophia Regina

I crumple the paper, balling it in my fist. "You have to hide him?" I say to her.

"I know where they won't look," Rémy calls out from the bed.

"And so do I," Bree replies.

I rush to Rémy's side and help him out of bed. He's groggy and slow-moving. "Where will you take him?"

"Somewhere safe, I promise," she says.

"I know how to hide," he grumbles.

"When you're not recovering. Please listen to Bree. You both know this palace well. And you're both so important to me." I take his hand.

He yanks me close, the strength of his motion a shock. Our foreheads touch. "Be safe. The Observatory Deck is on the top floor of the northern wing. Take one of the chariot lifts."

I kiss his cheek. "I will."

I turn to Bree. "I'll get ready for the party when I'm back."

She nods.

I pull on one of the simple day dresses in the apartment's dress salon, part of me wondering if these once belonged to Charlotte or if Sophia had all traces of her sister erased.

How can she so easily erase a sister?

The pain of losing Valerie—and now Arabella—is seared into my skin like an identification mark never to be removed. I squeeze any tears down inside me. They're quickly replaced with anger and determination.

Rémy and Bree are gone from the bedroom when I return. I snatch the voice-box from the side table and take it with me, then put the lace-skin over my face.

The hallways swell with bodies—servants toting gift boxes or pushing carts, attendants ushering excited courtiers in the direction of the festivities, royal sweet-vendors advertising their goods. And guards. Guards seem to be everywhere.

I join the chaos and grab one of the chariot lifts taking people across to the different palace wings.

"Where to?" a porter asks.

"Observatory Deck."

"That's for palace officials only," he replies.

"I am a guest of our future queen and I want to make sure her gift is delivered and placed with the others." I hold it up and lift my chin as if I'm the most important person in the world. "And I would *hate* to have to complain to her tonight of all nights." The confident threat beneath my words is enough to get him to close the door and shift the handle.

We sail over the belly of the palace. I keep my eyes down to avoid inviting more suspicion from the man. Below, I spot courtiers stealing kisses in dark corners and newsies rushing over gilded balconies and walkways with their navy story-balloons in tow and crowds of bodies making their way to the Imperial Ballroom. Mourning balloons putter about, complete with Charlotte's picture. They buzz along the corridors and walkways, leaving a sad trail of tear-shaped glitter and tiny wailing cries. Sophia's really added all the right touches to convince people of her lies. In a newsreel playing on the sides of the balloons, she describes how my experimentations led to her death.

One follows the chariot and the noise of it stokes my anger. Sophia must go. Our mission must succeed. Finally, the chariot stops at a platform near the very top of the palace.

"The Observatory Deck," the man announces, opening the door. "Ring the bell when you're ready to leave and I'll come back to get you."

I nod and thank him, then step off.

The deck is a glass bridge that smiles over the western wing of the palace. The walls are made of multicolored shards like a gigantic prism from the God of Luck. It catches the morning sunlight, shattering rays of indigo and ruby and turquoise and canary across a maze of gift boxes. Beyond the glass, post-balloons land on a balcony, one after another.

I scan the space.

Three guards. One on the deck itself. One beside the platform. One in the far corner.

Sweat beads in my temples. I didn't account for there being guards to watch over the gifts. But of course there would be. To watch for thieves.

I gulp down the sudden swell of nerves rising inside me. Another complication.

A woman with a parchment board and quill hunches amidst the sea of boxes. She glances up. "May I help you?"

"I have a gift for the queen. By the looks of things, it seems like she probably doesn't need another."

"Her Majesty loves presents above all else."

She loves beauty more.

"Guests are not allowed up here. There's a gift table in the Imperial Ballroom," the woman says.

I wait for the guards to turn in our direction, but they don't. Instead, they stand fixed in place. I walk in a zigzag, stepping over gift boxes both large and small, some covered in winter-season flowers and others exploding with velvet bows and silk ribbons.

"I am an important guest of Her Majesty. And I wanted to speak to you because I need my gift to impress. You must have the best sense of what she's gotten so far." I lift my royal emblem. I feel terrible about the fact that I'm going to need to hurt her, but I walk closer. A riot rises within me. My heartbeat overwhelms my entire body. My stomach twists with guilt and regret. A sticky sweat seeps out of my skin. "Can I show you the gift, and you'll let me know if it is good enough?" I ask.

Her blue eyes light up, and a primrose pink sets into the white of her cheeks. "Yes, it would be my pleasure. But quickly, I will get in trouble if you're found up here. I don't know how you got the porter to bring you up. It's forbidden."

"Our new queen said I could. He was following orders," I lie, and turn my back to her, set the box down, and remove the lid. She inches closer and leans forward. I wrap my finger around the voice-box, its brass edges warming beneath my fingertips. My hands itch with anticipation.

When I see the blond of her hair, I clobber her with it. She stumbles, croaks, touches her head, then collapses.

I hold my breath and wait a moment, hoping the nerves settle and that she isn't dead—just asleep for a little while. Enough time for the Iron Ladies to arrive.

One of the guards turns in my direction. "What's going on over there?"

His voice startles the others into action.

"She fainted," I lie.

"Show us your identification ink," one demands.

"You should call for a nurse from the Palace Infirmary."

They run in my direction.

I gaze down and grab a box covered in holly. Anger collects in my fingertips, the fire inside me loose and uncontrollable.

I grasp for the arcana, my three gifts just beneath my skin, at the ready. I stretch the waxy leaves until their edges are as sharp as Rémy's dagger at my hip.

These men will not get in my way.

Not now.

Not when I'm this close.

Two of the guards stumble backward with alarm. One clobbers his head and loses consciousness.

"Who are you?" the other one yells.

I catch the third as he tries to grab me, forcing the holly plant to coil around his torso. I press one of the thickened leaves at his throat, pushing the pointed edges into his skin. I tell the other guard, "Leave or I will kill him."

I let the holly plant dig a little harder into the man's flesh, and draw a teardrop of blood. The other guard's face pales and he puts his hands up. "I'm just here to watch the gifts. I don't even want to be a soldier," he stammers out, then scurries off like a coward.

I turn the holly leaves into a coffin, covering the guard's entire body until he resembles one of the hedges from the topiary maze on the palace grounds. No one will find him for a while or hear his shouts. I grab the woman's wrist and hunt for a pulse. It's faint. I exhale. She'll hopefully be out for a little bit.

I drop to my knees. The weight of what I've done couples with exhaustion from last night.

The sound of post-balloons bumping and thudding the glass is the only melody around me as they beg to be let in, their tail ribbons taut with the weight of their parcels.

I go to the Observatory Deck doors and slide one open a crack. Not enough for a passerby to notice. Not enough to cause alarm. A tendril of cold air cools the clamminess of my skin.

I look out at the horizon at a snow-white sky full of battalions of beautiful gift boxes and post-balloons. Many of the crates are so huge they require ten post-balloons to carry their weight. Ribbons in gossamer and amethyst and emerald and plum ruffle in the wind.

I hope they're full of Iron Ladies.

37

I walk with Bree to the Imperial Ballroom in the heavy gown sent by Sophia. The whole palace—its domes, gardens, turrets, spires, and pavilions—is aglow. Snow-lanterns bathe every possible corner with light. Gentle snowflakes dust the shoulders of men and women who dance under the snow-lanterns. People try to point out shapes before they shift into a myriad of new patterns. The cavernous room is thick with men in tuxedos and women in jewel-toned dresses.

With each footstep I take, I wonder what Sophia is going to do. Who is she going to present as Charlotte? Did she capture her sister? Did she kill someone? I push away any doubt. I have to believe our plan is moving forward.

"Did you find Amber?" I whisper to Bree before she leaves.

"No. Sophia must be hiding her. I'll keep looking."

I take a deep breath, touch the emblem around my neck, and hold the glamour in my mind. There's been no word from Padma or Auguste or any of the Iron Ladies in the last hour. But if Sophia can convince everyone that Charlotte is dead, she will be queen by the end of the day. I can't let that happen. Even if I have to stop her myself.

"Happy snow. Happy love." The cold-season blessing flutters through the room followed by kisses and the clinking of glasses. "May the Goddess of Love bless you. May you find sweetness in the new year. And most of all, may you always find beauty."

The ballroom is a jigsaw of bodies: men in top hats and women in gowns that swish and swirl as they spin in diagonals, dancing to a waltz being played by a small orchestra. Tiers of crème tarts and milk macarons sit on jeweled carts.

Courtiers pass by, locked in the fever of gossip.

"Did you see Colette Durand with her too-dark eyebrows? Looking just like the court jester. She thinks tinting them will work. That trend is long gone. Now, she just reeks of the elderberry juice she used to color them herself," one says.

"And Aimee Martin smells of skin paint," another adds. "She could've at least gone to the trouble of wearing a pomander or carrying a scent box. She's even gone and drawn veins onto her neck and face like she's a walking portrait or something."

The women burst with laughter.

"Inès Robert needs a skin treatment. She thinks taffeta patches will cover up those pocks," a third woman offers. "Thank god the teahouses will reopen soon. Our new queen will deliver on her promises."

"If I had Josette Agulliard's unfortunate bone structure, I'd have a Belle completely rebuild me from the bones out," the first says.

Black gossip post-balloons swarm overhead, listening to every word. Imperial attendants use tall poles and nets to swat them away, but they adeptly dodge and soar higher up to the grand ceiling, seeming to revel in a game of cat and mouse.

My nerves are on edge as I wait for Lady Arane, Surielle, Charlotte, and Auguste. I try not to fixate on the door for fear someone might ask me who I'm waiting for.

Sophia sits on a throne at the top of the room. Her teacup pets each have their own matching chair. Her ladies-of-honor sit at her feet on bright cushions.

An attendant announces me as I approach.

"And where are my teacup dragons?" Sophia whines to me.

"Resting. They don't like parties. Too many people cause anxiety," I improvise.

"A pity. We will have to train them out of it, now won't we?" She stares at me with a perfectly portioned smile on her face. "I don't think I'll be able to choose just one."

I bite down hard to avoid saying something nasty. When I look at her all I see are Remy's bruises, Arabella's dying breaths, a dagger in Valerie's neck. I don't know how long I can keep up this charade. Or this glamour.

Her attention flitters away from me and to the crowd. "I've always loved a ball at this time of year," Sophia says. "The cold weather is perfect for dancing."

"It's incredible tonight," Rachelle replies, gazing up at the snow-lanterns above her.

"Do you like it, Corinne?" Sophia pats a cushion beside her throne for me to sit on.

"Yes," I answer, sinking down beside her, hoping I can swallow my rage. "I can't wait to wander around and look at each snow-lantern. The newsies say each one is unique."

My body is alert with anticipation, hoping the Iron Ladies have come down into the palace. Any second now and the game will begin.

"It's a pity it'll turn into a funeral tonight," Rachelle says.

Sophia tries to hide a chuckle. "With the sweet comes the bitter."

I steal glances at her, wondering if she did capture Charlotte. I search for a sign, anything to know if Charlotte is all right, if she will show today as planned.

"We will dance and feast all day long, then you will say goodbye to your sister, and at midnight become queen," Gabrielle says proudly. "As it should be."

I pretend to watch the dancing as I keep my eye on the doors. Graceful dress trains swish and slap the floor. Men hold women's waists and turn them like pastel spinning toys.

The music shifts.

Sophia's old suitor, Alexander Dubois from House Berry, strides up. His jacket is lined with the brilliant silvers and reds of his house emblem, and under all the lights, his bald head shines like a copper ball. "Happy snow, Your Majesty."

"And to you," she says.

"May I have the next dance?" He presents his hand.

She glares at it.

"No," she says.

His face crumples with disappointment.

"I'll send for you when I'm in the mood."

He bows low and retreats.

"His hands used to get so wet they'd soak through my gloves," she complains. "And he always smells of cheese."

Her ladies giggle.

"And why is he bald at such a young age?" one asks.

Sophia shrugs. "I'll have my favorite Belle give him a tiny crop of hair."

Her words send a flicker up my spine.

"You are about to be married, anyway. He shouldn't ask you to dance anymore. You didn't choose him. Where is Auguste?" Rachelle asks. "Shouldn't he be here by now?"

I was just wondering the same thing.

Sophia stiffens. "My betrothed is on his way. I received his post-balloon not too long ago," she snaps. "And how dare you question it?"

Gabrielle glares at Rachelle. Anger stews inside me like a storm and triggers a headache to pulse in the back of my head. Pressure builds in my nose, signaling the start of another nosebleed. If I'm going to last all day, I need to take a break from holding the glamour.

I stand.

"Excuse me, Your Majesty. I am slipping off to the powder room," I lie with a quick bow. "Be back momentarily."

I don't wait for a response from Sophia or the others. My pulse flies as I weave in and out of the crowd. Before leaving the room, I stuff myself with tiny apple blossoms and fruit tarts and chocolate ganache from golden trays, hoping they will help reset my levels as I desperately hold on to this glamour.

Women steal glances at me. Snippets of gossip escape their carefully cupped hands. I rush past the windows, heading for the door.

A vendor hands me a cup with a hot sugared square of dough. "For you, my sweet."

I take it from him and force a smile. At that moment, the doors to the veranda are thrown open to let out a bit of the heat, and there it is—the Everlasting Rose. The building is massive. Its exterior glows, a sea pearl on a dark watery cushion. I crush the square in my hand like the head of a flower. The crumbs litter the floor beside me. The faces of my sisters and the other Belles flutter through my mind like the shuffling of a deck of cards.

Ivy

Edel

Hana

Amber

Delphine

Ada

Where are Charlotte and Padma and Auguste and the Iron Ladies? They should have been here by now. I duck through the crowds. I need to go back to the Observatory Deck. Maybe the woman woke up. Maybe she alerted other guards. Maybe they've all been taken.

A trumpet blares.

The room freezes.

"Ladies and gentlemen, please turn your attention to Her Majesty, Sophia, the next queen of Orléans," an attendant says.

Sophia stands. Everyone bows. I drop my head reluctantly.

"My loyal court, as we begin my Coronation and Ascension ceremony, I'd like to introduce you to several *loyal* people who made this whole thing possible. First, the newly titled Minister of Belles, Georgiana Fabry, and my *favorite* Belle, who will help me usher in this new age of beauty," she replies.

A chill wraps its arms around me.

The side doors burst open. Palace morning-lanterns rush in, scattering jewel-shaped shadows over the floor. Auguste's glamorous mother, Georgiana Fabry, strides into the room. Tall and stately, she towers over most in the crowd. Her yellow dress shimmers around her like sunlight woven into silk, and behind her, a rolling platform holds a life-size bell jar. Inside the jar is Amber.

38

The beat of my heart mirrors the rapid movement of the platform wheels. Amber's hands press against the walls of the glass; she's a trapped butterfly. Chains loop around her wrists like strands of golden pearls and her corseted dress holds her in place. Her pale and freckled arms wear jagged gashes.

I jerk forward, almost forgetting my disguise. The cold pain of the glamour pools with my rage. I duck and move through the crowd of bodies, trying to get closer to my sister.

Sophia springs up from her throne, her eyes wild as she gazes at Amber. "My favorite!" she taunts Amber, walking around the glass cage. "I have lots of new plans for the Belles, as evidenced." She motions to the veranda and the view of the Everlasting Rose. "Now, my petite Amber, if I take you out of this jar, you must promise to behave." Sophia traces her pointed nails along the glass, tapping it to make Amber flinch. "They're slowly learning their place."

The crowd chuckles.

Amber nods. "I promise." Her eyes spill over with tears, and are ringed with bruises.

A single guard removes the glass. Another hands Sophia a silver whip. She snaps it at the courtiers and several of them yelp. Sophia laughs, a deep belly laugh.

Angry tremors work their way through every part of my body as acid rises up my throat.

"Minister of Belles, tell this esteemed group of my most loyal courtiers some of the things they have to look forward to once my Coronation and Ascension are complete."

An attendant hands Georgiana a voice-box. "Good day to you all. I am so happy to join you on this auspicious occasion as we usher in this new age. Soon, I will set in place the Belle Codes, a new body of laws governing beauty work and—"

"Tell them about the facials," Sophia interjects with a squeal.

Georgiana purses her lips. "Yes, Your Majesty. We will offer Belle-blood facials as one of our newest treatments. We're unlocking the science of their blood. If you inject Belle blood into the top layer of your skin, you can defeat the gray."

The crowd oohs and ahhs.

My stomach dips and knots itself into a tangle. I must do something. I must help Amber. But what can I do? There are dozens of courtiers gathered about, and I can feel myself weakening after holding the glamour for so long.

Another door flies open. My heart jumps with hope that it's Padma and Auguste, Charlotte and Lady Pelletier, Lady Arane and her army of Iron Ladies.

Instead, more courtiers flood inside.

"Shall we demonstrate?" Sophia asks. "Wouldn't you all like to see how Belle blood transforms the skin?"

The crowd shouts with excitement.

Sophia pivots back to Amber. "We're going to show them our new trick."

Amber almost shrinks into herself. She pulls her arms in tight and drops her gaze.

Rage hums in my bones, urging me to help her. I step a little closer. Only a few paces more. Sophia motions for a nearby attendant, who steps up on the platform with my sister. Amber jerks away.

"I thought we were going to be agreeable today." Sophia twists the whip, then slaps it on the ground.

The sound reverberates through the room, the noise cutting deep inside me. My eyes burn with tears, my throat tight with disgust.

"I don't want to have to use this," Sophia says, but her anticipatory grin tells another story.

"Don't touch her," I shout.

The courtiers nearest me gasp and turn to stare.

"Who said that?" Sophia spins around.

I step out of the crowd.

We glare at each other. A knot coils tighter and tighter, the unspoken words between us twisting inside me like a set of knives.

"Corrine?" Her eyes flicker over me.

"Let her go," I demand.

A dead, haunting silence stretches through the room.

Amber stares at me.

The cold pain of maintaining the glamour sends blood pouring from my nose. I release it. I'm tired of holding on to it, tired of hiding. I want Sophia to know it's me. The disguise disappears.

Gasps explode in the room. The whole world seems to still.

"Camille?" Amber cries, that one word suffused with so much relief and anguish, hope and fear, it almost kills me.

A grin slowly curves along Sophia's mouth. "Dragon merchant." She begins to clap slow at first, then descends into a fervor. "Well done. You tricked me. I didn't know you could change yourselves."

"There's a lot about our gifts that you don't understand—will *never* understand and will *never* know!" I snap. "No matter how many of us you lock up or poke or prod."

I watch for the guards. They inch closer.

"Give me my sister."

"She is not my prisoner," Sophia replies, her eyes inspecting every inch of me.

"She is chained."

"Only because she tried to break our deal."

"What deal?" I spit.

Sophia jumps with glee. "Oh yes, oh yes. We have a deal, and deals are binding." Her gaze cuts back at Amber, who begins to sob. "Should I tell her? Or do you want to?"

She waits for an answer. Amber's cries deepen and her whole body shakes. I want to go to her. I want to tell her that everything is going to be all right, that I will get us both out of here even if no one shows up to help. She swallows over and over again like she has something stuck in her throat. Beads of sweat race down her face.

"This pretty little mouse sent me all sorts of messages about you," Sophia reports. "As soon as she told me what I needed, I staged her capture."

My pulse throbs, counting down the moments. Hate simmers inside me, sharp, hot, and pricking.

My fists ball. I clench my jaw.

I glare at Amber. She won't look at me. Edel's suspicions of her lock into place. The betrayal is thick and painful. I don't know why she would feed information to Sophia. Not even the hint of a reason can form in my head. It has to be something. Blackmail. Coercion.

Sophia motions to the guards. They unlock Amber's chains.

"After I caught this pretty little mouse, she promised to be my personal Belle until my new generation had reached maturation. She even said she'd give them lessons. Teach them everything those wretched Du Barrys taught you." Sophia's eyes gleam in the snow-lantern light. "Oh, and there's more." She pirouettes, her ballgown billowing around her slender frame. "She knew you'd come for her. She agreed to lure you here." She blows me a kiss. "Some sister that is."

"Amber, we're leaving. Let's go," I shout, not believing a word coming out of Sophia's lying mouth.

Amber gazes down at the platform.

"Amber?"

Sophia watches like a cat ready to pounce on its prey. "Amber, please bring me one of your flowers."

Amber sobs and hands one to her.

"Amber?" I say.

"Amber, bow to me."

Amber drops to her knees.

"Why would you do this?" I say, imploring her to look at me. The words taste sour as they leave my throat.

"Will you be going anywhere?" Sophia asks Amber, cupping her chin. Tears rush down my sister's reddened face. "So much for sisterly love." Sophia blows another kiss at me.

"I've seen *your* sister," I hiss at Sophia.

The crowd bursts again into a frenzy of whispers.

She frowns. "My sister is dead."

"She is not. She's alive and well, actually."

Sophia shrugs. "The gods will welcome her home soon, and I will be crowned queen."

"Whatever poor soul you'll be presenting to these people, her identification mark will prove she is no princess."

Sophia paces around me, then leans in to whisper, "To whom? No one in *my* cabinet. No one in *my* guard. I am adored. Any challenger, any usurper will be put down." She waves a hand in the air and turns back to the watching crowd.

The arcana is a small throbbing hum inside me, a reluctant ribbon buried deep, one I wasn't sure I wanted any longer, but I summon it to wake up again. The memory of what I did to the guards and the woman watching the gifts rushes back. I close my eyes and picture Sophia just as she is standing before me. My skin ignites, my limbs stretch, my curls straighten, and my dress changes to match hers.

"What are you doing?" Sophia yells. "Guards! Guards!"

We're identical now. I take a breath and attack, leaping on her with every ounce of my rage coursing through me. We toss and turn, thrashing across the floor. I slap her and shake her, and she bites and kicks.

The onlookers scatter to the edges of the room, cowering and screaming and trying to get away from us.

She shoves me away.

We scramble to our feet.

"Arrest her," Sophia orders, pointing at me.

"Arrest her," I parrot back, pointing at her. My first arcana—Manner—helps me perfect her pitchy voice.

The guards stand stunned.

"Did you hear me?" Sophia says, her voice now a shrill. "She's the fugitive Belle. A traitor."

They move in my direction.

I repeat her words.

They freeze.

Sophia's jaw tenses. "Fine! You want to play this game?"

I mimic her.

We circle each other, ready to fight again. I focus on holding the glamour and don't dare look away from my enemy. Her fingers twitch, and so do mine. I lick my lips, salivating to lash out, to end this once and for all.

I realize a second too late that our circling has brought Sophia within inches of her whip. Before I can move, she scoops it up and, with a flick of her wrist, it curls around Amber's neck, cuts a deep gash, and snaps it.

Amber doesn't even scream. Her eyes flutter, lashes batting like butterfly wings, and she tumbles forward.

"No!" I scream, falling to my knees.

The crowd erupts in horror.

39

"I win. I win. I win," Sophia says, parading around the now silent room.

I rush to Amber, cradling her head in my lap. Her vacant eyes stare up at me. My heart is still. Frozen in my chest. Maybe never to beat again. The glamour slides right off me, and with it more blood pours out of my nose and down onto Amber's forehead. I can't loosen my arms around her to wipe it.

"Now, take her, but don't be too rough. She's the one I really need," Sophia says.

The guards snatch me away from Amber. Her body slides off me and hits the floor again with a thud. A river of blood leaks from inside her. They loop chains around my wrists and lift me to my feet.

I can't fight them. My hands and arms are numb.

Sophia does a lap around me. "Now, I'm going to take all those teacup dragons of yours and add them to my collection. I'm going to keep you in my prison, for you will be *my* true everlasting rose, and I'm going to kill that traitorous guard you love so much. What's his name? Reim...no...Raine...no...Oh, Rémy. That's right."

The sound of his name hits me.

"You will learn to be loyal." I jerk forward, but the guards pin me in place. The edges of the room lose focus. "One way or another."

She laughs and I shiver. A cold settles into my veins like I'm about to create another glamour. But instead, Sophia and each guard appear in my head. The erratic beat of their hearts floods my ears. Their pulses are racing melodies. My anger mingles with the arcana twisting their portraits into unrecognizable shapes.

They all drop to their knees. Sophia screams. Her skin crinkles like parchment. Her eyes drift to the sides of her face like fish's. Her mouth is an O shape of anguish. I can't hear what she tries to say. I can't stop.

I focus on the hearts of everyone in the room. I slow them down, beat by beat, until there's only a faint murmur. The guards turn pale, and Sophia grabs at her chest. Her eyes begin to roll back. Everyone drops. Hundreds of people. Their screams are a chorus, echoing off the ceiling.

Blood rushes down my lips and chin and neck, the salt of it seeping into my mouth. My nerves are raw with power; all three arcana gifts sear through me.

I could kill them all. Not one of them helped Amber. Not one of them tried to stop Sophia.

The room almost dissolves around me. A carousel of light and shapes spinning as the heartbeats slow to a stop.

The door opens. "Stop!" a voice hollers.

It's Charlotte. She hobbles forward with a cane to support her. Her curly brown hair towers over her, thick with magnolia flowers, and her eyes hold strength. "You don't want to do this!"

The Iron Ladies stand proudly in their masks. Padma and Auguste edge into the room and stare at the horror I've unleashed.

"You aren't this person," Charlotte says.

"I am," I reply. "It needs to be over."

Sophia's body jerks forward and rolls around the floor. Her breath is ragged, and she starts to hiccup.

"Valerie is dead because of her. Arabella. Amber. She's hurt so many," I say. "She will keep doing it. She will never stop."

"And she hurt me," Charlotte says. "But I want her alive."

"Why? She poisoned you. Kept you asleep for six years."

"She's my sister." She looks down at Sophia with tears in her eyes. "Just like you forgive your sisters for their mistakes, I will forgive mine. Let me deal with her." She steps closer to me. Her hands reach out to touch my shoulder. "You don't want her death on your heart, and the rest of these people are innocent—complacent, maybe, but not evil. I need you to help me fix the problems she's created."

Padma cautiously approaches me and puts a hand in mine. "Just let go, Camille. Just breathe."

The rage inside me fights to get out. I close my eyes. I don't know if I can stop it. The portraits of the guards and Sophia are a swirling tornado. The blood is a river gushing from my nose still.

"You can," she whispers.

I release everyone in the room. All around me people gasp for air. I collapse forward. Sweat streams down my face and arms and legs. More blood pours from my nose and over my lips. All the light in the room disappears.

40

I'm swept into tumultuous dreams of our very last beauty session before the Beauté Carnaval. Back when we were still little girls. Back when we didn't know anything outside of the walls of the space we were born into. Back when we thought we were divine instruments to be treasured instead of used. Du Barry had us listen to visiting courtier women and their complaints about their bodies. We noted how they asked us to reset their insides, shifting the bone and marrow into new shapes more beautiful than their natural template.

My sisters and I hovered around a long treatment table like a ceremonial fan, gawking down at one woman's limbs. She'd traveled over six golden imperial bridges and on one canopied river-coach through the Rose Bayou to get to us from the Silk Isles. Tiny clusters of beauty-lanterns drifted over her like midnight stars. Perfect balls of light revealed how the gray of her skin made her look like a piece of fish that sat out all night.

We'd been so eager to use our beauty caisses for the first time and the items on the carts that the servants had wheeled in: tiered trays bursting with skin-color pastilles and rouge pots, brushes and combs and barrel irons, tonics and crèmes, bei-powder bundles, waxes and perfumes.

The woman's soft moans stretched out like an anxious bubble between us. Tensions were high during our final session before we traveled to the imperial island, before we displayed our talents for the queen, before we found out who would be named the favorite, before we were told which one of us was most important.

There was a woman waiting on the table. There would be people at court waiting to be changed, and anticipating perfect results. There would be expectations.

My sisters and I exchanged nervous glances. Edel had turned as pale as the white lesson dresses we all used to wear. Padi's black Belle-bun always caught the beauty-lantern light as she nosed around with careful and cautious curiosity. Hana had gotten in trouble for giggling when we'd catch a glimpse of certain body parts, and her long black braid hung down her back like a rope, swishing left and right as she trembled with laughter. Amber's cheeks had been permanently red from intense focus. Valerie always rubbed her hands together with a smile, antsy to make sure she did whatever she could to make someone's dreams come true.

We'd been all together. We'd worked together. We'd go through this experience together.

I'd felt like I had swallowed bayou butterflies that day.

The sound of humming pulls me awake, slow at first and then all at once. My eyes startle open, sore and watery as the light hits them through gauzy bed-curtains. The memories of where I am and what happened slide into my mind and a wave of nausea hits me. Sophia. Charlotte. The Iron Ladies. The Coronation and Ascension Ball.

I try to move, but my arms are threaded with needles and tubes, and my limbs hold the deepest soreness I've ever experienced.

I attempt to speak, but words come out in croaks.

"You sound terrible," a voice says. "You should just *not* speak."

I turn my head to the right and see Edel's grinning face. Tears spill out the sides of my eyes.

"Ugh, don't cry." She inches closer, then clutches onto my arm like it's the edge of a cliff and she needs to keep us both from tumbling off it. "I'm all right, and you're all right."

The bed-curtains open. "Did you wake her? You weren't supposed to," Padma says, carrying a morning-lantern. The beams illuminate the rich brownness of her skin like honey drizzled on a square of chocolate.

She climbs in on my left.

"Where's Hana?" I ask.

"I'm here. I'm here." She peeks her head through the bed-curtains. She looks different, so skinny she might be whisked away if a snowy wind became too strong. A soft day gown drapes her now wiry frame in the color of ginger and squash, and her black Belle-bun holds glass ornaments.

"Are you all right?" I reach for her.

She finds a space on the bed. "I will be. I arrived last night from the Fire Isles."

When we were little girls living at Maison Rouge with our mamans, we'd pile into bed together just so we'd be able to wake up near one another. We all had our positions: Edel would have to be on the edge so she could get out if she needed to, Hana loved being in the center, Padma along the foot, Amber in the middle where she could control everyone's movements, and Valerie closest to Edel, her favorite sleep partner out of all of us. I was happy wherever, as long as I was with my sisters.

The memory stings—the bed once snug with a tangle of legs and arms and warmth, and now, so few.

I start to ask them if they're all right and if we're going to be all right, but we each make eye contact and lie there in silence. I hold their hands and trace my fingers over their skin and gaze at them, ensuring that my few remaining sisters are intact. I am filled with regrets and unrequited wishes.

The doors open and Lady Pelletier pushes Charlotte in a wheeling chair followed by Lady Arane, Surielle, and Violetta.

Hana, Padma, and Edel sit up.

I struggle to rise.

"Please don't move, Camille," Charlotte says. "Rest."

Lady Pelletier pushes her close to the bed, then leans down and kisses my forehead. I swallow down tears. The softness of her lips reminds me of Maman.

"You look better," Charlotte remarks.

"Her levels are almost back to normal," Hana reports. "A few more days of rest, and she should be back to her old self."

I don't even know who that is anymore.

"You saved us," Lady Arane says to me. Her black eyes hold joyful tears as she gazes into the bed. "You opened the Observatory Deck and then created the perfect diversion."

"It didn't feel much like saving," I admit.

"But you did it," Charlotte adds, her voice strong and clear.

"What happened? How many days has it been?" I ask, trying to piece together the rest of the night after I fainted.

"It's been three days. I've freed all the Belles, plus the Fashion

Minister and Beauty Minister, from the Everlasting Rose and put my sister in her own prison, where she will stand trial for her crimes and get the help she needs. I don't know if she will ever truly understand the damage she's done, but I will spend my days impressing this upon her."

She purses her lips. "You missed my coronation," she teases.

"You are a beautiful queen," Lady Pelletier adds with a smile. "Your mother would be proud."

We all kiss our two fingers and tap our hearts to show respect for the dead. I let my hand linger there, thinking of Valerie, Amber, and Arabella.

"Where are the other Belles?" I ask.

"I've seen a few of them," Edel interjects. "They're here at the palace."

"We've released them from the teahouses as well and given them accommodations." Charlotte takes a breath. "And we'd love it, Camille, if you'd stay with us, and be our advisor on all matters related to Belles as we figure out what beauty work will look like going forward."

Lady Arane clears her throat. "Living without modifications does take adjustment and patience. The Iron Ladies will be moving our headquarters to Trianon to assist those who wish to make the change," she assures me.

The proposition stirs around inside my head. This last year I've felt like I've been trapped in a snow globe, shaken and jostled until the glass fissures and all the water leaks out. Before, all I ever wanted was to live at the palace forever in one of the beautiful apartments. But now, all I want to do is go home. Or to whatever is left of it.

"Your Majesty, it would be an honor to help you with this and to be here with you, but I don't believe it's the right path for me," I tell her. "I want to go back to Maison Rouge and take any Belles who want to come with me. While things are still settling across the kingdom, it will be a troublesome time for us. I need to be in a place that I know is safe, and I need to keep my sisters safe. And, if I may . . . I must also grapple with the things I've done—and the losses I've suffered."

Charlotte smiles knowingly. "I understand. I respect your decision. But I will still need your help. All of your help." She gestures at Hana, Edel, and Padma.

"I'll stay behind," Edel says, surprising us all.

"You will?" Padma replies.

"I won't ever return to another teahouse," she declares. "And if things are going to change in Orléans, I want to be a part of that change."

She reaches for my hand and for Hana's. I can feel her pulse thrumming beneath her skin.

"If I accomplish one thing in this life," she says firmly, "it will be to ensure that the old way of doing things is done."

41

A week later, the journey home from Trianon feels a thousand moments longer than the one that first brought me and my sisters to the imperial island. Our hearts buzzed with the promise of being true Belles, stepping into our destinies, being chosen and placed. The two days drifted past us before we knew it, our fates sprawled out before us like paths to unknown places, full of promise.

The horses' pace quickens as the carriages travel north across imperial bridges connecting the main island to outlying ones. The ride home is shadowed with worries, a tapering storm that may reignite at any moment.

We sit in silence. The noise of the road among us. Padma thumbs through Arabella's Belle-book. Hana reads a stack of newspapers and tattlers. Rémy sleeps, his arm in a sling and his foot propped up. Bree stokes a small fire. The absence of Valerie, Edel, and Amber is like a cold weight in my chest. At least Edel is well. She's taken her place at the palace at Charlotte's side.

I glance out the window at our procession—several carriages carrying Belles released from the Everlasting Rose and the teahouses—all those who wished to come.

The city of Trianon disappears in the distance, fading to a mere smudge. I crane to see its outline, wondering if I will ever return, if I'll ever want to. I wanted nothing more than to be the favorite and to stay in Trianon and the royal palace forever, but I had no idea what it would be like, all the horrors that would come to pass. A dream turned nightmare.

I curl into a little knot, limbs and body lost in the folds of my dress, and sink into the weight of all that's happened.

"More newspapers and tattlers," Bree says, sliding one stack into my lap and another into Hana's.

"Sit with me?" I ask her.

"I need to prepare tea."

"You're no longer an imperial servant."

"I know, but—"

I pat the cushion beside mine. "Just sit with me awhile."

She concedes.

We sit in the window and go through the headlines in the *Orléansian Times*:

MINISTER OF BELLES FLEES! GEORGIANA FABRY MISSING

THE LEADER OF THE IRON LADIES INVITED TO
MEET WITH HER MAJESTY QUEEN CHARLOTTE

LOCKED IN A TOWER OF HER OWN MAKING!
DISGRACED ALMOST QUEEN SOPHIA HELD IN
THE EVERLASTING ROSE TO AWAIT TRIAL

RIOTS AND UNREST SPARK IN THE SPICE ISLES!

"What do you think will happen?" Bree asks.

I turn the page and the headlines scatter. "I don't know."

"Will things go back to what they once were?"

"Can anything go back? All I know is that we will take care of one another and those with us, and help Charlotte." I trace my fingers along the underside of my wrist, the veins there a reminder of the arcana. And a choice.

She opens the *Trianon Tribune* and reads silently.

I close my eyes. Images circle inside my head with nowhere to go, like flies in a jar. I drift in and out of sleep. Time passes, more than three hourglasses' worth. The world outside the carriage gets quieter and quieter.

The wheels sink into soft earth. I recognize the feeling and know we're close to home. When I was younger, I loved the mud between my toes and the tiny worry that you might drift down and through the center of the world. If we were the slightest bit dirty, Du Barry would send us for a scrub treatment, and it was never pleasant. I miss those little-girl days before I was so excited to leave home—to crash into the world and discover its secrets.

We rattle along the wooden bridge to the carriage-house, and I hear the familiar late-night noises of the Rose Bayou—the hum of crickets, the bleat of frogs, and the buzz of fireflies. Above me a quilt of branches is heavy with snow-white moss.

The carriages are parked inside the brick carriage-house, which sits on a platform in the middle of the bayou. Behind me, the wooden bridge pulls away, returning to our closest island neighbor—Quin. During the warm months, rows of fruits and vegetables in every color, shape, and size grow along high hills and mountainsides, and we could see teams of workers tending to the millions of plants from my bedroom window.

Would everything settle back in place like a reset bone?

As the bridge disappears behind me, so does the path to the outside world. Maybe that's a good thing now. Maybe time away from the world will help.

I gaze ahead across the water. Home hides among the Rose Bayou's cypress trees. The newspapers used to say the Goddess of Beauty placed Belles on an island of milk and blood because of these white bark trees and their red leaves.

I wish the sight of them gave me the relief I crave, but it doesn't. What will it feel like to be here without Amber and Valerie? Will I be able to do all the things that need to be done?

Bayou boats arrive at the carriage-house pier.

We climb in.

Snowflies skip along the surface of the water, their little bodies white sparks brightening the dark. I want to plunge my whole hand in, like I did when I was a little girl. I want to see if the water is still the same.

The warning Du Barry used to give me rings out in my head: *"Sit up, Camellia, and hand out of the water. This bayou is full of the unknown."*

I leave a sliver of the window open to watch as we pass through a dense thicket of cypress trees where the boats slow to curve around their trunks. I want to reach out and pluck one of the roses growing out of the dark waters, but the feeling of Du Barry's eyes upon me lingers. Even if she isn't here.

Maison Rouge appears ahead. The pointed roof rises above the trees. Sill-lanterns sit in each window and cast red light over the island. Stone crypts freckle the land, and the Belle-graveyard seems endless, spilling into the dark forest that lurks in the mansion's shadow. Maman and I used to play hide-and-seek in the graveyard when she wanted alone time for us away from the other mothers and little girls. We'd zip around those vaults and fill the space with laughter instead of death. Back then, I wasn't afraid of dying, and I never thought there'd be a day when Maman would be placed in one of the graves. They were just stone pyramids to hide behind until my mother found me. Now, they feel real and used. Ready to receive the bodies of my sisters.

The boats are tethered to the dock, and the servants help us onto the platform. We follow a path of stepping-stones along the walkway to the house. Twisted cypress trees block the stars. The noise of our feet adds to the melody of the bayou. I jam a key into the lock just as Du Barry once did.

I slide the entryway doors open with both hands. The floors are warm beneath my feet, and the walls and corridors and rooms carry the scent of charcoal and flowers. The familiar smell of home.

Ivy stands there waiting. Her face has settled back to its original shape. She opens her arms, and I fall into them.

"It is so good to see you," I say. "How did you get here before us?"

"Always asking questions."

Her words make me smile. "It's good to see you, too."

"Welcome home, my little fox."

"Are we going to be all right?" I ask.

"Yes," she replies. "Together we will."

Epilogue

I open the double doors of Du Barry's office. The wood whispers beneath my feet, and I'm a little girl again, bracing myself to get in trouble, waiting for her to step out of the circuit-phone booth in the corner, expecting her to appear behind me, and say, "What do you think you're doing in here? Fetch your parchment and write fifty lines."

The scent of her lingers—rose water, cloves, and a touch of sugar—and it makes me wonder where she might be now. The windy season is here, and it's been three months since Charlotte locked Sophia in the Everlasting Rose.

Du Barry's high-backed velvet chair is still creased with the memory of her shape. Her abacus perches on the side like a tanager bird. The walls boast portraits of her ancestors—eight generations' worth, all stemming from the grand-mère who found the first Belle as she emerged from the dark forest.

Nothing has changed. All of it is frozen in place, anticipating her return, anticipating all things to settle back into place like they once were.

But everything is different now.

I sit at her desk, my legs finding the grooves left behind by her body.

The house bell rings. I glance out the window that faces the front. Padma ushers in more of Sophia's pods. The growing Belle babies slosh in their cradles as they're lifted inside. Hana follows behind, her arms full of supplies.

I step into the hallway. The lesson rooms are filled with small Belles examining flowers and products, the pitch of their voices bordering on squeals. Day-lanterns sail over the room like floating stars.

The foyer buzzes with activity as the nursery chamber welcomes the Belle-pods from the palace. Nurses rush in and out, following Ivy's orders.

I leave the house through the back doors. The dark forest lies ahead, spread out across the rest of our island like a blanket of night. The Belle-graveyard sits along its edge, headstones poking like thumbnails from the rich soil. The three freshest graves hold the bodies of Amber and Valerie and Arabella, but already the earth around them has settled. They barely look new anymore.

My heart pinches.

I glance up at the sky, wondering if new Belles will actually fall from it one day. Will my sisters be replaced? What will happen in the weeks and months and years to come?

A warm and familiar hand slips into mine. I look up and meet Rémy's eyes. "When did you get back?"

"Just now."

"How are your sisters? And mother and father?"

"Better," he says with a sigh of relief. He presents a ruby post-balloon. "This arrived from the palace."

I rip open the back of the balloon, fish out the letter holder, and unroll the parchment. Rémy reads over my shoulder.

Camille,

I hope everything is all right at home.

I have news that you should know in case it leaks to the papers. I still don't trust anyone here at court. Charlotte plans to abdicate the throne once things settle down. She wants to call for a new Beauty Trial.

It could be two months or two years from now. I don't know.

But I'm looking forward to what comes next.

Be safe, and write me.

Love,

Edel

PS: Hi, Rémy!

Rémy and I exchange glances.

"What does that mean?" he asks.

"Maybe chaos. Maybe an end to beauty work for good." I glance back at the house. "I don't know. One can only hope our new leader will be wise and just, and nothing like Sophia."

I look up at the post-balloon, and then at the sky as a streak mars the blue.

His hand finds mine.

"What would you say if I asked you to go into those woods with me? Would you be afraid?"

He turns my face toward him. "Anything for you."

We walk forward into the shadows, hand in hand.

ACKNOWLEDGMENTS

I have so many people to thank for helping me cross the finish line with this book. It was a struggle and a roller coaster, because during the writing of this book I was diagnosed with a very large, noncancerous liver tumor. Through numerous medical appointments, biopsies, and MRIs, I wrestled with this book and its plot and all my deadlines, and the reality that my quest for perfect skin was the reason I had this medical emergency. After spending several decades on oral contraceptives to control my cystic acne, I discovered it gave me a parting gift—a tumor the size of my hand. Beauty has a price, and I am learning the cost now.

It took a team to help me get this book to be its best. A list of thanks in no particular order:

My badass agent, Victoria Marini. Thank you for keeping me together. You are a superhero!

My amazing editor, Kieran S. Viola. Thank you for rescuing me. Always. Thank you for your patience as this medical crisis interrupted our normal editorial process. Thank you for helping me organize the chaos.

My amazing champion, Emily Meehan. Thank you for your vision and your support. I love being part of the Freeform family.

Marci Senders, brilliant cover wizard, you continue to amaze me with your cover-making powers. They just get better and better.

Maz Zissimos, best publicist in the freaking world, thank you for keeping me all together and making sure I get cool opportunities to talk about my world. You are amazing, and I feel lucky to also call you a friend.

Thank you to the whole Freeform team—Seale Ballenger, Holly Nagel, Dina Sherman, Mary Mudd, Shane Rebenschied, Elke Villa, Andrew Sansone, Patrice Caldwell. You are the dream team.

Thank you to my friends, my love nests, my group chats, my Slack channels, my covens. All those who keep me human. You know who you are. This was a tough year, and I barely made it through. Thank you for listening to me complain and whine and cry, and for keeping me all stitched together. Thank you for the chicken broth and the flowers and the tea and the steak. ☺

Thank you, Mom and Dad, for everything. Always, and forever.

And thank you to the readers. Thanks for coming down this dark rabbit hole with me.